Praise for Max Barry's

COMPANY

"Smart and fast-paced. . . . Make[s] topics like outsourcing, mission statements and H.R. come alive, breathe fire and vomit all over your in-basket."

—Douglas Coupland,
The New York Times Book Review

"A terrifically funny skewering of modern strategic management techniques and the people who cook them up. . . . Anyone who has worked for a large corporation . . . [will] read this with savage pleasure."

—*The Boston Globe*

"Max Barry establishes himself as fiction's most insightful and devilish satirist of corporate culture. . . . If you're reading a management book right now, any management book . . . put it down and get this instead."

—*Forbes*

"Darkly funny. . . . A scorched-earth assault on corporate culture. . . . You'll find plenty to laugh and cheer about."

—*The News-Press* (Fort Myers)

"Hilarious. . . . Barry has packed these pages with . . . vignettes of corporate characters you may find all too familiar."

—*Fortune*

"Intriguing and extremely funny. . . . An entertaining page-turner that is sure to have readers looking at their own place of employment in a new and critical way."

—*Bookpage*

"Biting, edgy, and downright wicked. . . . A chillingly funny look at corporate ethics."

—*Tucson Citizen*

"Inspired. . . . Compelling. . . . Hilarious."

—*The Portland Mercury*

Max Barry

COMPANY

Max Barry spent the best years of his life in the bowels of Hewlett-Packard, conducting secret research for this book. This is his third novel, following the cult hit *Syrup* and the bestselling *Jennifer Government*, which was chosen as a *New York Times* Notable Book. He was born on March 18, 1973, and lives in Melbourne, Australia. He writes full-time, but enforces a strict dress policy, requires that his desk be kept tidy at all times, and asks that he limit personal calls to less than two minutes.

ALSO BY MAX BARRY

Syrup

Jennifer Government

COMPANY

A Novel

MAX BARRY

VINTAGE CONTEMPORARIES
Vintage Books
A Division of Random House, Inc.
New York

FIRST VINTAGE CONTEMPORARIES EDITION, MARCH 2007

 Published in the United States by Vintage Books, a division of Random House, Inc., New York, and in Canada by Random House of Canada Limited, Toronto. Originally published in hardcover in the United States by Doubleday, a division of Random House, Inc., New York, in 2006.

The Library of Congress has cataloged the Doubleday edition as follows:
Barry, Max.
Company : a novel / by Max Barry.
p. cm.
1. Young men—Fiction. 2. Corporations—Fiction.
3. Business ethics—Fiction. 4. Work environment—Fiction.
5. Corporate culture—Fiction. I. Title.
PS3552.A7424C66 2005
813'.54—dc22
2005048498

Vintage ISBN: 978-1-4000-7937-7

www.vintagebooks.com

Printed in the United States of America
10 9

For Hewlett-Packard

COMPANY

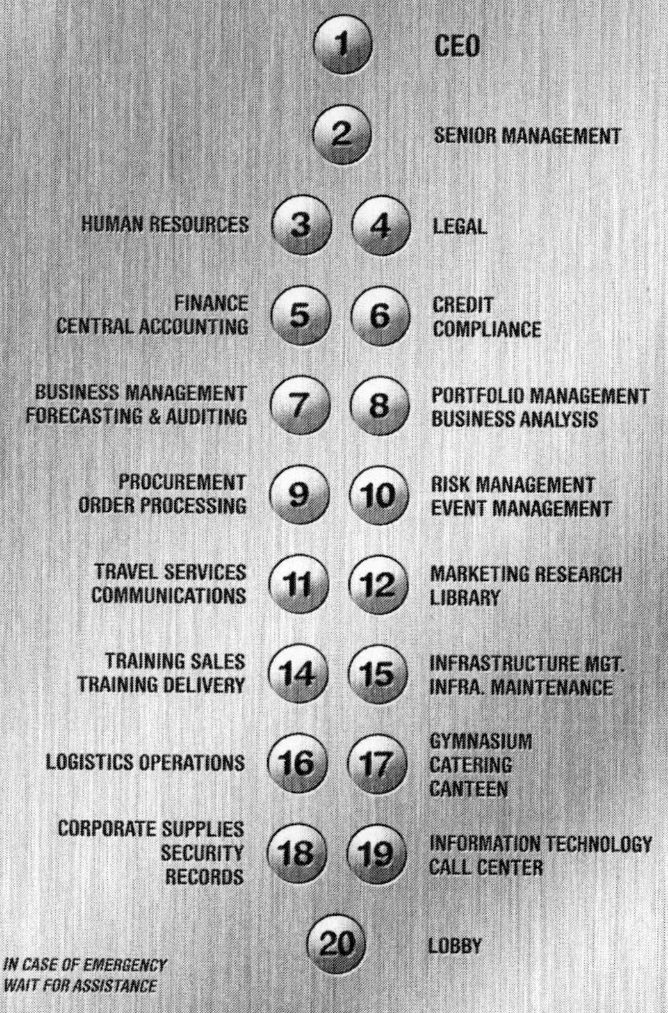
ZEPHYR
HOLDINGS,
INC.
1 CEO
2 SENIOR MANAGEMENT
HUMAN RESOURCES 3
4 LEGAL
FINANCE
CENTRAL ACCOUNTING 5
6 CREDIT
COMPLIANCE
BUSINESS MANAGEMENT
FORECASTING & AUDITING 7
8 PORTFOLIO MANAGEMENT
BUSINESS ANALYSIS
PROCUREMENT
ORDER PROCESSING 9
10 RISK MANAGEMENT
EVENT MANAGEMENT
TRAVEL SERVICES
COMMUNICATIONS 11
12 MARKETING RESEARCH
LIBRARY
TRAINING SALES
TRAINING DELIVERY 14
15 INFRASTRUCTURE MGT.
INFRA. MAINTENANCE
LOGISTICS OPERATIONS 16
17 GYMNASIUM
CATERING
CANTEEN
CORPORATE SUPPLIES
SECURITY
RECORDS 18
19 INFORMATION TECHNOLOGY
CALL CENTER
20 LOBBY
IN CASE OF EMERGENCY
WAIT FOR ASSISTANCE

TRAINING SALES DEPT.
MANAGER
Sydney Harper
x766
PERSONAL ASSISTANT
a
Megan Jckson
x767
SALES REP. 1
Elizabeth Miller
x701
SALES REP. 2
Wendell Hartford
x702
SALES REP. 3
Roger Jefferson
x703
SALES REP. 4
Jen Davies
x704
SALES ASSISTANT
Holly Vale
x711
SALES ASSISTANT
Freddy Carlson
x712
SALES ASSISTANT
Jim Wong
x713
James
SALES ASSISTANT
Nick Dash
x714

Q3/2: AUGUST

MONDAY MORNING and there's one less donut than there should be.

Keen observers note the reduced mass straightaway but stay silent, because saying, "Hey, is that only six donuts?" would betray their donut experience. It's not great for your career to be known as the person who can spot the difference between six and seven donuts at a glance. Everyone studiously avoids mentioning the missing donut until Roger turns up and sees the empty plate.

Roger says, "Where's my donut?"

Elizabeth dabs at her mouth with a piece of paper towel. "I only took one." Roger looks at her. "What?"

"That's a defensive response. I asked where my donut was. You tell me how many you took. What does that say?"

"It says I took one donut," Elizabeth says, rattled.

"But I didn't ask how many donuts you took. Naturally I would assume you took one. But by taking the trouble to articulate that assumption, you imply, deliberately or otherwise, that it's debatable."

Elizabeth puts her hands on her hips. Elizabeth has shoulder-length brown hair that looks as if it has been cut with a straight razor and a mouth that could have done the cutting. Elizabeth is smart, ruthless, and emotionally damaged; that is, she is a sales representative. If Elizabeth's brain was a person, it would have scars, tattoos, and be missing one eye. If you saw it coming, you would cross the street. "Do you want to ask me a question, Roger? Do you want to ask if I took your donut?"

Roger shrugs and begins filling his coffee cup. "I don't care about a missing donut. I just wonder why someone felt the need to take two."

"I don't think anyone took two. Catering must have shorted us."

"That's right," Holly says.

Roger looks at her. Holly is a sales assistant, so has no right to speak up at this point. Freddy, also a sales assistant, is wisely keeping his mouth shut. But then, Freddy is halfway through his own donut and has a mouthful. He is postponing swallowing because he's afraid he'll make an embarrassing gulping noise.

Holly wilts under Roger's stare. Elizabeth says, "Roger, we saw Catering put them out. We were standing right here."

"Oh," Roger says. "Oh, I'm sorry. I didn't realize you were staking out the donuts."

"We weren't *staking them out.* We just happened to be here."

"Look, it doesn't bother me one way or the other." Roger picks up a packet of sugar and shakes it as if it's in need of discipline: *wap-wap-wap-wap.* "I just find it interesting that donuts are so important to some people that they stand around waiting for them. I didn't know donuts were the reason we show up here every day. I'm sorry, I thought the idea was to improve shareholder value."

Elizabeth says, "Roger, how about you talk to Catering before you start making accusations. All right?" She walks off. Holly trails her like a remora.

Roger watches her go, amused. "Trust Elizabeth to get upset over a donut."

Freddy swallows. "Yeah," he says.

The Zephyr Holdings building sits nestled among the skyscrapers of Seattle's Madison Street like a big, gray brick. It is bereft of distinguishing features. You could argue that it has a certain neutral, understated charm, but only if you are willing to apply the same logic to prisons and 1970s Volvos. It is a building designed by committee: all they have been able to agree on is that it should be rectangular, have windows, and not fall over.

Perched at the top is the word ZEPHYR and the corporate logo, which is an orange-and-black polygon of foggy intent. Orange and black crops up a lot at Zephyr Holdings; you can't walk down a corridor, visit the bathroom, or catch an elevator without being reminded whose turf you're on. There's a logo on each panel of the lobby's sliding glass doors, and when you're through them, logos adorn the walls at intervals of three feet. A water feature of dark stones and well-tended ferns is a small, logo-free oasis, but to make up for this, the reception desk is practically a logo with a sign-in sheet on top. Even under soft, recessed lighting, the reception desk delivers such a blast of orange to your retinas that long after you've left it behind, you can still see it when you blink.

On one side of the lobby is an arrangement of comfortable chairs and low-slung tables, where visitors browse Zephyr's marketing literature while waiting for whomever they're meeting. Sitting there with his hands in his lap is young, fresh-faced Stephen Jones. His eyes are bright. His suit glows. His sandy-brown hair contains so much styling mousse it's a fire risk, and his shoes are black mirrors. This is his first day. So far he's been shown a series of corporate induction videos, one of which contained glowing buzzwords like TEAMWORK and BEST PRACTICE rocketing at the screen, and another of which featured actors from the late 1980s talking about customer service. Now he is waiting for someone from the Training Sales department to come and collect him.

He accidentally catches the eye of the receptionist for about the fourteenth time and they both smile and look away. The receptionist is GRETEL MONADNOCK, according to her nameplate; she's quite young, has long lustrous brown hair, and sits on the right side of the desk. On the left a nameplate says EVE JANTISS, but Eve herself is absent. Stephen Jones is a little disappointed about this, because while Gretel is nice, when he was here for his job interview and first saw Eve, he almost dropped his brand-new briefcase. It would be an exaggeration to say he took a job at Zephyr because of the beauty of its receptionist, but during his interview he was very enthusiastic.

He looks at his watch. It is eleven o'clock. His videos finished twenty minutes ago. He folds his hands back in his lap.

"I'll try them again," Gretel says. She smiles sympathetically. "Ah . . . sorry, it's going to voice mail again."

"Oh. Maybe something urgent came up."

"Ye-e-e-s." She seems unsure if he is joking. "Probably."

"The thing you have to remember," Roger says, "is that it's all about respect." Roger has one elbow on Freddy's cubicle partition wall, his lean frame blocking the entrance. "The donut itself is irrelevant. It's the lack of respect the theft implies."

Freddy's phone trills. He looks at the caller-ID screen: RECEPTION. "Roger, please, I have to pick up the new grad. They keep calling."

"Just a moment. This is important." Roger knows Freddy will wait. Freddy has been a sales assistant for five years. He is quick-witted, inventive, and full of ideas, so long as that's okay with everybody else. Freddy is a participant. A member. He is happiest when he's blending in with a crowd. In any group of people, the one you can't remember is Freddy. He has wriggled so far inside Zephyr Holdings that Roger sometimes has difficulty telling where the company ends and Freddy begins. "I'm explaining why I want you to go to Catering and find out exactly how many donuts they gave us."

Desperation enters Freddy's eyes. "If I get this new grad, he can do it. He's your assistant."

Roger ponders this for a moment. "He may not appreciate the need to treat a situation like this delicately." This means: *Keep it from Elizabeth and Holly.*

"I'll tell him. Please, Roger, you're getting me in trouble with reception."

"All right. All right." Roger holds up his palms in surrender. "Go get your graduate, then."

"*Your* graduate."

Roger looks at him sharply. But Freddy is not being disrespectful, Roger realizes; Freddy is just being accurate. "Yes, yes. That's what I meant."

Stephen Jones ignores the *ding* of the elevator, because it has dinged plenty of times over the last twenty-five minutes, and none of those ended with him meeting new coworkers. To stretch his legs, he has taken to wandering around the lobby and reading the plaques and framed photos. The biggest of the lot is a huge, gleaming thing complete with its own light and glass case.

MISSION STATEMENT

Zephyr Holdings aims to build and consolidate leadership positions in its chosen markets, forging profitable growth opportunities by developing strong relationships between internal and external business units and coordinating a strategic, consolidated approach to achieve maximum returns for its stakeholders.

This isn't the dullest thing Stephen Jones has ever read, but it's close. Oddly, it makes no mention of training packages, the selling of which is, as he understands it, Zephyr's main purpose. Then he realizes that a short man with dark hair and glasses is standing a few feet away, staring at him. "Jones?"

"Yes!"

The man's eyes flick over Jones's new suit. One of his hands wanders down to where his own shirt is stuffed awkwardly into his pants and tries to fix it. "I'm Freddy. Nice to meet you." He extends his free hand, and they shake. Freddy's watery blue eyes look huge behind his glasses. "You're younger than I thought you'd be."

"Okay," Jones says.

Freddy looks at his shoes. Then he glances at the reception desk, at—if Jones is not mistaken—the empty chair behind the EVE JANTISS nameplate. "Do you smoke?"

"No."

"I do." He says it apologetically. "This way."

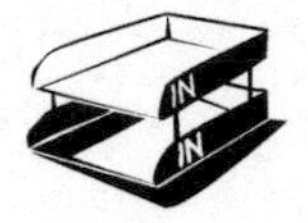

"It's a good department." Freddy sucks at his cigarette. It is a fine day: the clouds are high, there is a light breeze, and the gray Zephyr tower even seems to be emitting reflected warmth from the grid of tinted windows. Freddy's eyes follow a blue convertible inching toward them through traffic, then jump to Jones. "I mean, once you get used to things."

"I'm ready for a steep learning curve," Jones says, employing a phrase that came in handy during his job interviews.

"You're Roger's sales assistant. You have to process his orders, type up his quotes, file his expense forms, that kind of thing."

"What's he like?"

"Roger? Oh . . . nice." Freddy's eyes shift.

"Ah," Jones says. "So . . . he's not?"

Freddy glances around. "No. Sorry."

Jones snickers. "Well, I don't plan on being a sales assistant forever."

Freddy says nothing. Jones realizes that Freddy has probably been a sales assistant forever. "Roger's got a job for you, actually. He wants you to ask Catering how many donuts they gave our department this morning." In response to Jones's expression, he hurries on: "See, we get morning snacks; some days it's fruit, some days cookies, and occasionally, *rarely*, donuts. This morning there was an incident."

"Okay. Sure thing." Jones nods. This may not be a glamorous assignment, or make much sense, but it is his first task in the real business world, and by God, he's going to perform it well. "So where's Catering?"

Freddy doesn't answer. Jones follows his gaze until it intersects a midnight blue Audi sports car entering the Zephyr lot. The bulk of Zephyr's parking is subterranean, but there are a few valuable ground-level spaces, and the Audi slides confidently into one of these. The driver's door pops open and a pair of legs climb out. After a moment, Jones registers that the legs are attached to something. The something is Eve Jantiss.

She looks as if she is just stopping off at Zephyr on the way to an exclusive nightclub opening. Her hair, long, tousled, and honey-brown, bounces off exposed tan shoulders. Two delicate straps appear to play no functional role in suspending a thin, shimmering plum-colored dress; more mysterious forces are at work. She has lips like big sofa cushions, the kind of ancestry that probably includes nationalities Jones has never heard of, and liquid brown eyes that say: *Sex? Why, what an intriguing idea.* In the nights between his job interview and now, Jones has occasionally wondered if he wasn't building Eve Jantiss up in his head, remembering her as more attractive than she really is. Now he realizes: no.

"Morning," she says, clacking past on high heels. "Hi," Jones says, and Freddy says something like, "Muh." Jones turns and sees Freddy practically dribbling love. Freddy's gaze is fixed on the back of Eve's head, not flicking up and down her body. Jones feels suddenly sordid. He was checking her out: Freddy's infatuation is pure.

When the sliding doors block their vision of Eve, or at least tint it, Jones says, "The receptionist has a sports car?"

"What?" Freddy says. "You think she doesn't deserve it?"

Jones's business shoes squeak as he and Freddy cross the lobby. It sounds as if he is conducting a mouse orchestra, and he feels the eyes of the two receptionists, Eve and Gretel, swing onto him. "That's him," Gretel says to Eve. "His name is Jones."

"Ah." Eve smiles. "Welcome to the *Titanic,* Jones."

Corporate humor! Jones has heard about this. He would like to respond in kind, but is too self-conscious about his shoes. He settles for: "Thanks."

They reach the bank of elevators at the lobby's rear and Freddy pushes for UP. "People say she's Daniel Klausman's mistress." Klausman is the Zephyr CEO. "But that's just because she's hardly ever in reception."

Jones blinks. "Where does she go?"

"I don't know. But she's *not* his mistress. She's not like that." The elevator doors slide closed. "So anyway, Catering's on level 17. When you're done, come on up to 14."

"You mean come *down* to 14," Jones says, but even as the words come out, he sees the button panel. The floors are numbered top down: level 1 is at the panel's apex, marked CEO, while level 20, LOBBY, is at the bottom.

Freddy snickers. "Reverse numbering. It throws everyone at first. But you get used to it."

"Okay." Jones watches the numbers click over—20... 19... 18—while his body tells him he's rising. It feels unnatural.

"They say it's motivational," Freddy says. "As you move into more important departments, you rise up the rankings."

Jones looks at the button panel. "What's so bad about IT?"

"Please," Freddy says. "Some of them don't even wear suits."

On level 14, Elizabeth is falling in love. This is what makes her such a good sales rep, and an emotional basket case: she falls in love with her customers. It is hard to convey just how wretchedly, boot-lickingly draining it is to be a salesperson. Sales is a business of relationships, and you must cultivate customers with tenderness and love, like cabbages in winter, even if the customer is an egomaniacal asshole you want to hit with a shovel. There is something wrong with the kind of person who becomes a sales rep, or if not, there is something wrong after six months.

Elizabeth doesn't rely on the usual facades of friendship and illusions of intimacy: she forms actual attachments.

For Elizabeth, each new lead is a handsome stranger in a nightclub. When they dance, she grows giddy with the rush of possibilities. If he doesn't like her product offering, she dies. If he talks about sizable orders, she feels the urge to move in with him.

Elizabeth's love affairs are purely internal: no one else knows about them. But they're real enough to her, which is why she's so stressed: she's currently involved in eighteen long-term, on-off, hand-wringing relationships and last Thursday she spied somebody new across a crowded meeting room.

On the phone now, her customer is trying to scale back an order. Last week she sold him two hundred staff hours of training, but now he's trying to backpedal. As she sits in her cubicle, her back to the other two sales reps, the phone growing slippery in her hand, Elizabeth bites down on her lip. *Why can't he commit?* she wails. *What's wrong with me?*

"It's no biggie, Liz," the customer says. "I just checked our schedule and found we don't need to do so much at once. We'll take the package, we just need to scale back the numbers."

"But we talked about two hundred hours. That's what I thought we were talking about."

"We were, Liz. I'm just changing my mind."

"I..." Elizabeth's throat thickens. She fights to keep her voice steady. Men don't like clingy, needy women; she read that in one of the relationship books she owns that double as sales manuals. Men like to be challenged, so long as—so long as!—you never show disrespect. You have to set the challenge and at the same time imply that he is up to it. "But Bob, we had a commitment. You're not one of those guys who makes promises he can't keep. You're my rock. I love that about you. I *rely* on that with you. You know what I'm talking about."

A sigh from the phone. Elizabeth's heart leaps. "Okay, okay. We'll keep it at two hundred hours. But it's really more than I need, Liz."

"I appreciate that, Bob. You're a wonder."

"Well, you've always been good to me..." Elizabeth feels herself tuning out. Bob is under control. Bob is becoming less interesting by the second. Her thoughts drift to the man she saw in the meeting room. He was short and overweight; from the look of his shirt's armpits, he has some kind of sweat problem. She bites her lip, dreaming. She wonders if he is interested in some training.

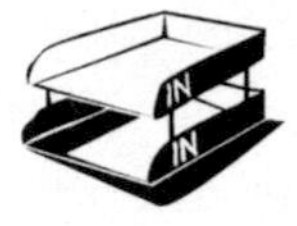

Training Sales has eight staff: three sales reps, three assistants, a manager, and a personal assistant. Each rep has a sales assistant. Elizabeth has Holly, who is a young, athletic blonde renowned throughout several floors for her obsession with the company gym and lack of any detectable sense of humor. Roger has, or is about to get, Jones. The third rep is Wendell, a large man who drives the rest of the department crazy by clearing his throat before he says anything, plus when they least expect it.

Like every other department in Zephyr, Training Sales has an open floor plan, which means everyone works in a sprawling cubicle farm except the manager, who has an office with a glass internal wall, across which blinds are permanently drawn. Open-plan seating, it has been explained in company-wide memos, increases teamwork and boosts productivity. Except in managers, that is, whose productivity tends to be boosted by—and the memos don't say this, but the conclusion is inescapable—corner offices with excellent views.

The Training Sales cubicle farm is bisected by an eight-foot-high divider with sales reps on one side and sales assistants on the other. To the untrained eye the two halves are identical, but to those in the know, the rep side has a subtle, fluorescent glow. That glow is status. The residents of the rep side possess much better numbers: they have six-figure salaries, seven-figure quotas, and single-digit golf handicaps.

During the last office relocation, a plan was mooted to seat each rep beside his or her assistant, in the interests of efficiency. Fierce lobbying led by Elizabeth and Wendell dismantled this proposal within a day. So the assistants get a lot of exercise. They call the cubicle divider the Berlin Partition.

Wendell stops at Roger's desk, folds his arms, and lets out the little barking cough that signifies he is about to speak.

"Roger. It pains me to raise this, but you've parked in my space again."

Roger holds up a finger. He is on the phone to Catering, waiting for a transfer to the Snacks and Desserts division. But it would be unwise to let Wendell, a fellow sales rep, know this, so Roger tells the phone, "I recommend the complete package, which gives you all the benefits at lower total cost of ownership. Yes... of course. Excellent. I'll put that through immediately." He hangs up. Wendell towers above him, blocking out the fluorescent lighting. "What?"

"Your car. Despite our previous conversations, it is yet again occupying my space."

Roger pinches the bridge of his nose. "Wendell, there is no allocated car parking on the second subfloor. It's first in, best dressed. You don't have an allocated car space. None of us do."

Wendell reaches into his jacket pocket. *"Hak-kah."* This is Wendell clearing his throat. "So you said last time. I have, however, taken the liberty of contacting Infrastructure Management for a parking plan. If I may direct your attention to this particular space *here,* the one your vehicle is currently occupying, you'll see it's marked TRAINING SALES DEPARTMENT—SR 2. That, Roger, is me. You have the next space along." He stabs the paper, at a space five feet farther from the elevator.

Roger waves the plan away. He has been a sales rep just six weeks; previously he was a customer. But he is terrifically talented, which makes Wendell nervous. Roger is too confident, his dark brown eyes too piercing. His hair is obviously executive material. Lately Wendell has been working ninety extra minutes a day and skipping lunch. Elizabeth has been affected, too; she's now constantly out on sales calls. But this is because being close to Roger makes her want to strangle him with his tie. "Infrastructure Management doesn't have the authority to appoint individual car spaces. It's up to each departmental manager. In our case, Sydney hasn't announced a system, so it's laissez-faire."

Wendell hesitates, unsure exactly how the balance of power works between Infrastructure Management and departmental managers. "In the absence of a decision from Sydney, we'd default to Infrastructure Management's allocation, surely."

"If you want to argue that, take it up with Sydney," Roger says. "Until then, it's laissez-faire."

"If it's *laissez-faire*," Wendell says, his voice rising, "*why do you always park in the same spot?* You never take Sydney's or Elizabeth's space. Everybody parks in the same spot every day, except *you always take mine.*"

"That's just coincidence." Roger allows this absurdity to hang in the air for a moment. "But I tell you what. I'll try not to park in quote your unquote space if you tell me why you took my donut."

"I didn't take your damn donut! Don't change the subject."

"Did you think it was some kind of revenge? Really, I'm just curious."

"I have no idea what happened to your donut, Roger, and I'm not going to discuss it. Just stay out of my parking space. Or I *will* go to Sydney." Wendell storms off to his desk, which is the next one along and shares a low wall with Roger's. When they're both seated, they stare at each other over the top of their docked notebook computers, their teamwork and productivity—if you believe the memos—steadily increasing.

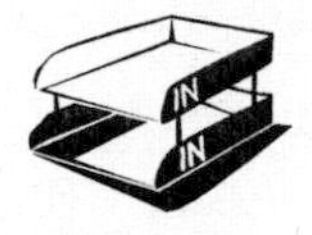

Jones walks down the orange-and-black carpeted corridor and pushes through the glass doors to Training Sales. He stops and looks around his new corporate home: at the cubicles, the Berlin Partition, the framed motivational posters (IT'S NOT HOW LONG YOU WORK, IT'S HOW SMART), the coffee machine, the complete absence of natural light. He spots Freddy, who gestures to the other side of the Partition (the rich side, West Berlin). Jones follows directions. Three people are there, all on the phone and none paying him any attention. He peers at their nameplates until he finds ROGER JEFFERSON, then waits by his desk. Roger says to his phone, "But I can't get the forms to Order Processing until they're approved by Legal. Well, you tell that to Credit. Until they release the hold, Marketing won't sign off." He frowns at Jones. "What do you want?"

Jones points to his ID tag. "Hi! I'm your new grad."

Roger tells his phone, "Hold on a second." He covers the mouthpiece. "Six or seven?"

"Six or seven wha—" Jones realizes. "The Catering department says Training Sales got seven donuts this morning."

"Are you sure?"

Jones is sure. Catering had a formal snack delivery

process, complete with charts. Next to TRAINING SALES DEPARTMENT was a 7 and a tick. They stood behind their chart. Jones felt awkward questioning them, because of the chart and because they were cleaning out the whole area in preparation for being outsourced, and Jones was holding them up to discuss donut numbers.

"Okay. Good work." Roger uncovers his phone. "Now, look, we can go to Human Resources to resolve this if you want. Is that what you want?"

Jones realizes he's been dismissed. He walks back to East Berlin, where Freddy and a girl with alarmingly toned arms poking out of a summer dress have wheeled their office chairs into the aisle between their cubicles. "Here he is," Freddy says. "Jones, this is Holly. She's Elizabeth's assistant."

As she and Jones shake hands, Holly says, "Is it true, you went to Catering?"

"Catering called Sydney and complained you were badgering them," Freddy explains. "Now she's mad."

Jones lets go of Holly's hand. "What? I just did what I was told."

"The Nuremberg defense," Holly says. "That's what Roger's *last* assistant said."

"Poor Jim," Freddy says. "I was just starting to like him, too."

"I'd better go see Sydney." Jones looks around for her office.

Freddy laughs. Then he realizes Jones is serious. "Jones, you don't *go see* Sydney."

"Why not?"

Freddy looks lost for words. He turns to Holly.

"You just don't," she says.

Jones spies an office at the far end of the cubicle farm. "Is she in there?"

Freddy and Holly exchange a glance. "Yes, but seriously—"

"I'll be back in a minute." Jones walks between Freddy and Holly, who wheel their office chairs apart to make way for him. Sydney's office is guarded by a large woman behind a tiny desk: Megan, the department PA. Megan, Jones sees, collects ceramic bears. She has bears dressed to go fishing, bears with T-shirts that say I LOVE YOU, bears with hard hats, and bears with Wellington boots. There are dozens of them, as if Megan's desk was the stage for an all-bear musical. An in-box is perched precariously on one corner, with several bears leaning against it as if they are trying to shove it off.

Sydney's door is closed. Jones tries to peer through the little square of glass set into it. "Can I . . . ?"

Megan stares mutely at him through brown glasses. Later Jones will realize that the only reason that Megan does not leap out of her chair and tackle him to the ground at this point is that she cannot believe he is actually going to walk straight into Sydney's office. He starts to turn the door handle, and by the time she realizes what he's doing, he's inside and gently closing the door.

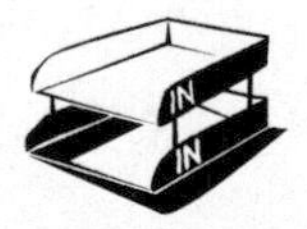

Wendell's and Elizabeth's heads appear above the Berlin Partition. Wendell says, "Did that person just go into Sydney's office?"

"He's new," Freddy says weakly. "That's our new grad. He doesn't know."

Nobody says anything for a moment. Megan's shocked face turns from Sydney's door to the other employees, then back.

"Well," Holly says, "he's gutsy."

"He's dead." Freddy sighs. "He didn't even have time to set up his voice mail."

"Pity," Elizabeth says. "He's cute."

"I *know,*" Holly says.

"What's his name?"

"Jones."

"Just Jones? What, like Madonna?"

"That's what his ID tag says."

"Intriguing," Elizabeth says.

"He's so young," Freddy says. "How can he know anything?"

"*Haaak-kah.* Clearly, he doesn't. He just walked into Sydney's office without an appointment."

"Hmm. Maybe the rumors are true," Elizabeth says.

They look at her. Freddy says, "What rumors?"

"Well... I'm not saying I believe it, but... some people say the company is running a secret project. On level 13."

Wendell snorts. There is no level 13: the elevator button after 12 is 14. But it is an old Zephyr joke that it takes a suspiciously long time to travel between those two floors.

"According to the rumors..." Elizabeth lowers her voice, "Human Resources is secretly scraping skin cells from successful sales reps and breeding clones in vats, to be released through the intern program."

Freddy and Holly crack up. Wendell rolls his eyes. "I have work to do." His head drops below the Berlin Partition.

"Don't take my word for it," Elizabeth says. "Check if Jones has a belly button."

"Mmm," Holly says. "Maybe I will."

"Better hurry," Freddy says.

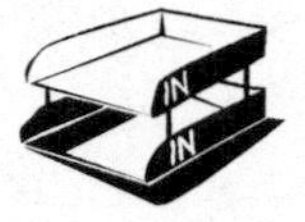

There's a small *clack* and Sydney's door swings open. It's as if the Training Sales employees' heads are connected to it by invisible strings: they all jerk around at the same time. Seven sets of eyes watch Jones walk all the way to his desk and sit down.

Freddy holds out for as long as he can. "Well?"

"Hmm? What?"

"What happened?"

"Oh. We talked. I think we got it straightened out." Jones shrugs. "She was kind of busy. Most of the time she was on the phone."

"You mean—" Holly starts, but Freddy cuts in: "To who?"

"Uh... somebody Seddon?"

Freddy rocks back in his chair. "Blake Seddon is in *Senior Management.*"

"So?" Jones is too new to Zephyr Holdings to see that a squall is developing here. The building is hermetically sealed, but Zephyr has its own weather: last Friday there was a high-pressure center over the telephone sales room; tomorrow a cold front of layoffs is predicted to sweep down from level 2. Right now a blustery rumor is gathering strength in the cubicle farm.

"Someone's getting fired," Freddy says.

Holly says, "You don't know that."

"Or maybe this is it. Outsourcing."

"They can't outsource us! Who would sell training?"

"Maybe Zephyr is getting out of training."

"That's crazy," Holly says, but her voice wavers. Holly is well protected from layoffs because Elizabeth is unsackable. But outsourcing, the nuclear bomb of Human Resources' arsenal, would spare no one. "If there was no training..." Holly trails off, unable to express the horrors of a world without training.

Freddy jumps out of his chair and heads for Megan, the PA. She confirms that Sydney has been exchanging calls with Senior Management, but refuses to tell him any details. This is because she doesn't know anything, but Megan sits away from everyone else in Training Sales and is lonely, so she drops hints that she's holding something back in order to encourage future visits.

"Megan knows something, but she's not telling," Freddy says grimly, walking through East Berlin without stopping. The turbulence from his passage causes a paper on Jones's desk to slide off, but in meteorological terms, Freddy is tearing up the carpet, pulling computers off desks, sending chairs spinning in a tornado.

"Who's getting fired?" Freddy asks Wendell in West Berlin, point-blank.

"What?" Wendell says, irritated. He was on zero points in hearts with Pauline about to go over the top, and had to close the program to stop Freddy from seeing it.

"Sydney's been on the phone to upstairs. It's about cost cutting, isn't it? Someone's getting canned."

"Sydney's talking to upstairs?"

"That's what Megan says."

"Well, that could mean anything. Don't jump to conclusions. *Hak-kah.*"

"Hey, guys," Elizabeth calls across the aisle. "Are you having trouble with the network? I just e-mailed Wendell and it bounced back."

"Haven't checked," Roger says, not looking up.

"What was your e-mail?" Wendell says.

"I'm selling raffle tickets for the Social Club. Want to buy some? You can win a set of golf clubs." Her eyebrows rise hopefully.

"Oh." Wendell's eyes lose focus. "I'll, *hak-kah,* consider that when I get your e-mail."

"They're only a dollar each," Elizabeth says, rolling closer. "And there are many secondary prizes. Want to see?"

"I'm busy right now, Elizabeth."

"Oh. Okay. Maybe later then." She rolls back to her computer.

Freddy says, "So you haven't heard anything?"

"No. Why, have the others?" Wendell looks at Roger and Elizabeth fearfully.

"I haven't asked."

"Leave it with me. I'll find out what's going on."

"Thanks." Freddy knows he can trust him. Wendell relies on Freddy to translate his outrageous expense claims into language acceptable to Central Accounting, a rare and valuable skill. Elizabeth and Roger are insanely jealous of Wendell in this regard. This year alone he has been compensated for parking fines, dozens of lunches, and a new suit, while Elizabeth's request for a new office chair was denied, forcing her to steal one late at night from Call Center.

Freddy heads out of West Berlin. Roger smiles at him as he passes by, which is so out of character that Freddy gets the heebie-jeebies. Roger is in the process of dialing someone, but he waits, his finger hovering above the number pad, until Freddy is gone.

"What's the story?" Holly asks.

"Nobody knows. Do you think we'd hear about it if we were being outsourced?"

"No idea... no one who's been outsourced has survived to talk about it."

Jones says, "Why would someone be sacked? You just hired me."

Freddy looks at him sympathetically. "You really don't understand this company."

"There's a hiring freeze," Holly explains. "Technically, we haven't hired you. We got you through the back door. See, toward the end of each financial year, Senior Management realizes we're going over budget, so they impose a hiring freeze. If an employee leaves, everyone else has to pick up their workload."

"Did you have spare time before?" Jones asks, lost.

Freddy laughs so hard that his nose touches his keyboard.

"This went on year after year, but the departments all realized they had to do their hiring before the freeze, so everyone was packing a year's worth of spending into the first six months. And that made Senior Management order the freeze *earlier.* Then about eighteen months ago, it became permanent."

"Permanent?"

"Well, they can't lift it now," Freddy says. "Every department would start hiring like crazy. We used to have eight reps and eight assistants."

"Also," Holly says, "Zephyr needs to show it's serious about cost cutting. If we started hiring people again now, our stock price would tumble. Further, I mean."

"Well, that's what they *say.* In my opinion, it's just an excuse to shovel work onto us guys in the trenches while Senior Management gets bonuses for meeting cost-reduction targets. Not to mention the golden handcuffs. You know about golden handcuffs?"

Jones nods. "Sure, the bonus an executive gets when he leaves the company."

"No, no, that's a golden parachute."

"Oh—right. The signing bonus, then."

"That's the golden handshake. Golden handcuffs are what they get for working in a company with low morale. First they screw up the company, then because it's hard to attract good staff, they pay themselves more."

"But that's wrong!" Jones says, shocked. "Did somebody take this up with Daniel Klausman?"

Freddy cracks up again. Even Holly smiles. "Remember when you first started here, Freddy, and you thought everyone was clever and helpful and only wanted to do what's best for the company?"

"Yeah. I used to shine my shoes."

Jones says, "So with this freeze, how did you hire me?"

"It was Freddy's idea. We process your salary as office expenses. Copy paper, specifically."

"That reminds me," Freddy says to Holly, "do you have to xerox all of Elizabeth's orders? Because the paper in that machine has to last until January."

"*We* probably won't last until January. I might as well xerox while I can."

"I'm *copy paper?*" Jones says.

"Don't worry, it's just a paperwork thing. It doesn't affect anything. Well, unless they cut our stationery budget. But there's nothing to sweat about, this is just a little creative accounting. It goes on all the time."

A wave of red light sweeps through the department. For a second Jones thinks he's fainting. Then he thinks the building has lost power and the emergency lights have kicked in. But it's the phones: all their voice-mail lights are suddenly blinking.

"Argh." Freddy picks up his phone. "I hate it when they do that." He tucks it under his ear. "All-staff voice mail. There should be instructions on your phone, Jones."

There are. Jones engages in a brief struggle with the voice-mail menu and comes out of it victorious.

"Click. Hi, it's Megan. Sydney asked me to pass this out. Click. Megan, this is Sydney. There's a message following from the CEO. Copy it to everyone, thanks. Click. Good morning, it's Janice... message following. Click. Hi, Janice... there's a message following this from Daniel Klausman. Please see that it gets out. Thanks. Click. Hello everyone, this is Meredith from Daniel Klausman's office. Please distribute the following message to all staff. Click."

A dramatic pause. Then: "Meredith, this is Daniel

Klausman. Please send this on to my department heads for distribution to all headcounts."

Jones blinks in surprise. He doesn't think it's a terrific idea for the CEO to call his staff "headcounts." That's not what they taught at business school. Jones feels a touch of excitement at spotting the mistake, like a chess prodigy who finds a flaw in Kasparov. He begins a few wild thoughts with: *If I was CEO*... These distract Jones from observing that it may not be a terrific idea to be employed by a CEO who calls his staff "headcounts," either.

"Good afternoon everyone. I hope you've had a positive start to the week and kicked a few goals for Zephyr. Today I want to address the recent movement in our share price. It's important for everyone to understand there's no need for panic. Share prices often rise and fall for reasons unrelated to a company's performance. The market can overreact to these changes and turn small swings into large ones. No one upstairs is panicking."

Jones nods to himself. He hasn't been at Zephyr Holdings long enough to realize that it's always a market overreaction to unrelated events when the stock price goes down. When it goes up, it's due to the brilliance of management, and rewarded with stock options.

"That said, dropping 18 percent in a quarter isn't great news. If we're to remain competitive, every department must continue cost cutting. It's essential that we strip out the fat, focus on our core competencies, and tighten our belts. If we do this, and stick to our guns, I'm confident we can avoid significant retrenchments.

"That's it for now. I won't keep you from your work any longer."

Freddy and Holly hang up together. "Ouch," Freddy says.

"That can't affect us," Holly says.

"He said every department."

"But there won't be sackings. No 'significant' retrenchments."

"It's significant if it happens to you," Freddy says.

Friday and Jones is heading into the bathroom when he bumps into Wendell. Jones is busting, because for the first time in his life there's free coffee available from a machine six yards away. It's four o'clock and he's had six coffees. The rest of the department is quickly learning that the best time to get a coffee is right after Jones, who doesn't mind replacing the filter.

He pulls open the bathroom's exterior door just as Wendell opens the interior one, so they face off in the tiny airlock, each with one hand on a door. Jones steps back to let Wendell pass, but Wendell doesn't move. *"Hak-kah."* He glances around. "Jones, you don't know what Roger's up to with this donut business, do you?"

"No." Jones can't help but notice that Wendell's hands are dry. He didn't hear the air blower.

"I haven't the foggiest idea who took his donut. But he's gotten it into his head that I'm somehow involved. He thinks I want to get back at him for taking my parking space."

"Okay."

"I've booked twelve hundred hours of training this month. That's more than Elizabeth. Roger's only got four hundred. If anyone should be nervous about getting fired, it should be him."

"Yeah, I guess."

Wendell fingers the door handle. "So if you hear anything, let me know, will you?"

"Sure."

"Thank you, Jones. I appreciate it." He puts a hand on Jones's forearm as he passes.

When Jones returns to his desk, his bladder relieved and his forearm washed and blow-dried, Freddy sidles over. "Did you hear? Sydney's called a meeting. To discuss 'organizational changes.' " He adjusts his glasses. "Look, if it's you . . . remember, it's nothing personal."

"*What?* Why would I be fired?"

Holly looks across the low divider. "Jones is getting fired?"

"No, *if.* I'm saying if Sydney's sacking someone, it's going to be Jones. You know, last in, first out."

"There's a *last-in, first-out policy?*"

"No," Holly says.

Freddy pats Jones on the arm. It is the most awkward thing Jones has ever seen. "She probably won't sack anybody," Freddy says, but this is clearly just for Jones's benefit.

Sydney, the Training Sales manager, enters the meeting room at two minutes past five. She is tiny. She has bright green eyes, little pixie features, and a nose like the Easter Bunny's. She surely cannot weigh more than thirty or forty pounds, and that's including her tailored business suit. Her hair is a neat blond bob. When she speaks, her voice is high and strained. When you see her, you want to pick her up and hug the adorable little thing tight.

But this would be a bad idea, because Sydney is a vicious bitch. You don't get to be manager of a sales department by the cuteness of your nose. Manager of marketing, yes; sales, no. In sales, you can't hide behind glossy brochures and manipulated reach figures. You either sell or you don't, and your performance is on display so everyone can tell which it is. To succeed in sales, you need skills—not skills entirely consistent with moral integrity and emotional well-being, but skills nevertheless. You must be able to sell things to people who don't want them. You must be able to sell more things to people who do want them than they need. And most important of all, you must be able to cajole your way into a lower quota and more gullible customers than your co-workers.

When she was a mere sales assistant, Sydney was an amusing oddity. When her elfin eyes narrowed, her little nose wrinkled, and her tiny mouth raged, people suppressed smiles. Her rants about people who failed to take her seriously were funny; you couldn't take them seriously. Then she was promoted to sales rep, which meant she couldn't be ignored anymore. That was less amusing. Sydney was bitter about pretty much everyone; there was nobody, it seemed, who had not done her wrong. The Training

Sales team suspects that a bitter incident lurks in Sydney's past, something involving faster-developing girls in the high-school locker room—or a series of incidents. If Sydney was male, they are sure that she would have a home gym and biceps the size of small children.

How she became manager remains a mystery. But there are only two possibilities. One is that Senior Management mistook her tirades for drive and a commitment to excellence. The other is that they knew Sydney was a paranoid psychopath, and that's exactly the kind of person they want in management.

Except for Sydney's office, the meeting room is the only place in the department with an exterior glass wall. At this time of the day, the sun streams in, bathing the room in delightful yellow warmth or fiery, retina-stabbing arrows, depending on which side of the table you sit. So the assistants are shielding their eyes while the sales reps quietly warm their backs. Except for Wendell: Wendell is nowhere to be seen.

Sydney takes a seat at the head of the table, which has been left for her. Not even Jones, new to these meetings, was foolish enough to drop himself into that seat. Today she is dressed from head to toe in black: black pants, black high-collared shirt, and black high heels tapering to a dangerous-looking point. Sydney has a variety of outfits, and they range in color from charcoal to jet. Freddy, the oldest surviving member of Training Sales, swears that one day she showed up in a gray knit, but nobody believes him.

Sydney's green eyes flick about the table. "How is everyone?"

"Great." Nobody mentions Wendell.

Sydney has papers. She smooths them as if they are very important, as if they are the bearers of great and terrible wisdom. "You all know the company is still cost cutting. Every department has to make more savings. And, well, I've looked at the alternatives. . . ." She shrugs. These alternatives clearly didn't impress her. "I'm dropping another headcount."

A low moan escapes from Jones. Elizabeth and Roger remain calm, at least outwardly. Megan, the department PA, is surprised; she had no idea anyone was getting sacked. Holly and Freddy glance at Wendell's empty chair.

Sydney says, "So that's that. It's always difficult for the rest when one person goes, but we just have to come together to make an even tighter team. Does anyone have anything else?"

There is silence. Megan, thinking she is the only ignorant one, says, "Sorry, who's been fired?"

"Oh. Wendell."

There is a collective exhalation like a punctured mattress—except from Freddy, who sucks in air. "But Wendell's the best-performing rep!"

Sydney's pixie features focus on him. Freddy involuntarily leans back in his chair. "Wendell's performance this month has been excellent, yes. His results should be a benchmark for you all. But it came to my attention that he was involved in some irregularities concerning morning snacks. There's no need to go into details. But I want to make this clear: I won't tolerate selfishness. This is a team. We pull together or we don't go anywhere. Is that clear?"

The team mumbles assent. "Absolutely," Roger says.

"Also," Sydney says, straightening her papers, "the commissions on all those orders of Wendell's would have put us way over budget."

Megan says, "Oh, I didn't know we cancel the commissions of reps who get fired." Everybody freezes. Megan has no idea how the department works, so occasionally comes out with something like this, which no one with a modicum of political knowledge would dare say out loud.

Sydney's eyes flick around the room. "That's . . . no, of course we don't. If a rep books an order, and we take the revenue, then obviously he's earned . . . look, you don't understand the technicalities. My point is that this is a *team.* And what's important is what's good for the team. Everybody should understand that already. Can you please stop interrupting the meeting, Megan?"

Megan reddens. "Sorry."

"Thank you." Sydney looks down at her papers. "Rather than distribute Wendell's accounts to Elizabeth and Roger, I've decided to promote a sales assistant." She corrects herself. "I mean, an assistant will look after his accounts. It's not an actual promotion. It's only until the hiring freeze is lifted."

Freddy sucks in his breath. If this was his first or second year in Training Sales, he would scorn such an offer, which obviously involves doing Wendell's job at a third of the salary, without commissions, and acting as his own assistant. But this is Freddy's fifth year, and he's desperate for vertical movement.

"And that person will be Jones," Sydney says. "Congratulate Jones, everyone, please."

Freddy makes a choking sound. The team claps. Elizabeth says, "Ah, excuse me—nothing personal, Jones—

but . . . Jones? Freddy knows those accounts, he's worked on them with Wendell for years."

"Well, maybe if Freddy was a little more proactive, like Jones, I would have considered him," Sydney says. "Frankly, Freddy can learn a lot from Jones, like how to come straight to me when he has an issue." Her eyes jump from one person to the next, daring them to argue, and nobody mentions the meeting two months ago when Sydney threatened to demote the next person to disturb her with trivia. "Freddy, you'll help Jones find his feet with those accounts."

Freddy says something like, *"Okay."*

"Good. Teamwork. That's what it's all about. Teamwork." She stands. "That's it."

Roger coughs into his hand.

"Oh," Sydney says. "Also, Roger gets Wendell's parking space."

Catering lugs equipment out through the lobby. Ovens, crockery, employees—everything must go. Gretel, the company receptionist, sits behind her orange desk and sniffles. The Catering staff are touched. They feel better about being fired—and although it's called "outsourcing," it's a sacking at heart; it's all various shades of dismissal—knowing they'll be missed, even if only by a receptionist. It is a terrible thing to be fired, like your parents saying you have to clean out your room and leave the family, and it's worse if the company happily continues on in your absence, not even noticing the difference. This is like passing your ex-family in the street and they're laughing and heading out to the movies. What you really want, following your sacking, is for the company to undergo a quick, public financial implosion directly traceable to your departure. But as a substitute, someone crying as you leave the building is pretty good.

"Come on, now," one of the Catering men says. "We'll be back tomorrow, running deliveries. We just don't work in the building anymore."

Gretel shakes her head, inconsolable. The Catering staff, or ex-staff, exchange sad, bemused smiles. They load their equipment onto the truck idling outside the lobby doors, and stand around, hands in pockets, as it drives off. There is a special truck for the equipment because it has been purchased by the company that won the bid to supply Zephyr; there is no special truck for the employees. They watch the truck until it vanishes into the traffic of Madison Street. Then they shake hands, hug each other, and head to their own cars. One of them ducks back into the lobby to say a final farewell to Gretel. "See you tomorrow, darling."

"No, no," she says. She knows she will never see them again.

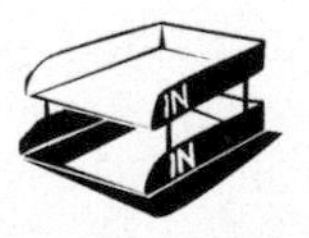

The following Monday, Jones arrives early, parks his clunker in the depths of the Zephyr employee lot, and heads to the local Barnes and Noble to browse the business section. He is looking for something called *The Omega Management System*, which is the latest management fad in a tradition stretching back through Six Sigma and Total Quality Management to the practice of bleeding sick patients and investing in tulips. OMS is very big lately; Jones even spotted a copy in Sydney's office. So as a method of providing visible evidence that he is an up-and-comer with management potential, Jones thinks he could do worse than an OMS book. And if he actually learns something, too, well, that's a bonus.

There turns out to be not just one book but three shelves of them. Jones sorts through the abridgments, revised editions, and fictionalizations until he finds one "For the New Executive," heads for the in-store café, and orders a latte. He is flipping through the book when a girl behind the counter catches his eye. She smiles at him and tucks a wisp of blond hair behind her ear. Jones sits up straighter. The girl serves a customer, but now Jones is completely distracted. When the line empties ten minutes later, he drains his coffee and strides up to the counter. The girl smiles at him. "Hi there."

"Hi." He hands over his book. She is very pretty.

"You looked like you were studying pretty hard over there."

She *was* watching him! Jones wonders if it's the suit. This sort of thing never happened to him before he bought a tie. "I just started a new job. I have to practice looking like I'm working."

She laughs. "Well, you were very convincing." She zaps his book with her wand and checks out the cover. "*The Omega Management System: Road-Tested Methods to Transform Corporate Duds into Superstars.* Which are you?"

"A dud. But an ambitious one."

"Ambition, huh? I could do with some of that." She cracks the book open at random. " 'Companies that require a doctor's certificate in all circumstances experience 6 percent fewer sick days than companies that do not require a certificate. This translates into a productivity gain of 0.4 percent for the average Fortune 500 company.' " She looks at him, uncertain. "Is this for real?"

"Well, that's interesting," Jones says. "It discourages staff from abusing the system, I guess."

"*My* manager makes me get a doctor's certificate for a single day off work. I end up being sick for twice as long because I have to catch the damn bus to the clinic."

"Yeah, that must suck. But they probably factored that in."

"Factored it in?"

Jones clears his throat. "I mean, companies need to get the most out of their workers. That's business. The more efficient the workforce, the better the company."

"I wish I worked for *you.*" She's no longer smiling. "Wow, you'd be a *great* boss."

"Just give me my book," Jones says.

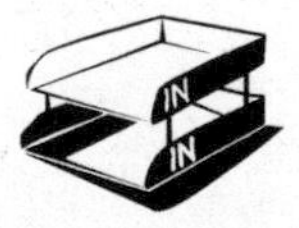

Jones gets three steps inside Training Sales before Roger's head pops over the Berlin Partition. "Jones. Jones. Got a minute?" He walks to the coffee machine. Jones follows, carrying his briefcase. Roger lowers his voice. "Have you heard anything about my donut?"

Jones blinks. "What, like where it is?"

"No. I mean, did Holly say anything about who took it?"

"I thought Wendell took your donut."

Roger shakes his head. "I bumped into him on the way out on Friday. He was a mess. He wanted to talk about old times . . . I got the impression maybe he hadn't taken it."

"Oh," Jones says bleakly.

"Now I suspect Elizabeth. You don't know the history, but this is exactly the kind of thing she'd do. Keep your ears open. Holly might let something slip. If she does, let me know."

"Okay."

"Good man." Roger winks. He looks at the coffeepot, which is empty. "Were you planning on making coffee?"

"Let me just put down my briefcase."

Jones walks to East Berlin, feeling unsettled. All of a sudden he can imagine Roger cleansing the entire Training Sales department, having one person fired after another in endless pursuit of this donut thief.

"Well well," Freddy says, not looking up from his computer. "It's the department's new top sales rep."

Jones hesitates. "Freddy, I feel awkward, too. But it's not really a promotion, is it? It's just a bunch of extra work for no pay."

"What? Oh, right. No, I mean you really are the top rep."

"What?" Jones moves over to look at Freddy's screen. He

is about to discover why he is the last person to arrive at work at eight thirty in the morning: Roger and Elizabeth have been hard at work backing out orders. Friday afternoon the reps heard Sydney say: *I'm sacking reps who earn too much commission.* Elizabeth has been here since seven thirty. When she arrived, Roger was already at his desk, leaving voice mails for clients to tell them the price he quoted earlier is wrong, *much* too low; also, it's looking as if Training Delivery won't be able to fulfill any orders for months. Elizabeth grabbed her phone and, her heart breaking, began telling customers in a low, pained voice that things just weren't working out; that it wasn't them, it was her; that she wasn't in a place where she could fulfill their needs.

"Roger's on minus eighty," Holly says from across the aisle. "Elizabeth's on minus three hundred. She got that big order from Marketing last month canceled." Holly can't quite keep the pride out of her voice.

"Looks like you've got a lot of work to do," Freddy says. "You don't want to make the other reps look bad. Could be tough explaining those canceled orders if you're bringing in new ones."

Jones's eyes flick helplessly between Freddy and Holly.

"It's okay," Freddy says. "I'll help you out."

"Thanks. Thanks." Jones exhales. "But first I have to make Roger a coffee."

A pair of beautiful eyes watch Jones walk to the coffee machine. They belong to Megan, the PA. Megan is overweight, her skin is a disaster zone, and no matter what she tries her hair looks as if she was caught without an umbrella while walking to work, but her eyes are gorgeous. People talk about bedroom eyes; well, Megan has the whole suite.

One of her hands takes hold of her computer mouse. The cord snakes between the army of ceramic bears, but doesn't disturb a single one. On her screen, she clicks a file called JACTIVITY.TXT. She scrolls down to 8/23 and carefully types: 8:49 COFFEE.

Megan is infatuated. With Jones's sandy hair, his lean body, his crisp, new, blindingly white shirts—she loves everything, the whole package. She loves how he strides from place to place. How he looks clearly and directly at things—but not in an arrogant way, like a manager (or a sales rep). He is not trying to impress people all the time, like Roger. He doesn't give you the impression that he thinks you've either done something wrong or are about to, like Elizabeth. He doesn't act differently depending on whom he's talking to. He is simply Jones: fresh, new, and utterly gorgeous.

She has taken to imagining erotic scenarios: Jones coming over to borrow a stapler and her grabbing his tie and pulling him close. His eyes widening in shock as their lips crush together, his hands touching her body, tentative at first, then with growing passion as they clamber onto her desk, sweeping the ceramic bears aside (carefully, none damaged), his eyes locked onto hers—yes! Yes!

When he sits at his desk, all she can see over the partition is his hair. Sometimes he stretches, and she sees his arms, maybe a flash of wrist, and her heart pounds; on these occasions she opens up JACTIVITY.TXT and writes the time and STRETCH.

She will die before allowing anyone to discover this. People would think it was creepy. They wouldn't understand: this is simply her way of being close to him. She has never spoken to him. Nobody bothered to introduce them; she was simply pointed out along with the xerox machine and other pieces of useful office furniture. PAs get no respect in Zephyr Holdings, Megan knows. They are the illegal immigrant laborers of the company; their existence is tolerated, but nobody bothers to get close. PAs are as interchangeable as Erector set components; they wheel one out and install someone else and hardly anybody notices the difference. Nobody looks at a PA properly, Megan has discovered. Instead, their eyes simply slide over you. And the biggest waste in the world is a PA with nice eyes, because no one ever sees them.

There are stories—legends, really—of the "steady job." Old-timers gather graduates around the flickering light of a computer monitor and tell stories of how the company used to be, back when a job was for life, not just for the business cycle. In those days, there were dinners for employees who racked up twenty-five years—don't laugh, you, yes, twenty-five years!—of service. In those days, a man didn't change jobs every five minutes. When you walked down the corridors, you recognized everyone you met; hell, you knew the names of their *kids.*

The graduates snicker. A steady job! They've never heard of such a thing. What they know is the *flexible* job. It's what they were raised on in business school; it's what they experienced, too, as they drove a cash register or stacked shelves between classes. Flexibility is where it's at, not dull, rigid, monotonous steadiness. Flexible jobs allow employees to share in the company's ups and downs; well, not so much the ups. But when times get tough, it's the flexible company that thrives. By comparison, a company with *steady jobs* hobbles along with a ball and chain. The graduates have read the management textbooks and they know the truth: long-term employees are *so* last century.

The problem with employees, you see, is everything. You have to pay to hire them and pay to fire them, and, in between, you have to pay them. They need business cards. They need computers. They need ID tags and security clearances and phones and air-conditioning and somewhere to sit. You have to ferry them to off-site team meetings. You have to ferry them home again. They get pregnant. They injure themselves. They steal. They join religions with firm views on when it's permissible to work. When they read their e-mail they open every attachment they get, and when they write it they expose the company to enormous legal liabilities. They arrive with no useful skills, and once you've trained them, they leave. And don't expect gratitude! If they're not taking sick days, they're requesting compassionate leave. If they're not gossiping with co-workers, they're complaining about them. They consider it their inalienable right to wear body ornamentation that scares customers. They talk about (dear God) unionizing. They want raises. They want management to notice when they do a good job. They want to know what's going to happen in the next corporate reorganization. And lawsuits! The lawsuits! They sue for sexual harassment, for an unsafe workplace, for discrimination in thirty-two different flavors. For—get this—wrongful termination. Wrongful termination! These people are only here because you brought them into the corporate world! Suddenly you're responsible for them for *life*?

The truly flexible company—and the textbooks don't come right out and say it, but the graduates can tell that they want to—doesn't employ people at all. This is the siren song of outsourcing. The seductiveness of the subcontract. Just try out the words: *no employees.* Feels good, doesn't it? Strong. Healthy. Supple. Oh yes, a company without employees would be a wondrous thing. Let the workers suck up a little competitive pressure. Let them get a taste of the free market.

The old-timers' stories are fairy tales, dreams of a world that no longer exists. They rest on the bizarre assumption that people somehow deserve a job. The graduates know better; they've been taught that they don't.

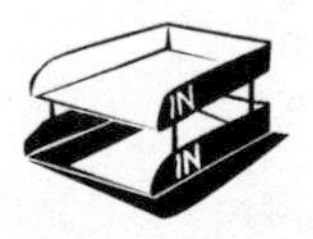

"The first thing," Freddy says to Jones, "is to get a list of your accounts. Do you have a list?"

"No."

"Holly can get that for you."

"Hey. Get your own assistant. I work for Elizabeth."

Freddy looks at her. "You're doing your hair."

"Some of us exercise in the mornings, you know." Holly's head is tilted all the way to one side so her hair hangs down in a single sheet. She attacks this with a brush and so much vigor that Jones winces.

"I thought you went to the gym *after* work."

"I do." Her eyes run critically over Freddy's body. "You know, you could stand to do a little exercise."

"I don't think I could."

Jones says, "Can we get back on topic?"

They look at him. "Check out business boy," Holly says.

"I just mean—"

"Fine, I'll print out your account list. Just let me finish my hair."

"That's my girl." Freddy maneuvers his office chair around the partitions and wheels into Jones's cubicle. "Now, I'll call one of Wendell's customers and you listen in. Try to pick up some strategies."

Jones nods enthusiastically. "Thanks. That'd be great."

Freddy punches for speakerphone. "Hi, this is Freddy Carlson from Zephyr Training Sales. You placed an order for eighty hours of training with us last week, right? Well, you need to cancel them."

"Why, what's wrong?"

"It's for, what, three people? That's just ridiculous. Why would you need eighty hours of training for three people?"

"Ah . . . there was a reason . . . the sales rep, Wendell, explained it to me."

"Was it total cost of ownership? Because we make those figures up. No, wait, did he say we've got a revamped product lineup? All we did is change the fonts on the brochures."

"Why do you want me to cancel my order?" The man's tone grows suspicious. "Are you overbooked?"

"I'm just looking out for you. Seriously, our courses are terrible. They're the same basic teamwork lesson packaged under different names."

"I didn't order anything about teamwork. I ordered Managing C++ Programmers in Time-Sensitive Projects."

"That's the teamwork course! They're all the teamwork course!"

"Maybe I should order more courses, if they're filling up so fast. Do you have something on workflow best practice for small groups?"

Freddy freezes. Then he stabs the TALK button.

Jones blinks. "Did you just hang up on that guy?"

"This is more difficult than I thought."

"Hey," Holly says, from her desk. "Check the printer behind you. List of accounts."

"Maybe this is why I'm not a sales rep," Freddy says. He chews his lip. "Could we just cancel orders and not tell anyone, do you think?"

"I doubt it," Holly says. "I bet there are checks. Balances, too."

Jones retrieves his printout. He holds it up for Holly. "Is this it?"

"Yep."

"But this can't be right."

"What's the matter?"

"These are my customers?"

Infrastructure Management—Building
Infrastructure Management—Fleet
Infrastructure Management—Interiors
Infrastructure Management—Acquisitions
Infrastructure Management—Fire and Emergency
Marketing—Corporate
Marketing—Branding
Marketing—Public Relations
Marketing—Internal
Marketing—Direct
Marketing—Operations
Marketing—Research
Infrastructure Maintenance—Control
Infrastructure Maintenance—Acquisitions
Infrastructure Maintenance—Clean Teams
Infrastructure Maintenance—Reporting
Infrastructure Maintenance—Softs
Infrastructure Maintenance—Climate Control
Infrastructure Maintenance—Large

It continues for another three pages. Holly says, "What's the problem?"

"They're internal departments."

"So?"

"You're telling me we sell training packages to *other Zephyr departments*?"

"You didn't know that?"

"No! I thought our customers were other companies!"

Holly and Freddy start laughing. Freddy says, "That's so funny."

"That's how Zephyr works," Holly says. "Infrastructure Management bills our department for parking and office space. Fleet bills us for company cars. We bill other departments for training. Well, actually, Training Delivery bills them. We just take a commission."

"It's all about efficiently allocating costs," Freddy says. "Or something."

"But I thought Zephyr was a training company. I thought that's what we did. What do we do, then?"

Holly says, "You mean, like, overall?"

"Yes!"

She shrugs. Jones stares. She crosses her arms defensively. "I know what our department does. But Zephyr's a big company."

Jones looks at Freddy. "Don't ask me. The company does a lot of things, Jones."

"Which of them involves selling things to people who don't work in this building?"

Freddy scratches his chin. Holly says, "I'm sure there's *something*."

Jones feels faint. He is realizing that he took a job at a company without knowing what it does.

Freddy says, "I know who our main competitor is, if that helps. Assiduous. Assiduous is always hiring our ex-employees."

Holly lets out a short, disgusted snort. "Traitors."

Jones has never heard of Assiduous. "What does it do?"

Holly and Freddy look at each other.

"Oh, come on."

"Well, you can't go around asking questions about Assiduous," Freddy says. "How would that look? Besides, when someone joins Assiduous, they're the enemy. You can't call them up and ask how they're doing. You have to protect company secrets."

"What secrets? You guys don't know anything!"

"Remember Jim?" Holly says to Freddy. "I was sad when he left. I would have liked to have kept in touch with him."

Jones's phone rings. He reaches over Freddy's shoulder for his handset, but Freddy beats him and pushes SPEAKER. Jones says, "Hello?"

"Hi. I've heard there's something of a run on the training courses. Can I still get an order in, or is it too late?"

Freddy frowns and leans close to the speaker. "Is this Procurement?"

"Ah, yes."

"You're Roger's account! Why are you calling this number?"

"Oh, I'm sorry, I thought I did call Roger."

"No! You didn't!" Freddy kills the call. He gets up and walks back to his desk.

Jones says, "Was that necessary?"

Freddy picks up his phone. "I want to try something."

Jones's phone rings. "Hello?"

Freddy yelps. Jones gets it in stereo: across the aisle and out of the handset. "Roger's forwarded his phone!" He hurries to Jones's desk and starts punching buttons.

"Hey, Jones," Holly says. "This thing about what the company does, don't let it get to you. I was the same when I first started working here. But you just get used to it. The thing is, there's plenty about Zephyr that makes no sense. Sydney got promoted to manager. One of the best parking spaces is always empty, I mean *always*, but we're not allowed to use it. Last month we had to sit through a presentation on eliminating redundancy, and it was a bunch of PowerPoint slides, plus a guy reading out what was on the slides, and then he gave us all hard copies. I don't understand these things. I don't really understand anything about this company. It's just how things are. Like that story, you know, with the monkeys?"

"Chimps," Freddy says. He stabs at Jones's phone. "A-*ha*. Jones, I've forwarded your phone to Elizabeth."

Holly folds her hands on her desk. "These chimps, they're in a cage, and the scientists poke in a banana on a stick. The chimps try to grab it, but as soon as they do, the scientists electrify the floor, so all the chimps get a shock. This goes on until the chimps learn that touching a banana equals electric shock. Right? Then the scientists take one chimp out and put in a new one. This chimp, when he goes to grab the banana, he gets beaten up by all the others, because they don't want to get shocked. You see?"

"That's a terrible story," Jones says.

"The scientists keep switching chimps, one at a time, until none of the originals are left. Then they add one more. The new chimp, he goes for the banana and the others jump him, same as before. But, see, none of them was ever shocked. They don't know why they're doing it. They just know that's the way they do things."

"So I'm the new chimp."

"You're the new chimp. Don't try to understand the company. Just go with it."

In the bowels of the company, a computer is about to be murdered. It's a simple computer, a PABX. Its job is to route phone calls. It is running software that was once as clean and functional as a mountain stream, but over the past decade has been patched, tweaked, and customized into a steaming, festering jungle, where vines snag at your feet and snarling, fanged creatures live in the shadows. There is a path through the jungle, a clear, well-worn path, and if you follow it you will always be safe. But take two misdirected steps and the jungle will eat you alive.

The software prevents two phones from forwarding their calls to each other, which would create what is known as an infinite loop, a particularly brutal way to kill a computer. In IT, infinite loops are the equivalent of manslaughter: death through foreseeable negligence. So at this point on the jungle path there is a strong wooden barrier. What the software does not prevent—not anymore, not after ten years of quick hacks to meet ever-changing departmental wish lists—is a forwarding circle, where person A (say, Roger) forwards his phone to B (Jones), who forwards his phone to C (Elizabeth), who forwards her phone to A (Roger). There is no barrier here, just a deep, dark ravine where things wait with glittering eyes and sharp teeth.

Right now a mid-level manager in Travel Services is dialing her Training Sales representative. She is thinking of ordering some training for her two telesales staff. They don't really need it, but she's caught wind that Training Sales is trying to cancel orders. This manager has been in Zephyr Holdings long enough to know that if someone doesn't want you to order something, you grab as much of it as you can and hang on tight. It was the same way with office chairs.

Her finger pushes the last digit, a six. The phone clicks in her ear. There is a pause. Then the building's lights go off.

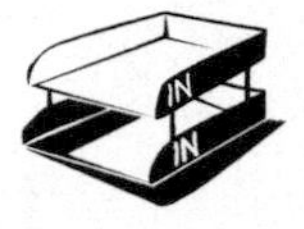

Jones, Freddy, and Holly are plunged into darkness as sudden and shocking as a slap. For two or three seconds, the loudest sound is the dying electric whine of printers and copy machines. The air-conditioning, which puts out a hum so low and omnipresent that the employees have never consciously noticed it, emits a throaty death rattle, and silence drops upon them like a collapsing marquee.

A few faint lines of light squeeze through the blinds

of Sydney's office, lending a silvery, dungeon-like ambiance.

"What's happening?" Jones says.

"Maybe it's a fire," Holly says in the gloom.

"Who said that?" Megan calls. "Did someone say there's a fire?"

"Fire!" Roger shouts from West Berlin. "Get to the elevators!"

"I didn't say there *was* a fire!" Holly shouts, but her voice is lost in an argument over whether it's safe to use the elevators during a fire. It is a loud argument, because everyone is sure it's not except Roger, and he is insistent. A chair is knocked over. Megan, trying to get out, bumps her desk and hears bears spill to the floor, just before something crunches underfoot. The lights flicker as the backup generator kicks in, long enough for Megan to see that she has crushed a mother-and-daughter bear set. Tears well in her eyes. Darkness descends again.

"Don't take the elevators!" Elizabeth shouts. She gropes along the wall until she reaches the door to the stairwell and tugs at the handle. But it won't move. For one insane second she thinks Infrastructure Management has locked the stairwell door. Then she realizes she must simply be lost in the darkness. Then she realizes she's not. This is the stairwell door, it is locked, and they are all trapped. "There's no way out!"

People panic, bumping into things and stepping on Megan's bears. Megan gets on her hands and knees, hysterical, trying to save them all; the bears, that is. Jones grabs Holly's buttocks in the dark but doesn't realize it: they're so well toned that he mistakes them for the back of an office chair. Holly is too shocked to say anything. Freddy becomes disoriented and, thinking a sliver of light is a corridor, runs into Sydney's office wall and rebounds from the glass.

Sydney's door pops open. Daylight streams into the department, dazzling them. Sydney's tiny body is framed in the doorway, like some kind of angel. "What the hell are you doing?"

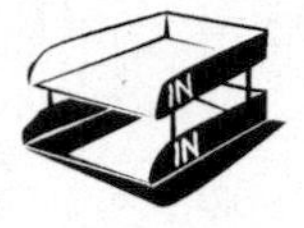

When the power is back and the phones are working—neither of which happen quickly—recriminations begin to fly. During the blackout, numerous departments discovered their stairwell doors were locked, and this has generated a certain amount of antagonism toward Infrastructure Management. People want the department to be reported to the police, or even outsourced. An emergency conference call between Senior Management and all departmental managers is arranged.

Infrastructure Management protests that it locks the stairwells for safety reasons—a few years earlier, a PA tripped and Legal went into conniptions, has everyone forgotten that? They installed a sophisticated system (at great expense) to automatically unlock the doors in case of emergency, but because of the blackout, it didn't work. And whose fault is that? Information Technology.

Senior Management's focus swings onto IT. Indeed,

what kind of department allows a telephone call to shut down the building? Information Technology hastens to explain exactly what kind. They have half the staff they did six months ago and keep getting lumped with new systems, like Infrastructure Management's emergency door opener, that require supervision, maintenance, and integration with everything else. It has twenty-four increasingly harried and sleep-deprived technical staff fighting to maintain digital life support to Zephyr's body, in between taking calls from senior executives who are sure they sent an e-mail to somebody last week but now the guy is saying he never got it. In this environment, less critical tasks, like simulating what would happen in the event of a PABX meltdown, have had to be postponed.

Less critical? *Less critical?* Senior Management hopes Information Technology is joking. The building shut down! What Senior Management wants to hear, right now, is that IT understands exactly what went wrong and can promise it will never happen again. You can say this for Senior Management: it knows how to articulate a goal. The strategy may be fuzzy, the execution nonexistent, but Senior Management knows what it wants.

IT does know what went wrong, down to the line number of the offending piece of code. It begins to explain several possible solutions. But these involve confusing phrases like "automatic fail-over switching," and Senior Management gets irritable. It skips ahead to the logical conclusion: Information Technology is a bunch of idiots who locked the stairwells. They put the wheels in motion: IT will be outsourced by the end of the week.

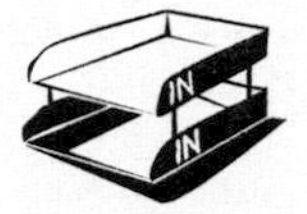

Jones flips through *The Omega Management System* over a microwaved TV dinner. Jones lives in a four-floor walk-up with crumbling plaster walls and life-threatening wiring. Until quite recently, he did so with Tim and Emily, classmates from the University of Washington—Tim was an incredible cook and Emily incredible all over, as far as Jones was concerned. One night he confessed his feelings to her in the hallway outside the bathroom, and she said he was sweet and she liked him a lot but they couldn't; how unfair would that be to Tim? This was four months ago, and Jones began to focus, laser-like, on the end of his student days, which would likewise terminate their three-way living arrangement. The day of his final exam, he came home to find Tim and Emily waiting for him on the sofa, holding hands. "We didn't tell you sooner," Tim said, "because we didn't think it would be fair on you." Now Jones lives alone and eats microwaved dinners.

He flips to the section on retrenchment. A sacking, the book says, is one of the most harrowing and stressful events you may ever experience—Jones assumes "you" means the person being sacked until he realizes it's talking about the manager. According to the book, sackings can be highly destabilizing: workers stop thinking about doing their jobs and start thinking about whether they'll still have them. It then describes a range of strategies managers can use to harness that fear and uncertainty and jujitsu-throw it into a motivating factor.

What Jones doesn't find in the book—and he doesn't notice this at first; he has to flick back and forth—is any mention of the retrenched employees. How they might feel, for example, or what might happen to them afterward. It's kind of creepy. It's almost as if once they are sacked, they cease to exist.

Q3/3: SEPTEMBER

JONES ARRIVES to find Freddy loitering outside the glass lobby doors, smoking. "Hey, Freddy. How come no one smokes out here but you?"

Freddy shrugs. "I like it here. Most people go out the back, or the side. Sometimes I do, too."

Jones peers in through the tinted glass. Neither Gretel nor Eve has arrived yet, but on Eve's desk is a towering stack of flowers. Jones looks at Freddy.

"What?"

"Are you sending the receptionist flowers?"

Freddy jumps. "Why do you say that?"

Jones snickers.

"What?"

"That's a yes. That's what guilty people say; they don't want to lie, so they say, 'Why do you say that?' "

"I..." Freddy waits for a janitor, an older man with a shock of silver hair and blue overalls, to pass. Jones classifies the man in his head: Infrastructure Maintenance department—Clean Teams division, one of Jones's potential customers. Freddy leans close, bathing Jones in his smoky cigarette breath. "Don't you dare tell her."

"You send them anonymously?"

"Of course! Have you *seen* her? She won't talk to me."

"I dunno, she seems nice enough."

Freddy shakes his head emphatically. "She can never know."

"If you're not going to tell her who they're from, why send them?"

"Because she's beautiful."

"Well, that's nice, but I bet she'd like to know who sent her those flowers. They must have cost you fifty bucks."

"Forty." He shrugs. "A week."

"A week?"

"I've been doing this for a while." He shifts his feet. "What?"

"Freddy, you have to tell her."

"She'll probably be disappointed. She probably thinks it's from someone else."

"No, look, we'll come up with a plan. Trust me. She'll be thrilled to find out you've been sending her flowers."

"Hmm." His eyes flick hopefully at Jones, then away. "I don't know about that."

Jones looks at his watch. "I'd better get inside. I want to catch someone from Senior Management before they start work."

Freddy takes a step backward in shock. "Senior Management?"

"Yeah. I want to know what this company actually does."

"Didn't you listen to the chimp story? It doesn't matter."

"But the company could be doing anything. What if it's unethical?"

Freddy looks at him blankly.

"I'd feel better knowing," Jones says. "So I'm going to talk to Senior Management."

Freddy shakes his head slowly. "You're so different, Jones."

On level 17—which is to say, not far above ground level—morning sunshine pours through the gym's floor-to-ceiling windows. Holly, entwined in a machine that facilitates bicep crunches, has struck up a conversation with a communications manager from Corporate Marketing. The communications manager is about twenty-five and has a jaunty ponytail that swings from side to side as she power walks on a treadmill. Holly is enjoying talking to the communications manager, but she is becoming jealous of that ponytail.

"First we had to cut out above-the-line advertising," the communications manager says. "Then we cut advertising altogether. After that we were down to market research and PR. But lately we don't even do those."

"Then what do you do?"

"Nothing. We don't have the budget."

"Nothing at all?"

"Not since June." The communications manager winks. "Don't tell anybody. So far, no one's noticed."

"Huh," Holly says.

"Before then, we were really under the gun. We got warned on expenses three times in a month. But now everyone's feeling really positive. Morale is way up."

"But what do you do all day?"

"Oh, we're still working. We're working harder than ever. Every day we identify new ways to lower expenses. Just yesterday, we boarded up our office windows."

"You have windows?" Holly cries.

"*Had.* Now they're covered in cardboard."

"Why would you do that?"

"Infrastructure Management bills for windows. Covering them up cut our overhead by 8 percent. But we're just getting started. Today we're getting rid of our desks and chairs. We figure we don't really need them anymore, since we're not doing any marketing. And it's way better feng shui. We'll put the computers on the carpet."

"What do you use the computers for?"

The communications manager's eyes widen. "Hey hey. That's the kind of thinking we could use in marketing. That's a great idea."

Holly stops crunching. "If you're not actually doing any marketing, aren't you worried they'll cut you?"

"With expenses this low? Which company do you work for?" She laughs. Her ponytail swishes.

Jones swipes his ID card through the elevator's reader and pushes 2, which is SENIOR MANAGEMENT. This is only Jones's fourth week at Zephyr Holdings, but he's heard about level 2. Nobody claims to have been there *personally*, but everyone knows somebody who has. If Jones believes the stories, when the elevator doors open on level 2 he will be confronted with rolling meadows, frolicking deer, and naked virgins feeding grapes to Zephyr executives reclining on cushions. As for level 1, the sprawling penthouse office where Daniel Klausman composes all-staff voice mails and receives strategic visions—that's different. Nobody claims to have been there.

The button for level 2 lights up, then goes dark. Jones tries again. He reswipes his ID. But the elevator does not want to take him to level 2. Across the lobby, he sees the front doors slide open and Gretel Monadnock walk in. Jones calls, "Hey, Gretel, how come the elevator won't go?"

"Um . . ." She puts her purse on the giant orange reception desk, eyes the enormous flower arrangement, and runs a hand through her hair. Jones feels a twinge of sympathy for Gretel, who would probably be considered beautiful if she didn't sit next to Eve Jantiss. "I guess you don't have the proper security clearance."

"How do I get that?"

"Where are you trying to get to?"

"Level 2."

She looks startled. "Why do you want to do that?"

"I want to talk to Senior Management." The lobby doors part again: this time it's Freddy, finished with his cigarette.

"How do I make an appointment with someone from Senior Management?"

Gretel looks at Freddy, uncertain. Freddy says, "No, he's serious."

"Um... can I get back to you on that? Nobody's asked me that before."

"You're kidding."

"No, she's not," Freddy says. "You're meant to send requests like this up through your manager, Jones. You don't barge in on Senior Management."

"This is ridiculous." Jones puts his hands on his hips. "I just want to know what the company does." Then he spots the coffee table for visitors, littered with marketing brochures and annual reports. *"A-ha."*

"He's happy, now," Freddy says to Gretel. "Hey, is Eve due in this morning or what?"

"Eve doesn't keep me up-to-date on her movements."

"Oh."

"Um... Jones?" Gretel puts out her hand to touch Jones, who is passing by with a handful of annual reports.

"I'll bring these right back, I promise."

She shakes her head. "No, I mean... I've wondered what Zephyr does, too. I've... well, we're not supposed to maintain contact with people who have left, but... I've been writing down their names." She looks embarrassed. "It's just nobody ever talks about them, and I think... someone should remember them. So I write down their names. I've got the name of everybody who's worked here in the last three years."

"Oh," Jones says. He's not sure what to do with this information. "That's... really nice."

"It's really *morbid*," Freddy says in the elevator. "It's *wrong*. What sort of person writes down the names of people as they get fired? It's like a *death list*."

Jones flips through the annual report. " 'Diversified product offering.' 'Vertically integrated distribution chain.' 'Chosen markets.' This tells me nothing!"

"It's Zephyr *Holdings*. I don't think we manufacture anything directly. We just control other companies."

"Mmm," Jones says, unconvinced. He flips the page and is confronted with a glossy photo of smiling employees underneath the words: NOT A JOB. A WAY OF LIFE. "Why are there no pictures of Daniel Klausman in this thing?"

"He's camera shy. There are no photos of him anywhere."

"None?"

Freddy shrugs. "He doesn't like to meet people face-to-face. Doesn't mean he can't do his job."

"Do you even know what he looks like?"

"Me? No. But some people say they've met him. Hey, check it out." He points at the button panel. "No more Information Technology."

Jones realizes that instead of the number 19, there is a small round hole. "They actually remove the button?"

"For security, I guess."

Jones looks at him.

"Chimps," Freddy says. "Think of the chimps."

"I don't want to be the new chimp." Jones snaps shut the annual report. "I want to know what the hell's going on."

Elizabeth sits on the toilet and stares at the stall door. There's nothing particularly interesting about the door. That's why she's looking at it. Elizabeth has had a rough morning. Her stomach is tight. She has vomited. But it's not the individual issues that bother her. It's the thought that they may be symptoms. This is the third morning in a row she has been sick.

The realization has been growing in a corner of Elizabeth's mind for some time. Now she faces it, this tiny, wriggling zygote of knowledge. She mouths: *I am pregnant.* The words taste alien. There is an invader in her uterus.

She knows who the father is. She closes her eyes and puts her hand to her forehead. Yes, she falls in love with her customers, but she doesn't make a habit of sleeping with them. She's interested in relationships, not one-night stands. Except... it was the last day of the quarter and they were hammering out details over pizza and wine stolen from Marketing, and she was already in love with him even before he started talking about a "second round" of training. He was the personnel development coordinator of Forecasting and Auditing, and he hovered his pen above the dotted line, smiling, and said, "Sealed with a kiss."

If he'd signed first, there would have been no problem. She found them less attractive once they signed. She would have shaken his hand, maybe kissed his cheek. But with the pen an inch from the paper, her adrenaline surging, and the wine buzzing in her brain, she kissed him, this man, who was then a customer and soon after transferred into Training Sales to become her colleague, and Roger kissed her back, and they had sex on his desk with her skirt bunched around her waist and the order forms scrunching beneath her buttocks. They didn't use protection, which seems idiotic now...but Elizabeth doesn't want to analyze this too deeply. She is single and thirty-six and was having sex for the first time in two years; it is not beyond the realms of possibility that a small, secret part of her—a part that has very little to do with selling training packages—performed an executive veto on the condom issue, striking it off the agenda, ensuring that the decision, much like Roger himself, slipped in without adequate review.

Near the end, she cried out that she loved him, and he said, "I love it, too," which should have told her plainly enough that it was going to end badly. But she ignored it because she did love him, at least for a while, even when it was over and he was pulling up his pants, avoiding her eyes.

"We shouldn't tell anybody," Roger said. "I'm not one of those men."

"What men?" But he was scribbling his signature on the

order and she felt the love draining out of her, dribbling away, even as an essential part of Roger did the same. Although, she realizes now, not *enough* of an essential part of Roger.

"You know. Men who do this."

"Do what?"

He handed her the order. "Have sex with sales reps."

He might as well have kicked her. She'd thought he was going to say "affairs." She'd thought he was going to say "lose control." She concentrated on tugging her skirt into place and let her hair fall over her face.

"Oh, don't be like that," Roger said. "Come on. It was good."

His transfer to Training Sales a few weeks later had nothing to do with her; she knows that. He is not pursuing her, hoping to make things right. At first she wondered, but then he arrived in the department and Sydney said, "This is Elizabeth," and Roger frowned. It was a small frown, a wrinkle, but it conveyed his attitude clearly enough. She snapped her mouth closed on a more exuberant greeting and grew another small scar on her soul. But that didn't matter. Elizabeth has plenty of scars already. Her whole job is rejection; Roger's was merely her first for the day. If he wants to be a jerk about it, well, fine. Of course, she didn't realize quite how much of a jerk he wanted to be, but even so, it's not costing her any sleep. It takes more than a petulant ex-lover to upset Elizabeth.

Like a pregnancy. Sitting on the toilet seat, she clenches her hands into balls. Roger has turned out to be not a clean sale; there is a support issue. Things will happen to her if she stays pregnant, she knows. Zephyr Holdings is not exactly baby friendly. It is not pregnant-sales-rep friendly, either. Accounts will be reassigned. Plans will exclude her. She will lose the customers she loves. Management will discuss her: Did you hear? Elizabeth got pregnant. It's a pity. She was a good rep.

"Did I tell you about my plan?" Freddy says, shrugging off his jacket. He goes to hang it on the coat stand, then stops and looks at Jones.

"What?"

"I don't want to seem petty, but you've taken my hook."

"*Your* hook?"

"It's not like it's a big deal," Freddy says, but thin lines of anxiety are spreading across his face. His feet shift nervously. "It's just that's the hook I've used the whole time I've been here."

"Well, if it's not a big deal..." Jones says, feeling perverse.

Freddy's hands tighten on his jacket collar.

"Okay, I'll move my jacket."

"Thanks." Freddy gushes relief. "It's just a funny thing, you know, you get, well, not exactly attached to these things, but used to them."

Jones finds the idea of becoming emotionally involved with a hook profoundly disturbing. He hopes he never becomes sentimental about inanimate objects in the workplace.

Freddy wanders into his cubicle and sits down. "Anyway, my plan. Last week I filed an application for disability."

"Disability? For what?"

"Stupidity."

"Stupidity!"

"Think about it. If I'm born stupid, is that my fault? No, I'm just an honest, hardworking Joe, doing my stupid best. And the company can't sack people who have a disability. It's a fact."

"Wow. That's clever."

"Thanks." He smiles. "See, you just need to know how to work the company."

Jones sits. He is interested in finding out how the company works. But there's something wrong with his computer. "Freddy . . . can you connect to the network?"

"Ah . . . hey, no."

"Damn, that's a pain."

Freddy rises slowly to his feet. "Wendell . . . the day Wendell got canned, Elizabeth tried to e-mail him and it bounced back."

"So?"

"This is what they do just before they fire you. They cancel your account. They don't let you—" His hands dance about in the air. "There was an incident a few years ago, a guy in Public Relations got told he was fired, and he walked straight back to his desk and e-mailed a video of his boss giving a blow job to the whole company." He sees

Jones's expression. "I mean, he e-mailed the whole company. The video was just of those two people."

"Oh, thank God."

"But the point is it's an early-warning system. I wasn't thinking with Wendell, I didn't realize..."

"You think we're being sacked?"

Freddy walks briskly to Megan's empty desk and grabs her mouse.

"Well?"

"The same." Freddy hurries past, into West Berlin. After a minute, he calls over the divider, "The reps too! No one can connect!"

"So it's just a network problem," Jones says.

"No. No." Freddy's head pops over the Berlin Partition, his face pale and moonlike. "It's happened! It's finally happened! The department's being outsourced!"

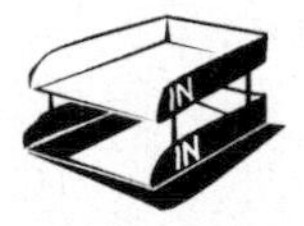

Training Sales is not being outsourced. Throughout the building, employees try fruitlessly to log on to the network. They click their mice. They hammer at their keyboards. Finally, they pick up their phones and dial the IT help desk. Their calls race through the wiring of the Zephyr building to the nineteenth floor. There, rows of cubicles stand mute and empty. The lights are off. Office chairs sit vacant. Nothing moves. On empty desks, so thoroughly cleaned that you would think no one had ever used them, the phones ring and ring.

Elizabeth is missing and no one dares to disturb Sydney, so Roger takes charge. He orders Freddy and Jones on an exploratory mission to establish whether the whole building has lost its network connection (which would be good news), or just Training Sales (very bad). First stop is level 15, Infrastructure Management and Infrastructure Maintenance, both of which are cube farms surrounded by real offices—but of course, *all* the floors are cube farms surrounded by offices. Freddy and Jones peer over the dividers. There are a lot of people playing solitaire on their computers. One gives them a fright by having an open Web browser, but he is just clicking the REFRESH button over and over, getting network errors each time. *Addict,* Freddy mouths, making a *click-click* mouse motion with his hand.

So Infrastructure Management has no network. They go down a floor: Logistics has no network. They visit level 17, and—well, whoever those people are, they have no network. They barely have computers. "Amazonians," Freddy whispers. "Lost tribe." The level-17 people wear casual clothes and stare at Freddy and Jones as if they have never seen suits before. Freddy and Jones scurry back to the elevators. When they're safe, Freddy exhales. "Did you see those monitors? Those guys haven't requisitioned anything for a long time."

Freddy and Jones aren't the only explorers doing the rounds; little teams crawl throughout the building. By noon, everyone but Senior Management knows the network is down. Senior Management remains ignorant because nobody on level 2 uses a computer except the PAs, and if a PA is having computer trouble, well, that comes as no surprise to Senior Management. To them, the capacity of PAs to ensnare themselves in computer problems is a source of endless amusement. If it's not the printer, it's the mouse, and if it's not either of those, it's—you know, one of those software things. Senior Management knows very little about computers, but it feels confident that most "computer problems" could be more accurately described as "unintelligent PA problems." Senior Management may not use a computer, but they use toasters and microwaves, and worked out how to program their car's stereo—well, not worked out, but the dealer showed them how to do it—so how much more complicated could a computer be?

The departments don't report the problem because a good manager knows the only reason to call Senior Management, ever, is to deliver good news. People who ring Senior Management with problems do not have much of a future at Zephyr Holdings. Senior Management is not there to hold departmental hands. It is there to dispense stock options. So it's three in the afternoon before word filters up.

The only reason it happens then is because eight departmental managers gather on level 19 and wander between the empty desks. There is no help desk. There are no pale, floppy-haired tech-support people. There are plenty of computers, though, and the managers peer at their screens, looking for problems. "Over here!" calls Risk Management, and they all hurry to a tiny monitor that sits on a table outside a glass-encased room full of fat, beige computer cases and a web of colorful cables. The monitor is black except for a single line in glowing green: 04:04 NETWORK ERROR 614

The managers look at each other, just in case anybody knows what this means. When it becomes clear that no one is entirely sure what those beige things in the glass room even are (let alone what they do), they decide to call Senior Management. This is a viable option because reporting problems in someone else's department isn't nearly as bad as reporting problems in your own. So they get a PA on the phone, and she promises to pass on the message as soon as Senior Management gets out of a meeting. The managers hang up, satisfied. They mill around for a few minutes, chatting about cars and golf handicaps—it's not so often that the departmental managers get to hang out together—then reluctantly head back to their own crummy departments, their lazy, stationery-stealing, unproductive employees, and their hopelessly unattainable productivity goals.

Seventeen floors up, Senior Management begins to stir. It gathers in the boardroom. At first, confusion reigns. Is this something to do with IT being outsourced? Is the new provider not honoring their contract? Who is the new provider, anyway?

No one is quite sure. There is a scandalous lack of documentation, due, one suspects, to lack of initiative on the part of the PAs. But Senior Management knows there's no point in playing the blame game. Its role is to identify solutions, not culprits. Or at least solutions first, then culprits. Gradually it emerges that in the aftermath of last month's blackout, the task of expunging incompetent goons in IT was assigned a higher priority than organizing an appropriate replacement. Zephyr has no IT people.

A snap decision is made: everyone laid off is to be immediately rehired. They are to get the network running again as a matter of urgency. Then, once a proper outsourcing plan is in place, they can be terminated again.

Senior Management relaxes. Crisis over! The order is passed to Human Resources for implementation. But here it strikes a snag. Human Resources' files are all on the network. Without them, it has no idea how to contact the ex-employees. It doesn't even know who they were. The call goes out, echoing plaintively around the building: Does anybody remember who we used to employ in IT? But no one does. Zephyr departments barely mingle at the best of times; those odd, T-shirt-wearing IT employees were actively avoided. There is only one person in the building who could supply the information Senior Management needs: Gretel in reception with her piece of paper. But nobody asks her.

In East Berlin, Holly carefully touches up her nails. She wonders if she could sneak off to the gym for a while; she's not doing anything useful here. She twists around in her seat to see the wall clock, and is surprised to discover that Megan is standing right behind her. Holly sits with her back to Megan, so she never sees her coming.

"Sorry," Megan says. "Sydney asked if you could summarize the reps' sales reports onto a page for her. She needs it by twelve."

Holly leans to one side. The wall clock says eleven thirty-five. Holly would bet a lot of money that Sydney has known about this task for several days. To Holly, it seems that Sydney's main job is to transform routine tasks into urgent ones by concealing their existence until the last possible moment. "Okay. Thanks."

Megan moves off. Holly flicks through the reports. Part of her whines: *Why doesn't Sydney just ask the reps for shorter reports in the first place?* But she firmly represses this. It is the sort of question she would have asked three years ago, when she was as fresh as Jones. Understanding of such things would, she imagined at the time, be accompanied by the gaining of rungs on the corporate ladder and the purchasing of ever-finer shoes and shirts. Today Holly has neither rungs nor comprehension. Instead she's got a permanent frown line, a reputation for being unsociable, and a growing addiction to the gymnasium. She loves the gym's simple, immutable rules: if you run, your butt will tighten. If you lift, your arms will tone. It is so different from her life in Training Sales.

She slogs through the summary and is heading for the

PRINT button when Jones and Freddy return from their expedition. She sits up. "Well?"

Freddy shakes his head. "Network's out everywhere. So it's just an IT problem, thank God. What are you doing?"

"The usual. Wasting my life."

Freddy drops into his chair. Jones looks around. "Maybe now's a good time to speak to Sydney."

"Gahh," Freddy says. To Holly: "Jones is obsessed with finding out the company's *true purpose.*"

"Oh. I worked that out for you, Jones. It's a big psychological experiment into how much pain and suffering human beings can tolerate before they quit." She turns to Freddy. "Which reminds me. You know how people have been complaining to management about work-life balance? Well, they've agreed to hold an all-staff meeting about it next Monday. At 7:30 A.M."

Freddy starts laughing. He wipes his eyes. "Which would be worse, do you think: that this kind of stuff is deliberate, or they're just clueless?"

Holly shakes her head. "I think maybe Wendell was lucky. Did you hear he got a job at Assiduous?"

Jones jumps. "Who told you that?"

"One of the girls at the gym. Why?"

"Don't you find it the tiniest bit suspicious that everyone who leaves Zephyr seems to join Assiduous?"

"Not *everyone.*"

"Name one person who's left that you still keep in touch with."

"Um..."

"*I* think," Jones says, "that there's no such company as

Assiduous. It's just an excuse. A reason to stop you from getting in touch with anyone who's left."

Holly looks startled. "Why would they do that?"

"Because," Freddy says, his voice dropping, *"they haven't really left at all."* He laughs.

"I don't know why. But I'm right, I bet I am."

Freddy says, "*I* bet that if you keep poking around, you'll get fired." To Holly, he says, "One day Jones just won't turn up, and they'll tell us he's left . . . for Assiduous."

"Don't," Holly says. "You're giving me goose bumps."

"I'm so sorry," Penny says, dumping herself into a chair. Penny is Jones's sister. She slides her black leather bag under the table, pushes her sunglasses onto her forehead, places both hands palm-down on the table, and exhales dramatically. "Court ran until one fifteen. It's unheard of, but the witness was crying, it's a sexual assault . . . if George hadn't cut her off, she might never have gotten it out." She looks around for a waiter. "Have you ordered?"

Penny clerks for a judge in the family court. She is always coming out with little stories like this, which make Jones feel small and pointless. It is not easy, being the younger brother of a rising star. "Yeah. I got you the usual."

She smiles. Since she started clerking, Penny has taken to wearing snappy jackets and shirts with big, sharp collars. This always looks to Jones like she has been playing dress-up in Mommy's closet. "Wow, it feels like I haven't seen you for a year. How's the new job?"

"It's good. I mean, it's great. I'm starting on the ground floor, but it's a big company, so there's a ton of potential."

"Yeah? Which industry?" She begins to tug shiny black hair out of a ponytail.

"Well . . . it's a holding company."

"What does it hold?"

Jones looks around the café. "Ah, you know . . . various stakeholdings. It's a diversified portfolio."

"Why don't you want to tell me? What is it? Porn?"

"No! It's not porn." Penny stares at him until he cracks, a tactic that has worked since he was nine. "Look, the thing is, I don't really know. I thought it was selling training packages, but that's just my department. The company as a whole . . . I'm not actually sure."

"Wow," Penny says eventually.

The waiter arrives with their coffees. "I know. I know. I'm going to find out, it's just . . . it's a big company. They do things differently there."

"What do you do?"

Jones hesitates. "See, last week the network went down, and without that there's not much you can do. So we . . . well, until they fix that, we're mostly just . . . talking."

"What company is this again?"

"Zephyr."

"I haven't heard of it."

"It's very big, in . . ."

"In whatever field it's in."

"Right."

"Stephen," Penny says, "you realize this is nuts."

"Is it?" he says anxiously. "Because it's hard to tell. Nobody at Zephyr seems to think anything's unusual."

"No. Trust me. You don't know what the company does. That's unusual."

"Well," Jones says, sitting back, "this isn't the court system. This is the real world." A certain amount of relish leaks into his voice. When he was a student and Penny was new at her job, she breezily dropped phrases like "real world" at family dinners. "Maybe this is how big business works."

Penny doesn't say anything for a moment. Then she picks up her coffee. "Sure. Okay, yeah, that could be it."

Jones sighs. "I have to find out what's going on."

"I think that would be good," Penny says.

In the lower levels of Zephyr Holdings things scuttle and crawl, like Corporate Supplies employees. In many ways Corporate Supplies is a zoo: its staff spend all day shoveling materials they barely recognize into animals they don't understand, and when they're done, the animals want more. Corporate Supplies considers itself something of an engine room at Zephyr Holdings, and from time to time its employees dream about what would happen if they simply closed their doors and deprived Zephyr of embossed letterhead, Post-it notes, and bottled water: the company would collapse, that's what. In the glory days, Corporate Supplies spanned three floors and had its own elevator;

old-timers occasionally put their feet on their desks and bend the ears of interns about it. To hear them tell it, requests for materials by other departments were once just that, requests, and Corporate Supplies acquiesced if and when Corporate Supplies was good and ready. They made things to last in those days; if you ordered a pen, the ink would last for eight years. And graduates had more respect; they knew their fancy book learning wasn't worth spit on the floor. They were golden days, all right, before ugly words like "cutback" and "rationalization" and "reorganization" were invented. Now Corporate Supplies is half of one measly floor. There are a quarter as many people doing four times as much work. When a department orders something—*orders*—it wants it delivered that day and gets aggrieved if it's not. And they don't even call anymore, so Corporate Supplies can't suggest alternatives or advise of delays; instead their requests ("5 × box blue pens ballpoint, need bfore 10 A.M.") just pop up on Corporate Supplies computers via the network.

That is, they did. Since the network went down, the phones have begun to ring again. Things have changed, Corporate Supplies is realizing. They are still a twelve-person department with a laughable budget, but it may just be that the glory days are here again.

Throughout the building, Zephyr Holdings is slowly getting back to full operating speed. Not because the network has been fixed; oh no. The east wing of level 19 remains a barren wasteland. No server lives there. No hub can flourish in 19's harsh, inhospitable conditions. Dry, gasping network cables search for data they will never find. IT is dark and dead and will not recover.

But there is work to be done, network or no network. Two weeks ago the network went down; soon after Senior Management assured the company it would have the problem fixed within a few days; now everyone is realizing it is never going to happen. Work-arounds are springing up everywhere you look, like new grass after rain. In the absence of e-mail, employees are discovering the art of speaking into phones. They are realizing that discussions that previously required three days and six e-mails can, with phones, be settled in minutes. Spam and computer viruses, both of which IT claimed were unsolvable problems, have vanished. The plague of e-mail jokes, funny at first and then not, has been eliminated. The pressure to forward chain letters under threat of personal catastrophe has lifted. In-boxes no longer fill with desperate sales pitches from co-workers trying to shift their cars, or kittens.

To transfer documents from one location to another, workers tighten their shoelaces and stretch their legs. People pass each other in the corridors, papers in hand, exchanging happy greetings. Their brains dizzy from unexpected exercise, they stop to chat and laugh. No one realized there were so many people in Zephyr. Until now, you never saw them. Until now, most people arrived at work, planted their buttocks in a chair, and the twain didn't part until five thirty. Now the corridors are like maternity ward waiting rooms, filled with excited voices and good cheer. Lower-back pain is clearing up. Color is rising. Workers find each other more physically attractive. And nobody receives suspicious looks for leaving the department anymore, not so long as they're clutching a sheaf of papers.

Network—what was that thing ever good for? The

workers shake their heads in amazement. Good riddance! Zephyr Holdings may not be the world's greatest employer, the workers agree; it may have a sadistic Human Resources and an incompetent Senior Management; the company's purpose may be a complete mystery and the CEO an out-of-touch eccentric whom no one has seen in person—all this may be true, but at least it doesn't have a network.

Q4/1: OCTOBER

FREDDY RETURNS from running a set of folders up to Business Management and starts doing stretches. "Anyone want to go to lunch? I'm so hungry lately. Do you think it's the extra exercise?"

Holly says, "Just let me finish these printouts for Sydney." Holly's computer is the only one connected to the departmental printer, so whenever anyone else needs to print, they have to see her. Her computer has developed dark smudge marks around the disk drive's eject button and the CD drive is making an odd, tired whine.

"Hey." Freddy stops stretching. "You know what we should do? Start a dead pool. Everyone can put in ten bucks."

Jones says, "A what?"

Holly says, "Are you serious?"

"Why not?"

"It's sick, that's why not."

"What's a dead pool?" Jones says.

"We bet who's getting fired next. Come on, it'll keep things interesting. I'll even let you have first pick, Holly."

She hesitates, and glances at Jones. "Hey," he says. Then Roger arrives from West Berlin with a floppy disk in hand. Holly reflexively puts out her hand, but he makes no attempt to give it to her. "Having some kind of bet, are you?"

"A dead pool," Freddy says. "Ten bucks and you're in."

"Sold." Roger flips open his wallet. "Who's taken?"

"Nobody yet."

"Wait," Holly says. "You said I could pick first."

"So you're in?"

"I—well, if everyone else is doing it. I'll take Jones."

"Why *me*?"

"Because... no reason."

"I'm going to pick myself," Freddy says. "If they fire me, I'll have something to take with me."

"I'll choose Elizabeth," Roger says.

There's an awkward silence. Freddy says, "Why Elizabeth?"

Roger shrugs modestly. "Just a guess."

Sydney's door *clacks* open. Everyone's head turns. Sydney, wearing an ensemble that is so dark it is difficult to make out individual pieces of clothing, stomps into East Berlin and up to Holly's desk. "Have you got that report?"

"It's in the printer."

Sydney pulls Holly's report out of the tray, then notices Freddy and Roger frozen in the act of exchanging money. "What's going on?"

Freddy clears his throat. "It's a dead pool. We're betting on who leaves Zephyr next."

Sydney's green eyes fix on Freddy. "Who told you someone was leaving?"

"No one. No, it's just a game. It's just... if someone does."

"Oh. I see. In that case, can I join in?"

Freddy looks at Holly, then Roger, then, hopelessly, at Jones. "Well... it might not be... I mean, since you can fire people, that might not be fair."

Sydney looks amused. "You're not suggesting I'd fire someone just to win your game."

"No! Of course not."

"So?"

Freddy swallows. "Yes, sure. Sure, then, that's fine. It's ten dollars."

"This sounds like fun. All right, then. All right. I'll choose Jones."

"Actually... Holly's already picked Jones."

Sydney's button nose wrinkles. Roger winces. "So?"

"Everyone has to choose someone different."

"Why can't Holly pick someone different?"

"Well, she already picked, so that wouldn't really... be... fair."

"Oh. I see. I see. Well, then, has anyone chosen Holly?"

"No."

"Then I'll take Holly." Sydney smiles, first at Freddy, then at Holly. She digs into her black pants and produces a note. Freddy takes it as if it might bite his fingers. No one says anything until Sydney has gone, and no one says anything for a while after that, either.

"Thanks a lot, Freddy," Holly says.

"It's just a game," Freddy says. "She probably... it's just a game."

Jones hurries after Sydney. Roger wanders back to West Berlin. Holly blows air out of her mouth and says, "I'm going to lunch."

"I'll come with you," Freddy says, rising. "Just give me a second—"

"I said *I'm* going to lunch." She walks away.

Freddy deflates back into his chair. He looks around, not sure what to do, and notices that his red voice-mail light is blinking. This is odd, because it wasn't blinking a minute ago. Someone has sent him a recorded message.

He picks up and presses for access. A deep, liquid voice spills into his ear:

"Good morning. This is Human Resources. We have received your disability application. We have some questions. Report to level 3 at your earliest convenience. Thank you."

Freddy goes to put back the handset, fumbles it, grabs it again, and slams it down. His hands tremble. His application was meant to disappear into the bureaucratic pit: to slip through the cracks and be processed without adequate review. Instead he's attracted HR's attention. He has fallen under the beast's scorching gaze. Pretending to be stupid suddenly seems like a very stupid idea.

For a second, Freddy thinks about ignoring the summons—maybe he can claim his voice mail didn't work! But this is madness. Nobody escapes Human Resources. He can only face his fate like a man.

He decides to leave his suit jacket on. He'd climb into a suit of armor if it was available. He scribbles on a Post-it note and sticks it to his monitor: GONE TO HUMAN RESOURCES.

This way, if anything happens to him, people will understand. Holly will know. Freddy forces himself to walk toward the elevators. He feels tears prick his eyes. Dead man walking! We've got a dead man walking here!

The elevator doors are closing by the time Jones gets there, and he has to lunge forward to stick his arm between them. The doors crash to a halt and reverse direction, revealing the tiny, imposing form of Sydney, standing with her arms folded. "In a hurry?"

He steps inside. "I'm sorry, I didn't know you were in here." Which is a lie, of course, but Jones has realized that you don't get anywhere with Sydney by disrespecting her. In this way she is similar to Roger... and, now he thinks about it, pretty much every manager he has met so far. Does this mean that Roger is destined for management? Is it possible to predict who will rise up the corporate hierarchy simply by picking out the people most desperate for public recognition? This train of thought distracts him until Sydney pulls out her cell phone and begins pushing buttons. "Oh!" She looks up at him expectantly. "Sorry. The thing is, I've been wondering what it is that Zephyr does. I mean overall, as a primary source of revenue. I can't find that out from anywhere. Isn't that weird?" He laughs.

Sydney looks back at her phone. "That's the thing with cogs, Jones. They don't need to understand the whole machine. They just need to turn."

"Right. I see what you're saying. But if one of those cogs *wanted* to understand the whole machine, and got so distracted about *not* knowing that it stopped turning properly—"

"That would be a very bad idea," Sydney says. She still doesn't look at him.

The elevator doors slide apart. Sydney begins to cross the lobby, her heels *clack-clack*ing rapidly across the Zephyr logo tiles, but Jones has a good ten inches on her in height and easily keeps pace. "It's not a secret, though, right? What the company does?" They pass the reception desk—Gretel, Eve, Eve's tower of flowers—and Jones begins to sweat. "Is it?"

"Of course not. Have you read the mission statement?"

"Yes, but—"

"You do realize we're a holding company?"

"Yes," Jones says, getting frustrated, "but that tells me *nothing*. Look, if it's not a secret, why can't you just tell me what Zephyr does?"

Sydney stops walking so unexpectedly that Jones nearly collides with her. The lobby doors jump apart anyway. It's a warm day outside, and a taste of it blows into the lobby and over Jones's face. "Jones. You're not listening to me. It's not a secret. But asking that question betrays a lack of focus. Think about it: What happens to this company if every employee wants to understand our strategic direction? If they want to second-guess Senior Management decisions? We can't run a company with eight hundred CEOs. It's not your job, or my job, or the *janitor's* job"—here she gestures to a man with a mop in one hand, who is leaning over the reception desk to chat to Eve Jantiss—"to formulate corporate strategy. If you can't understand that, you can't be a team player."

This accusation, Jones knows, is as vicious as it gets. He has seen the motivational posters.

"All right?" Her sharp green eyes flick between his.

"Fine," he says, and before the word is completely out of his mouth, Sydney is out the lobby doors. Deflated, Jones drifts back toward the elevators. Then he remembers something, and detours to the reception desk. Eve Jantiss and the janitor look at him with some interest, but Jones's question is for Gretel. "Did you find out how I could get an appointment with Senior Management?"

"Oh, yes! The answer is you can't."

"I can't," Jones says heavily.

"They suggested you speak to your manager, or, failing that, use the suggestion box. Do you know about the suggestion box?"

"So, let's see." Jones drums his fingers on the counter. "I can't get to level 2 without an appointment. I can't get an appointment because I should speak to Sydney. And Sydney *could* answer my question, but she'd sack me for asking it. Have I got that right?" Jones hears his voice growing loud. No one answers him: not Gretel, not the beautiful Eve Jantiss, not the silver-haired janitor. "What do you think would happen if I camped out in the parking lot until someone from Senior Management arrived? They have reserved parking spaces, right—what would happen if I went down and sat on a BMW?"

"I think they'd call Security," Gretel says.

"Ah! Of course! And while the guards dragged me away, they'd probably lecture me about proper channels. Meanwhile, nobody in this company has *any idea what it does*!"

The janitor says, "There's a mission statement hanging right on that wall, son."

"Sssss," Jones says, which is the sound of air whistling between his clenched teeth. Then he spots something: across the lobby, the stairwell door is wedged open by the janitor's trolley of cleaning products. The stairwell doors are normally locked—Jones knows this as a result of the August blackout. His eyes flick between it and the janitor. He begins to walk toward it.

He makes most of the distance before anyone reacts. It's Eve who seems to realize what he's up to first. "Where are you going?" There is something strange in her tone, something not quite like fear and not quite like menace, and it inflames Jones's determination. When the janitor says, *"Hey!"* Jones breaks into a run. He kicks the trolley out of the way, which bounces off the wall and topples over, sending plastic bottles of colorful liquid spinning across the tiles. Entering the stairwell is like stepping into a freezer; it's a good twenty degrees colder than the lobby, is full of deep echoes, and smells like concrete. Jones pulls shut the door behind him, which makes the kind of satisfying *click* that tells him it'll take the janitor a lot of fumbling around with keys to get it open again. Then he begins leaping up the concrete steps two at a time. It's funny. He doesn't *feel* like he's destroying his career.

Freddy arrives on level 3. It's so high in the building he feels a rush of vertigo and his knees tremble. Or maybe it's not vertigo. Maybe it's the sign before him:

HUMAN RESOURCES

Everything looks different here. The lighting is muted. The walls are a dark blue, not the ubiquitous cream. There are no motivational posters, no orange-and-black logos, no taped-up printouts of pie graphs. Everything is soft and shadowy. As Freddy walks down the corridor, his footsteps completely swallowed by the carpet, he could almost believe the walls are breathing in and out.

There is a reception desk, but no one staffing it. It is black and smooth, devoid of clutter. There's not a phone, nor a notepad, nor a ceramic bear in sight. No RING FOR SERVICE bell. Freddy looks around nervously. Two identical doors lead off from reception, one left and one right. Maybe this is some kind of test. Maybe one leads to Heaven and the other to Hell. Or, since this is Human Resources, maybe they both lead to Hell. Freddy bites his lip. He thinks he'll just stay where he is.

The door on the left clicks and swings open.

"Hello?" He walks up to the door and peers through it. It opens onto a long, empty corridor with half a dozen identical doors on each side.

He clenches his jaw, puts one foot in front of the other,

and walks through the doorway. He half expects the door to swing shut behind him—*snick*—and the lights to go out and someone (or something) to begin cackling maniacally in the darkness, but, of course, none of these things happen. He is simply walking up a corridor in Human Resources. Still, he has to fight against the urge to flee back to the elevators.

All the doors are closed. None are labeled. Then one to his left clicks, and Freddy stops. The door swings open. Beyond it is a dark meeting room. But there's no table, just a plastic chair in the center of the room. Freddy steps inside warily. "You want me to sit in the chair?" There is no response but silence. He walks over and sits. He realizes he is facing an enormous mirror.

The voice comes out of nowhere, the one from the voice mail. "Your name," it says. "State your name."

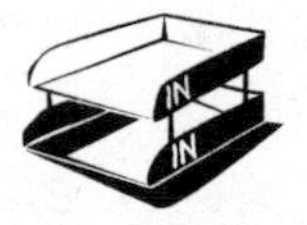

Passing by a stairwell door marked 15, Jones notices a certain weakness entering his legs. By the time he reaches 10, his legs are visibly shaking and his shirt is stuck to his back. At 5, he misses a step and decides to go with it: he half sits, half falls onto a concrete step, and takes the opportunity to suck air into his burning lungs. As if waiting for this, his forehead jets sweat, which Jones tries, mostly unsuccessfully, to mop up with his sleeves. He realizes he is not going to make the best impression on Senior Management.

A sound bounces up the stairwell from below. Jones sits up. It comes again (or is that an echo?), then he hears voices. One says something like, "Up or down?" and the other replies, "Gotta be up." Jones wonders if this might be Security, tracking him down, and then one of them yells, *"Mr. Jones? You're not permitted in the stairwell. We need to take you to Human Resources. Are you there? Mr. Jones? It's best if we get this done quickly."* This settles the issue, and Jones hauls himself to his feet and starts climbing again.

A few minutes of Herculean effort later, he is face-to-face with a stairwell door marked 2. The Security guards are still behind him, but at least five floors lower. Jones reaches for the bar to open the door . . . then hesitates. He looks up. Level 2 is Senior Management. But level 1 is Daniel Klausman, the CEO. Jones thinks: *Why settle for second-best?* He has come all this way.

His legs lodge an objection, but Jones overrules them: he staggers up one more set of concrete steps. And then he is facing a door marked 1 with nowhere else to go.

It looks just like all the other stairwell doors. He's a little disappointed; he was half expecting golden gates, fluffy clouds, and bright light spilling out. Oh well. He puts his hands on the metal bar and pushes it down. *Ker-lack!* In the stairwell, it sounds like a gunshot. Down below, the Security guards start shouting. Because of the echoes, it's hard to make out individual words, but Jones gets the impression that there are dire consequences in store for him. Jones knew that already. He just hopes there are no Security guards on level 1. If he's gone through all this for nothing, he will be very disgruntled. He shoulders open the door.

The wind nearly pulls him onto his face. He has to grab at the door for balance. It's so different from what he expected that for a second his brain fails to comprehend it; he just hangs there, gulping air, his eyeballs struggling for focus. His first stupid thought is: *His office is huge!*

Jones is on the roof.

"You know my name," Freddy says. "You asked me to come here."

"State your name," the voice says again.

He swallows. He guesses this is for the record. Whatever record that is. Or maybe—another idea occurs to him—it's to calibrate their equipment. When you have a polygraph test, Freddy has heard, they ask simple questions first, to get the parameters right. They save the real questions for later.

"Freddy Carlson."

"State your employee number."

"It's 4123488."

"State your department."

"Training Sales. Level 14." He clears his throat. "All this is on my application."

"You have a disability."

Freddy shifts on the chair. In the mirror, his reflection does likewise. To Freddy, his reflection looks very guilty. "Yes."

"Your disability is stupidity."

"I can't help it. I mean, I tried hard at school and everything, I'm just not naturally bright."

"It seems there is an error on your application."

"Probably," Freddy says. "I'm such a doofus, there are probably several."

"Your application states that you are stupid."

"Right."

"We think you mean to say that Human Resources is stupid."

"Oh, no. No, of course not."

"You know Human Resources' policy on disabilities."

"I . . . might have heard it somewhere."

"You know Human Resources complies fully with state and federal law."

"Well, I assume."

"You know Human Resources is proud to ensure that Zephyr Holdings is an equal opportunity employer."

"Sure."

"You know no employee of Zephyr Holdings has ever been discriminated against on the basis of a disability."

"I didn't, no, but that's great."

"You know that an employee with a recognized disability limits Human Resources' natural ability to terminate that employee."

"I guess it does," Freddy says.

"What's seven times three?"

"Tw—" Freddy catches his tongue. That was crafty! It was Human Resources' first question. "I'm not sure, I don't have a calculator."

"What's the opposite of east?"

"Left."

"Which go up, stalactites or stalagmites?"

"No idea," Freddy says, truthfully.

"Teamwork is the lifeblood of the company, true or false?"

Freddy hesitates. This feels like a trick question. No one, no matter how mentally deficient, could not know Zephyr's position on teamwork. "True."

A pause. When the voice resumes, it is deeper, even angry. "You know no disabled employee of Zephyr Holdings has ever been discriminated against on the basis of disability."

"You just said that."

Silence.

"Yes," Freddy says.

"They have been *transferred.*" The voice adds a slight but clearly detectable emphasis. "They have been *passed over.* They have been *demoted.* They have been *docked.* But they have not been *discriminated against.*"

He swallows. "Oh."

"They have received promotions that carry increased responsibilities but no extra pay. They have been integrated into teams with incompatible personalities. They have been assigned projects with mutually exclusive goals. They have been made supervisor of the Social Club's finances. They have been put in charge of cleaning up the customer database. They have been asked to train graduates."

"Okay. Look—"

"They have failed to receive recognition for their accomplishments. Rumors have sprung up about them and unattractive co-workers. Their monitors have begun to strobe. The spring-loading on their chairs has failed. Their pens have gone missing. They have been given multiple managers. They—"

"Enough!" Freddy says. "I get it, all right?"

There is a pause. A pause to savor the moment.

"What is seven times three?" the voice says.

Holly returns from lunch (a salad eaten alone at the counter of the local deli) to find East Berlin deserted. Jones is nowhere to be seen, and Freddy has vanished, too—GONE TO HUMAN RESOURCES, according to the Post-it on his monitor, but she assumes that's a joke. She sighs. She feels restless.

She gets up and walks to the watercooler. Holly is at the tail end of an eight-week aerobic plan; it's important to keep hydrated. She tugs out a paper cup, fills it, throws back her head, and keeps swallowing until she's drained it. When she lowers the cup, she is treated to the sight of Roger walking past, looking at her breasts. His eyes flick up to her face. He winks. "Holly."

"Roger."

He walks away. Holly puts down her cup. This is something she cannot get used to: the sheer shamelessness of businessmen. Holly doesn't want to be a bitch about it, but she doesn't understand why sagging, pot-bellied, out-of-shape assholes with overinflated senses of their own importance should think that they have a chance with her. Except that's the whole problem: within the company they *are* important, or at least more important than her. So a creepy, wet-lipped manager in Order Processing is entitled to flirt with her. Not to come right out and proposition her—that would be a gross violation of the company's policy on inter-employee relationships (short version: they're banned)—but that almost makes it worse. She has to pretend it's all friendly, harmless banter, when if the environment permitted a more honest response, she could tell them to go screw themselves.

If she was higher up the corporate ladder, this wouldn't happen: she would be too important for men to dare to flirt with her. And if the men were better-looking (or, in Roger's case, not such a complete prick), maybe she wouldn't mind so much. But they all think the best way to deal with a bulging belly is not to spend thirty minutes a day on the treadmill but to stretch a thin business shirt over it. (Sometimes there is a gap, the belly dragging the tie away from the shirt; sometimes the tie practically lies horizontal.) If they choose to take no pride in their own appearance, why are they entitled to enjoy hers? There is a lot Holly doesn't understand about Zephyr Holdings, but the rules of the corporate flirtation game irk her more than anything else. She can't accept them. Now people say she's unfriendly.

She walks back to her desk and pulls a couple of pages from her in-box. It seems that Elizabeth dropped by. She wants Holly to compile a summary of the summary she wrote for Sydney a couple of hours ago. Holly feels a migraine coming on. She wonders what would happen if she just walked out and went to the gym for the rest of the day.

Freddy arrives and collapses into his chair. She looks at

him, waiting for an explanation, but he just stares at his keyboard. "What's the matter?"

"Didn't you see my note?" He pulls the Post-it off his monitor and begins slowly tearing it into strips.

"Yeah, but seriously."

Freddy doesn't say anything.

"You really went to Human Resources?" She sits up. "What was it like? What do they do? Do they have cubicles?"

"I don't want to talk about it."

"Oh. Okay, be that way." Freddy remains silent. "Come on, tell me *something.*"

He shakes his head.

"Oh, *fine,*" Holly says. She turns back to her computer.

Jones takes a few tentative steps out onto the roof, letting the door rest gently against the frame so it won't close and lock him out. He is standing on a gray concrete slab stained with the excrement of about a million pigeons, many of whom are currently observing him from the tops of various aerials and vents. The upper sections of half a dozen skyscrapers that are particularly tall or situated farther up the hill or both are visible to one side, each window a tiny, tinted glimpse into a miniature corporate world. He walks to the barrier at the roof's edge and finds himself looking down at lunchtime traffic crawling along First Avenue. At this altitude, it's surprisingly quiet. Jones stares at it while the wind pulls at his hair and freezes the sweat on his back.

It's a minute before his brain starts to work again and points out that if he's quick, he can make it back down to level 2 before Security arrives. He can return to the original plan, modifying it only slightly to add asking Senior Management why the hell Daniel Klausman's office is the roof. He hurries back to the door. As he does, he sees there's a service elevator right beside it. He also hears suspiciously loud noises from the stairwell, and tugs the door open to find himself facing two sweaty, red-faced men in blue Security uniforms.

"You," one of them says. Jones gets the feeling this is the start of a two-word sentence, but doesn't wait for the denouement. He slams the door and slides the bolt home, locking it. He stabs at the elevator call button (which is red and made of rubber) and waits. "Mr. Jones," one of the guards says through the door, "if you don't leave Mr. Klausman alone right away, there will be serious repercussions."

The elevator arrives. Jones jumps into it. He stabs 2—SENIOR MANAGEMENT—and to his great relief the doors ease closed.

He exhales. He checks his cuffs and straightens his tie. He raises his chin. He may currently be in breach of any number of HR and Security policies, but the company is clearly practicing some kind of vast deception on its workers, so Jones figures that makes them even. He waits for the *ding*, for the doors to open.

They don't. He looks up. The elevator screen says 4, and even as he watches, ticks over to 5. Alarmed, he reaches for 2 again and realizes it's not illuminated. He presses it: it lights up, then goes dark. He tries 5, then 6, then he runs his hand up and down the columns of buttons. All illuminate for no longer than a second. He puts his hand on the elevator wall to steady himself. Is this thing accelerating? In a flash he realizes that this must be how Zephyr disposes of employees who are no longer useful: the elevator free-falls them into the basement.

He feels the elevator begin to slow. So maybe not. The screen shows 11. That winks out and is replaced by 12. It appears he is headed for 14: Training Sales. He exhales in disgust. Security is probably waiting for him there with all his possessions in a cardboard box.

The number 12 blinks out, and the elevator comes to a complete stop. There is a curiously long pause. Then two things happen at once: the elevator goes *ding* and the screen shows 13.

Jones looks at the button panel, just in case he has recently lost his mind. But no. As he thought, there is no button for 13.

The doors slide open.

The first thing he notices is the lighting. It's not fluorescent and stabbing at his retinas, oh no; this is a soft, muted light that glows from invisible recesses in the ceiling. Second: the carpet is not the usual violent orange but a gentle, soothing blue. Third: the elevator opens onto a corridor—no surprise there—but this corridor is made of glass, and beyond it Jones can see glass-walled offices everywhere, *offices with walls.* These are the things that really grab his attention. It's only when he has recovered from the shock of these that he notices less significant things, such as the group of people standing in front of him. Front and center is the janitor. Beside him is Eve Jantiss.

"Mr. Jones," the janitor says. "I'm Daniel Klausman. Welcome to Project Alpha."

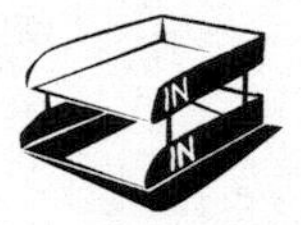

"Standard procedure, of course, is to throw you out of the building." Klausman is still wearing his gray overalls, but it's his shock of steely-gray hair that Jones can't stop looking at. That's enough to convince him that this man really is the CEO of Zephyr Holdings: he has management hair. Klausman puts a hand on Jones's arm and steers him down a corridor. "We'd be spreading the word that you'd been caught stealing a computer and that'd be the end of you. Wouldn't be the first time."

Jones glances at Eve, who smiles brilliantly. The sight of all those gleaming teeth makes him more nervous.

Klausman stops walking, and, dutifully, so does everybody else. "But there's something about you, Mr. Jones. Something special. We noticed it right from the start, didn't we?" He looks at Eve. She nods, then, when Klausman turns away, winks. "But this roof thing clinched it. Nobody's ever made it that far before. Curious fella, aren't you? We like that, Mr. Jones. We like it a lot. It would have been interesting to study you. But since that's no longer possible... we're going to make you an offer."

"You pose as a janitor," Jones says. He realizes this is not particularly insightful, but he needs to establish some facts they can all agree on.

"Some executives, they make a big show of working on the front lines every now and again. You see those McDonald's managers? They flip burgers one day a year, taking breaks every five minutes to call back to the office, and think they're getting frontline experience. I, Mr. Jones, live in the front line. No one's closer to his employees than me." He smiles, as if expecting Jones to say something appreciative.

"And Eve is not really a receptionist."

"She is as much a receptionist as I am a janitor." A smile twitches around the corner of Klausman's lips.

"She *is* a receptionist, but she's mostly something else."

"Keep going."

Jones looks around. Through the glass walls, he sees banks of monitors, displaying pictures from around the company. "You're watching. Everything that goes on in the company."

"Almost there. Can you hit a homer?"

He takes a breath. "The purpose of Zephyr Holdings..." He hesitates. If he's wrong, everybody in this room is going to kill themselves laughing. Eve nods encouragingly. He decides: *What the hell.* "Zephyr is a test bed. A laboratory, for trying management techniques and observing the results. Zephyr's an experiment."

Nobody laughs. Klausman looks around. "What did I tell you? Huh?"

"You've done it again," one of the suits says.

Klausman spreads his palms. "I am the Alpha and the Omega."

Now they laugh. Eventually, Jones gets it. "The Omega Management System." He feels unsteady. "You created it. This is where you come up with the techniques."

In Training Sales, something terrible is happening to Elizabeth: she is finding Roger attractive. It must be a joke, arranged by her treacherous body and pregnancy-fueled hormones. But Elizabeth is not laughing. *Roger?* Anybody who would set her up with Roger doesn't know the first thing about her. Elizabeth is shocked by her body's opinion of her.

She hasn't decided what to do about her situation. At first it seemed obvious. There's no place in her career for a baby. But that initial reaction has tempered. A hidden, furtive part of her mind, the part that vetoed the condom, perhaps, is growing in influence. It is seeping into her marrow. Elizabeth is losing ground to it. It is a shocking process, or would be if it weren't so anesthetizing. She only glimpses the true extent of its power at moments like this, when she realizes that she is gazing across the aisle at Roger with her mouth hanging open.

Roger catches her gaze. He blinks in surprise. Elizabeth snaps her mouth closed and wheels around to her desk. She clenches her hands into fists. *No! Please, God, not that!*

"I don't know why it's such a surprise to everyone," Klausman says. He is seated behind the biggest desk Jones has ever seen. Two walls of his office are glass, and low-lying clouds drift by. Jones feels as if the building is in the process of toppling over; he keeps realizing he's leaning to the left, seeking balance. "I'm simply applying scientific methods of investigation to a business environment. We don't expect scientists to work on live human beings. They use labs. They experiment in controlled conditions. It's the exact same concept."

Jones says, "But you are practicing on live human beings."

"No, no, no. Zephyr Holdings is an entirely artificial company. It has no actual customers. Oh, wait, I see, you're saying the staff are live people. Yes, that's true. But it's not as if we're hurting them. We give them jobs—essentially pointless jobs, yes, but they don't know that. And when you get right down to it, most jobs are pointless. Pick any single position in a company and eliminate it, and the remaining staff find a way to cover. It's true. We proved it in Logistics."

"Still... isn't there some kind of ethical—"

"In fact, Zephyr employees are better off *because* they don't have to deal with customers."

"What's wrong with customers?"

Klausman laughs. The suits behind Jones chuckle. "Forgive him. He's young." He leans forward. "Customers are vermin, Mr. Jones. They infect companies with disease." He says this with complete solemnity. "A company is a system. It is built to perform a relatively small set of actions over and over, as efficiently as possible. The enemy of systems is variation, and customers produce variation. They want special products. They have unique circumstances. They try to place orders with after-sales support and they direct complaints to sales. My proudest accomplishment, and I am being perfectly honest with you here, Mr. Jones, is not the Omega Management System and its associated revenue stream—which, by the way, is extremely lucrative. It is Zephyr. A customer-free company. Listen to that, Mr. Jones. *A customer-free company.* In the early days, you know, we tried to simulate customers. It was a disaster. Killed the whole project. When we started again, I cut every department that had external customers. It was like shooting a pack of rabid dogs. Now, I'm not claiming Zephyr Holdings is perfect. But we're getting there, Mr. Jones. We're getting there."

Jones says, "This is a lot to take in."

"I wish I could give you a few days to consider it. But I can't. You're either with us or against us, I'm afraid."

"You're offering me a job? As what?"

Klausman holds up his palms. "I just do vision. Eve, take Mr. Jones somewhere and fill him in on the details, will you?"

Eve tips Klausman a wink on the way out, and Klausman says, "Be gentle with him," and they both laugh, which concerns Jones somewhat. Eve slips her arm through Jones's and marches him down a corridor. "Want to get some sun? A few hours in this place at a time is about all I can stand."

Jones says something in response, but can't remember what, because Eve's left breast is snuggling up against his bicep. When she reaches for the elevator button, her honey-brown hair brushes past his face, and the scent invades Jones's nostrils, heads straight for his brain, and starts fooling about with his controls.

"Sometimes you can wait here for five minutes," Eve says, looking at the screen. "They won't stop unless they're empty. At lunchtime—ah, here we go." She steps inside. Jones follows. In the elevator's mirrored walls, he can see himself and Eve, Eve and him, all the way to infinity. "I have to say, I am deeply impressed by how quickly you found us out. Most people who work at Zephyr are dumb as cattle. I mean that. It's numbing. Some nights I go home and just stare at myself in the mirror until I remember I'm not one of them." She grins.

"What are you? What's your position?"

"Well, what do you think? How do we control Zephyr Holdings?"

Jones thinks. Then he catches sight of the button panel, and the answer is obvious. "Human Resources. They're not a real department. They're part of Alpha."

Eve smirks. "Actually, no. Human Resources is just like that. We gave them a lot of freedom to evolve on their own, and this is what happened. You should read the reports;

they're fascinating. HR staff actually grow to hate people. No, Alpha works by placing agents throughout the company. There's only twelve of us. Most of the time, all we do is watch. But when we want to study something in particular, we pull a few strings in the background to make it happen."

"And nobody in Zephyr knows."

"Right." Her teeth gleam. "Now, if you see anyone you know, act natural."

"What?"

The elevator doors slide open.

Eve starts across the lobby floor, her heels *clack*ing. Jones hurries after her. He feels incredibly self-conscious. Gretel gives him a smile and a wave, and Jones is too rattled to return it properly. Does Gretel know? He catches sight of the security cameras in the corner of the ceiling and suddenly understands how pervasive they are. They are in every room in the building. Until now, he never thought twice about them.

The lobby doors whoosh apart. Eve digs in her purse and then the beautiful Audi convertible is *boop-boop*ing and Eve is throwing the keys at his face. Jones catches them, startled. "You can drive a shift, right?"

"You're not serious."

"I am serious." She unlatches the passenger-side door, levers her long legs into the car, and drums her hands on the dash. "Come on, gawky."

Jones takes a moment. He thinks: *Am I really about to drive this car?* Then he thinks: *Yes. I am.*

He opens the driver's-side door and slides his butt into the seat. The leather whispers approvingly to him. He puts his hands on the steering wheel and takes some deep breaths.

"Are you one of those people who are really into cars?" Eve says.

"I had thought not," Jones says.

She laughs. "Let's go."

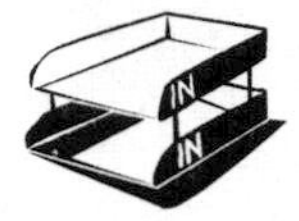

"I'm not talking yet," Eve says, "because you seem preoccupied with the car."

Jones shifts into fourth and the car leaps forward. What impresses him is how much the Audi trusts him. His old Toyota, currently parked on sublevel 2 of the Zephyr lot, doesn't respond to the controls so much as take their advice on board for consideration. This car reads his every twitch as gospel. Jones is having trouble maintaining a steady speed because it is listening to the thumping of his heart through his business shoes.

"Interesting, isn't it?" Eve says. "How you need to be more disciplined to operate a high-performance piece of machinery. More machinelike yourself." She stretches in the sun. Jones wants to glance at her, but doesn't trust himself not to wrap the Audi around a street sign. "Damn, this is a beautiful day. Someone tried to tell me the other day that the only habitable place in America is California. But I just don't understand how you could spend your life restricted to summer outfits." She slides something onto her hair, pulling it into a ponytail that leaps and twists in the wind. "Okay, let's get down to business. You seem like a smart guy, so I'll spare you the sales pitch, all right?"

"Thanks."

"If you don't join Alpha, your career is over."

Jones swerves a little. A white Ford honks at him. "Can I have the sales pitch?"

She laughs. "If you join Alpha, you'll start at $125,000 a year, be on the cutting edge of global business management practices, and get the kind of experience money can't buy. Instead of spending your days with the pencil pushers and clock-watchers, you get to play with the big boys. You get to have fun."

Jones risks a glance at her. "What do you mean, my career would be over?"

"What happens if people find out Zephyr is fake?"

"I guess... the experiment is ruined. You'd have to shut the company down."

"So we can't have you telling anybody. We would take steps to ensure you didn't."

"What sort of—"

" 'Stephen Jones was a competent and productive member of staff, except when using the Internet to download animal-related pornography.' "

"Jesus!"

She laughs. "I'm kidding. Kind of. But you get the idea. You wouldn't want to put us on your CV. You can come up with some story to explain the gap in your employment history, but still, that's the kind of thing that makes employers wary. If it comes down to you and someone who didn't mysteriously miss out on every major graduate intake program, I know who I'd hire."

"What if I just promise not to tell anyone about Project Alpha?"

"We prefer to play it safe," Eve says. "There's a lot at stake."

Jones doesn't say anything.

"But don't focus on the negatives. The important thing is the opportunity. So just say yes."

"To what? I don't know what you want me to do."

"Same as the rest of us: become an agent. You keep your official job, but you also run projects for Alpha. If Klausman likes your ideas, you get your own project. Maybe it even goes into the next edition of *The Omega Management System.* It's very rewarding. Occasionally we go into other companies to present our findings, tailor a solution for their special circumstances. That's the best. You fly around the country, stay in five-star hotels, bill everything to the client... I'm telling you, Jones, it beats the crap out of filing someone else's expense forms."

"But no one in Zephyr would know what I'm doing."

"No." Eve snickers. "No, Jones."

He pulls up at a red light and looks across at her. She has one arm hanging out of the car and is looking at him through dark sunglasses and smiling. Despite this, Jones says, "I don't know if I feel comfortable spying on my co-workers."

"Urrrr," Eve says, as if she has heard this a million times before. "Okay, look. Companies spy on their workers. They have security cameras. They monitor e-mails. Employees know they're being watched. We're just more organized about it than most companies."

"There's a difference between a security camera and sitting next to someone pretending to be their colleague." She doesn't say anything, so he adds, "Don't you think?"

"Honestly? No. If you see a co-worker ripping off the company and report it to your manager, is that wrong? That's what we're doing: we're looking out for unproductive situations and trying to fix them."

"But—"

"Do you want the ethics speech? Because we have one. It's on video, this whole spiel about how we're improving business efficiency, creating jobs, and building a stronger America. By the time it's over, you'll think anyone who doesn't like what we're doing is a Communist. We hand them out to our more religious investors. You're not religious, are you?"

"Well, not really—"

"It's kind of a joke. When someone asks for the ethics tape, we know they've already decided to invest. They just want some reassurance so they can feel good about it, too. That's the thing you learn about values, Jones: they're what people make up to justify what they did. Did you take business ethics in college?"

"Yes."

"They teach you people's behavior is guided by their values, right? That's a load of crap. When you watch people like we do, you find out it's the other way around. Look, I believe in what Alpha does, I really do. But do I worry about whether every little thing we do is ethical? No, because you can rationalize anything as ethical. You talk to a criminal—a tax dodger, a serial killer, a child abuser—and every one of them will justify their actions. They'll explain to you, totally seriously, why they had to do what they did. Why they're still good people. That's the thing: when people talk about the importance of ethics, they never include themselves. The day anyone, anywhere, admits that they personally are unethical, I'll start taking that whole issue seriously."

Someone honks. Jones realizes the light is green. He jumps the car forward, almost stalls it, then gets it under control.

"You know, I'm surprised," she says. "I don't understand why you're not jumping at this. Are you afraid of challenges? I guess that would explain why you took a job at Zephyr, a company you'd never heard of."

"No, I took the job because—" Jones starts, but this is not a sentence he wants to finish. "I'm not afraid of challenges."

"Then say yes. I mean, come on, what else are you going to do with your career? Do you really want to spend the next ten years working your way up to a middle-management position? Ninety-five percent of all jobs suck, Jones. That's why people get paid to do them. We're offering you one of the 5 percent. This work is exciting. And it pays really well. Anyone in Training Sales would slit your throat for it. What's to think about?"

The phrase "ten years" gets him. This is scarily plausible: Jones can imagine himself slogging through a decade of corporate politics and day-to-day drudgery, steadily losing his enthusiasm until he is experienced and mercenary enough to qualify for the kind of position that Eve is offering him right now.

"Heh. You're cute," she says. "It's like you're broadcasting your thoughts right there on your face."

Jones gets flustered. He pulls the Audi over to the side

of the road. He actually feels bad about having to kill the engine. After a minute he says, "Okay. I'm in."

Eve grins. "Good. I'm pleased." She puts one hand on his thigh and squeezes. "Now we'd better get back. I need to cancel the computer-porn story."

At 4:00 P.M., the Credit department implodes. Until now, Credit's job has been to make sure that before any Zephyr department accepts an order, the customer has both the means and the inclination to pay. The customers are all other Zephyr departments, of course, but some manage their finances better than others. There have been cases where departments—there's no need to name names—ordered something then tried to delay payment. These are Credit's mortal enemies. To defeat them, it wields a terrible weapon: the Credit hold.

When successfully deployed, it cripples the victim, leaving it unable to carry out the critical, life-supporting task of buying things. Poison floods through its fiscal veins. The only known way for a department to cure a Credit hold is to persuade Credit that its finances are in terrific shape—which is difficult to do while its operations are paralyzed. Every department ever infected with a Credit hold has perished. Which, as Credit has pointed out, proves how prescient it was to deploy it in the first place.

A lot of money has been wagered around the company

on which will happen first: whether Credit will strangle Human Resources or Human Resources will sack Credit. This battle of the superdepartments has been a long time coming, and warning shots have been fired over the bows of both sides. Last month, Credit issued a warning on certain bloated Human Resources expense accounts; in response, Human Resources trimmed Credit from twenty-eight employees to twenty-six. Tensions escalated. Alliances formed in darkened meeting rooms. A rumor began circulating: Senior Management was thinking about downgrading the Credit hold from company policy to a simple advisory. If true, war was inevitable, because Credit would have no choice but to attack Human Resources while it could. A lot of annual leave was being hastily arranged in the Credit and Human Resources departments.

But all this is now moot, thanks to two hundred missing sheets of letterhead. On Monday morning, these sheets, fresh from Corporate Supplies, vanished. They could be replaced for a little under three dollars, but Credit's manager declared the theft to be not merely criminal but an assault on that most sacred of principles: teamwork. He issued a department-wide demand for the return of the pilfered papers. Inquiries began. Staff were called in for one-on-one discussions. Work records were studied. Desk drawers were opened and their contents carefully sifted through. As the investigation heated up, careless accusations were thrown. Employee morale, already strained from tensions with Human Resources, fell to bitter new lows.

This morning, Credit employees arrive at their desks to find a memo from the manager. It upbraids three people for shoddy work practices, which were uncovered as a by-product of the recent investigation. It stresses the importance of completing two major projects. And finally, offhandedly, it says the manager has located the missing stationery, which he misfiled in his desk, so that matter is closed.

Enraged Credit employees storm the manager's office. The manager is lucky to get to the door in time; he locks it and takes cover behind his desk. As the workers outside shout and bang on the glass wall, he stabs at his phone for Human Resources. He wants to lay off the whole department, he says: all of them, all of them! Human Resources is happy to oblige. Within two minutes, a dozen blue-uniformed Security guards step from the elevators.

By the time the last employee is dragged away and Security has begun to clean up, Human Resources has issued a company-wide voice mail. It announces that Credit has chosen to lay off all but one employee as a cost-saving measure. And since a group of fewer than ten people does not qualify as a department, the entity Credit no longer exists. Forthwith, Credit holds will be issued by Human Resources.

"Where did you go?" Freddy says. "Someone came around to look at your computer. We thought you'd been sacked."

"Someone looked at my computer?"

"Yeah, some guy from Security. But it turns out he was just installing new drivers."

Jones says, "How do you know?"

"That's what he said."

"Did he install anything on your computers? Holly?"

"You know, Freddy's right," Holly says, heading for the watercooler. "You *are* getting paranoid."

"Don't you think it's weird that—" He stops himself. "Sorry. You're right. Sorry."

Freddy waits until Holly's left. "Speaking of weird, I heard you went for a ride with Eve Jantiss!" He smiles. It looks painful.

"Uh, yeah."

"Wow." Freddy shakes his head. "I have no idea how you managed that."

Jones realizes that this is as close as Freddy can bring himself to asking what the hell Jones is up to. "Oh, I just, you know, we got to talking about those flowers, and she thought maybe I'd sent them to her, and I said no—"

"She thought *you'd* sent them? But I started sending her flowers before you even got hired."

Jones starts to sweat. "Oh. Well, that's weird."

"How could she think they were from you?"

"I guess—anyway, I said they weren't, but I might know who sent them. And she was like, 'You *have* to tell me.' I didn't, of course"—Jones injects, because Freddy now looks to be on the verge of a heart attack—"but she wanted to find out, and she offered me a ride in her car, so . . . that's how that happened." Freddy doesn't say anything, so Jones adds, "She's really intrigued by the whole flower thing. I think you should tell her it's you."

Freddy stares. "Maybe I should speak to her."

"Exactly. Exactly. Get to know her a bit, then when you

tell her about the flowers, she already knows you're a nice guy."

Freddy nods slowly. "Thanks. Thanks, Jones. You know, at first . . . I thought maybe you were moving in." He laughs.

"No, no! Come on."

Freddy smiles: genuinely, this time. "You're a good man, Jones."

"Come on," Jones says. "Come on."

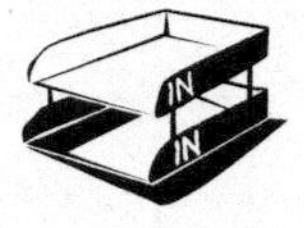

At seven fifteen in the morning the lights of the Zephyr building burn in the fog like the port windows of a sinking ship. Tendrils of dawn sunlight leak into the night sky, but it makes no difference to Zephyr Holdings: inside, thanks to the eternally vigilant fluorescents, it's always 9:00 A.M. Turning off the lights, after all, would imply that employees are expected at some point to leave. So at Zephyr the lights stay on regardless of whether anybody's home.

Jones walks across the parking lot, gravel crunching under his shoes. He is surprisingly alert for this time of the day, considering he hasn't had a coffee yet—but then again, he is en route to his first secret Project Alpha meeting. He enters the lobby and squeaks his way across to the elevators. All four cars are open and waiting for him.

Jones steps inside and sets down his briefcase. Eve gave him specific instructions on how to reach level 13, these being: (1) choose an empty elevator, (2) swipe his (upgraded)

ID card, (3) press the 12 and 14 buttons simultaneously, and (4) press DOOR OPEN when the elevator is roughly level with 13. This doesn't sound too complicated in theory, but Jones expects to spend a bit of time bouncing between floors before he's nailed step four, which is why he's here fifteen minutes early. But he gets it right on his first attempt: the screen flashes up 13 and the doors open on blue carpet and muted lighting. Jones feels mildly proud of himself.

He walks down the glass corridor, following the sound of voices, and enters a meeting room. There are half a dozen people already here, including Eve Jantiss, who is leaning against an oak table roughly the size of Jones's apartment. This table can't be a single piece of wood, because that would be ridiculous, but it certainly looks like it. It is a rich, warm brown, not so much reflecting the recessed lights as gently spreading their luminence around; it is a table so beautiful that Jones actually notices it despite the fact that Eve is right in front of him in a short black skirt and buttoned shirt. "Jones!" she says. "You just won me fifty dollars." She points through the glass wall to a bank of monitors. "Level 13 on the first try. Tom thought we'd need to go fetch you."

"Hi," says Tom, a middle-aged man with a bright blue tie who is browsing the buffet table on the other side of the room. Jones nods hello.

Eve says, "You know, one time I tried that trick at the Hyatt in New York, pressing 12 and 14 then DOOR OPEN at 13, and I surprised a bunch of FBI agents. I swear I'm telling the truth."

The room chuckles at this, so Jones wipes the amazed

expression off his face and replaces it with a smile. He looks around for somewhere to stash his briefcase.

"Under the table," Eve says. "And help yourself to a pastry."

This occupies Jones for the next few minutes, along with introductions to the other agents of Project Alpha. They all seem reasonably sociable, but the common thread is that they are clearly very smart. Jones realizes he will be running along behind these people for a while.

"Ah, the wunderkind," a voice says behind him. Jones turns to see Blake Seddon grinning at him from the doorway. Blake is Alpha's plant in Senior Management. He is deeply tanned, in his late thirties, wears pinstriped suits, and has teeth so bright that Jones finds himself squinting. Did his parents just take the gamble that he would turn out a square-jawed hunk with great hair, Jones wonders, or was that brought on somehow by his name? There's a whole nature-versus-nurture debate right there. "You know, if you're meant to be the hot new thing here, you should get yourself a new suit."

Jones realizes he's been insulted. He looks down at his suit, which is two months old and cost four hundred dollars.

"Oh, fuck off, Blake," Eve says amiably. Blake laughs. Eve takes a seat and gets to work on her croissant. "Jones," she says, through a mouthful. "Come sit."

Jones obeys. The chair surprises him, giving in some places and supporting in others. This, he realizes, is an expensive chair. He experiments, moving his butt and arching his back. It gets better. Jones had no idea that chairs could do this. To think, all his life he has accepted that chairs provide a certain standard level of comfort, while society's elite were enjoying *this.*

"Ignore Blake." Eve doesn't deliberately aim this at Blake, but she doesn't lower her voice, either. "He's just threatened."

"Why?"

She looks at him. "You don't know? Wow. You *are* cute."

Jones feels thrown. What do you say to that? He settles for a mixture of smiling and looking doubtful.

"What a beautiful morning!" Daniel Klausman exclaims, striding into the room. From the general reaction, Jones gets the impression that this is a standard greeting. He's wearing his overalls, which is going to take Jones some getting used to, and he drops into an enormous leather chair at the head of the table. The agents take this as a signal to get organized, but Jones notices they are not exactly rushing, in the way they would if, say, this was Training Sales and Sydney's meeting. So Klausman is fairly relaxed about protocol.

Klausman leans to his right and peers at a pastry on a napkin in front of a young woman wearing delicate glasses. "What is that, Mona? Cake?"

"Mille-feuille," Mona says, covering her mouth daintily. She swallows. "It's a French pastry. Custard, filo, and, if I'm not mistaken, a hint of almonds."

"Nice?"

"Very nice."

"Good. The company's prices are outrageous, but they promise quality."

"They deliver," Eve says. "I had a pastry last week that was positively orgasmic."

"Well," Klausman says. "They are *exceeding* expectations, then." He looks around the table. "Shall we begin?"

"Project 3811," Blake says. "Training Delivery. We're experimenting with endurance limits in floating-deadline environments. Basically we've recruited four volunteers for what we've told them is a task of critical importance, put them in a meeting room, and every few hours we change the task's goals in minor but significant ways that require them to keep working."

"Hmm," Klausman says. "You're getting them food and water?"

"Oh yes. They order in pizza, and so forth. It's very interesting. They've been in there for twenty-eight hours and no one's left. The dynamic seems to be that no one wants to let the others down, even though they all want to go home. I don't need to point out the potential here. But there are some side effects: shouting, increased aggressiveness, declining conformity to company dress code, that sort of thing."

"I bet you can't keep them in there for more than two days," Eve says.

Blake raises his eyebrows. "I'll take that bet."

"Bottle of Dom Pérignon?

"I believe you still owe me a bottle from our last bet."

"So you'll have two."

"If I don't have *one now*," Blake says, "why should I believe you'll deliver *two later*?"

"Touché," Eve says.

"Children," Klausman chides. "Take this off-line, if you please. Tom, how are you going with the depersonalization project?"

"Well, mixed results. Although..." He clears his throat, glancing at Jones.

"Ah," Klausman says. "Of course. Mr. Jones, you are unwittingly part of this project. We're experimenting with eliminating first names, encouraging employees to refer to each other by surname only. That's why your ID tag doesn't have your first name on it."

"Oh," Jones says. "I was wondering about that."

"My theory is it encourages focus on job function rather than personality," Tom explains. "The military does it. Can I ask: What did you think? When I was observing you, you didn't seem to raise any objections."

"Uh... I guess, no. I thought it was strange... but everyone was calling me Jones, so I just went with it."

Tom nods, satisfied. "It's early days yet. But we are seeing potentially significant downward trends in nonbusiness watercooler and phone chatter."

There is an approving murmur at this. Jones sees Eve smile at Tom appreciatively and feels a stab of surprising, stupid jealousy.

"Good, good. Mona, make a note of that?"

"Got it." She begins to murmur into something that looks a little like a tape recorder but, Jones has no doubt, is probably also able to organize her calendar, unlock her car, and place phone calls.

"Next. Jones. Jones?"

"Yes, sir."

"What have you got for me?"

Jones feels everyone's eyes on him. "You mean like, a project idea?"

There are a few chuckles. Blake, across the table, laughs

a little louder and longer than Jones feels is really necessary. "Yes," Klausman says. "That's what you're here for."

Jones clears his throat. "Well, obviously I'm new to all this, so I don't know exactly what you're after... but I was thinking of doing something about smoking." He leaves a little pause, just in case anyone wants to jump in with, *We already have a project on smoking, Jones,* or *Not again, every damn new guy wants to do something about smoking.* "As I'm sure you're aware, the average company loses 5.7 days per year for every employee who smokes, due to the additional breaks they take. It's illegal to discriminate against them, but companies that reduce smoking in their workforce will see a productivity increase. Not to mention, of course, the health benefits."

"Right," Tom says. "We pay higher premiums for smokers."

"Ah, yes, there's that, too," Jones says. "So my first idea is to reward nonsmokers with additional vacation time for not taking smoking breaks—say, a day per year."

Across the table, Blake interjects, "Or we could just penalize smokers a vacation day. Or make them work overtime."

"Well... no. Because that would be illegal." Jones doesn't want to get into a pissing match with Blake, so resists the impulse to add something inflammatory, like: *obviously.*

Eve says, "Zing!"

"Also," Jones says, pressing ahead, "this way you get buy-in from the staff. Plenty of nonsmokers feel aggrieved that smokers get extra breaks during the day. This will make them feel justified about their outrage, and more willing to speak out about it, which increases peer pressure on smokers to quit. It's kind of inflammatory, but given the benefits, including to the smokers themselves, I think it's justified."

Eve smiles. "Is this guy good or what?"

"My other thought," Jones says, gaining confidence, "is to create a designated smoking area. Currently people hang out in two or three groups near the exits."

"Wait," Tom says. "How does this help discourage smoking?"

"We put up little mock fences and a sign that says Smokers' Corral," Jones says. "So it's socially embarrassing."

There's a ripple of laughter. "I like it," Klausman says. "I can see you'll fit right in here, Jones." He ponders for a moment. "I want you to do it. But with the vacation days, don't make an official announcement. We'll just spread the rumor that the company is considering it. As for the Corral, I think we should be able to set something up near the backup generator, yes?"

Blake says, "I can put a request in to Infrastructure Management."

"Excellent!" Klausman smacks his lips. "Now, all this talk of smoking is giving me cravings."

"Me, too," Eve says. "And I quit a year ago."

"What say we take a recess," Klausman says, standing, "and pick this up in ten."

Megan, the Training Sales PA, staggers through the glass doors of the level 17 gymnasium. She's wearing a big, baggy tracksuit that's stuck to her skin with what feels like a gallon of frozen sweat. Her heart is thumping so hard she can feel it in her ears. This morning Megan decided to walk to work. When the Zephyr building drew within sight, she picked up pace; then, at the very end, she broke out into an actual jog. It is the first time Megan has run since high school, and it nearly killed her.

But she feels happy. Last night Megan was channel surfing, zapping from one stupid show to another from the comfort of her sofa, when she hit a motivational speaker on an infomercial. "*Your* goals are within *your* reach," the speaker said, the squareness of his jaw brooking no argument. Megan's finger hesitated on the remote. "The only thing holding *you* back is *you*."

Lying alone in bed that night, Megan wondered if that wasn't true. Why is she, a reasonably intelligent twenty-four-year-old woman, spending forty hours a week sitting at a desk against a wall with nobody to talk to and nothing to do more interesting than rearrange ceramic bears? Why is she keeping careful notes on the movement of Jones (who is away from his desk a lot lately; she hopes he doesn't have medical trouble), instead of talking to him? Yes, Sydney makes her sit away from everybody else, and yes, people in Zephyr Holdings are generally oblivious to the lives of PAs, but *Megan has the power to change this.* If she was more confident, she might get into more conversations. If she lost some weight and bought some better clothes . . .

This was fantasy. But the man on the TV said *the only*

thing holding Megan back was Megan, and if he's right, then Jones is within her reach, too.

She can't even think it without flushing like an idiot. It is ridiculous to imagine that Jones could fall in love with her. He is young and dynamic and surrounded by girls who are effortlessly more attractive than Megan, people like Holly Vale (blond, slim, athletic) and Gretel Monadnock (beautiful) and Eve Jantiss (depressingly beautiful). Megan has stood in the shadows of girls like that all her life, as they tossed their shiny hair and flashed their perfect smiles, touching their necks as they laughed at the jokes of all the boys Megan has ever liked. She knows how it works. They flirt, even though they already have boyfriends (they always do, and always the best ones), and whether they mean to or not they exert a gravitational pull on every man around, reminding them that this is what a desirable woman looks like, *this,* not like fat, bespectacled Megan, who might as well belong to a different species.

She heads into the gymnasium shower room. Every step hurts, but her body feels as if it is singing. Megan is amazed. So this is why people exercise! If it works like this, instead of being a constant battle against pain and exhaustion, well, Megan can see herself doing it. She could run to work every day. She could (eventually) become one of those people like Holly, who is thin and attractive and—emerging from a shower stall right in front of her.

Megan stops dead. Holly, wearing just a white towel, sees her and blinks with surprise.

"Hi," Megan says, but only her mouth participates: her throat fails to get organized enough to supply it with sound. She clears her throat to try again, but thanks to the jogging emits a thick, wet noise that sounds like someone blowing their nose. She is too mortified to speak.

"I didn't know you worked out." Holly walks to the bench, puts one foot up on it, leans forward, and begins to dry her hair with a second towel.

"I'm just starting." Megan's voice comes out strained. She cannot bear to stand here and watch the muscles work in Holly's tan shoulders—shoulders that look nothing at all like hers. The idea of walking past those shoulders to the showers is so daunting that it takes her a second to force her body into motion. Her hand grips her bag of work clothes so hard that her fingers ache.

As she's squeezing past, Holly says, "Well, good for you, Megan."

Megan is shocked. It sounds like Holly really means it.

Level 14 is split into two halves: Training Sales when you turn right from the elevators and Training Delivery when you turn left. They are exact mirror images. Most of Zephyr is like this, and there are several amusing stories of burned-out employees wandering into the wrong department, settling down, and complaining about being unable to log on to their computer.

In the Training Delivery meeting room, blinds are drawn across both the internal wall and the windows. Four people sit around a table, not speaking. One, Simon Huggis, is staring at Karen Nguyen's face—or, more specifically, at the mole beside her nose. Simon has worked with Karen for two years, and in all that time her mole never bothered him. But he's been in this meeting room for thirty-four consecutive hours, and now it's all he can think about. He loathes it. When he closes his eyes, he can still see it, nestled in under the curve of one nostril. Over the past couple of hours, an idea has been forming in his brain: Karen knows exactly how annoying it is, and that's why she leaves it there.

Across the table, Karen looks up from a list of action items. There are deep, dark troughs under her eyes. Her hair is frayed. "What?"

"Nothing." Simon reaches for a mint. As he does, everybody else exhales sharply.

"Simon," says Darryl Klosterman. His voice is gentle but pained, like a doctor explaining that the cancer is inoperable. He is sitting beside Karen Nguyen. *Everybody* is on the opposite side of the table from Simon, because, allegedly, Simon smells. That's what they said, ten hours ago. Another explanation is that they are plotting against him. "Please. No more mints."

Simon slowly unwraps the mint. The plastic crackles.

"Simon," says Helen Patelli. She is a tall woman with graying hair, which is all Simon can see at the moment, because she has her head in her arms, resting on the table. "If you have one more mint, I swear, I'm going to slap you so hard."

Simon pops the mint in his mouth. He sucks on it more vigorously than is really warranted, making little smacking noises.

"Please. Please," Darryl says. "We're almost done. This

is it. Let's just keep it together for one more half hour, then we can all go home."

"That's what you said yesterday," Helen says into her arms. "*Yesterday!*" Her voice cracks.

"But we've agreed. This is it, no matter what. This is our last revision. We made that perfectly clear. If they want more changes, they can get someone else to do it. So let's just pull together for this one last—"

The meeting room door cracks open, spilling light into the room. Everyone looks around, dazed. Even Helen's head comes up. Standing in the doorway is a tanned, handsome man in a beautiful pinstriped suit. Simon doesn't recognize him.

"Not interrupting, am I? Blake Seddon. Senior Management." He smiles. His teeth leave an afterimage on Simon's retina. "Just wanted to duck in and say what a fantastic job you're doing. Everyone in Senior Management is aware of the sacrifice you've made. Including Daniel Klausman."

This gets a murmur from the group. Helen says, "Daniel Klausman . . . knows about us?"

"He's very impressed. He told me to make sure that when all this is over, you get whatever you want. Vacation days, a bonus—you name it."

Simon sees his co-workers' mouths split open and their teeth emerge. It takes him a moment to realize what's happening, because it's been at least a day since he's seen any of them smile. Even Karen Nguyen's mole briefly disappears behind her nose. The tightness in Simon's chest eases a little.

"Now," Blake says, looking at a piece of paper in his hand, and Simon's gut spasms. This is what happened two hours ago, and three hours before that, and so many times before that that Simon can't remember them all: someone comes in to deliver praise, then . . . "I want to make sure you know these figures need to be plotted out over five years. Right?"

They stare at him. They are, of course, aware of no such thing; nobody mentioned five-year projections last time their objectives were updated, or the time before that, or *ever,* not even back when this nightmare began and they were all human.

Darryl clears his throat. Simon knows what's coming. Darryl will explain their position, and this pinstriped man will frown and say he can't understand how this happened, and after five minutes of excruciating dialogue, during which it will be explained that their work of the last thirty-four hours is basically useless without five-year projections, they will agree to keep working, *just this one more time.* To cut this short, Simon stands up. His pants make a peeling sound as they separate from his office chair. Everybody looks at him, dull surprise on their faces, as he walks unsteadily around the table.

"Yes?" Blake says.

The feeling starts in Simon's calves and comes scampering up through his legs. It floods his torso. He doesn't completely identify it until it hits his right shoulder and funnels into his arm, then he realizes: it's violence. He has about a quarter of a second to think, *Do I really want to punch this guy in the face?* and the answer is nonverbal: his fist rocketing out and smashing Blake's face. Blake yelps, pinwheels back, bounces off the door frame, and sprawls on the carpet. Simon just stands there. He is quietly prepared to go ahead and kill Blake, but this punch feels so good he takes a few moments to savor it.

"*Simon!*" Helen shrieks. He turns. They're a line of circus clowns, their mouths all hanging open.

"Ug! Ug! Jeebus *Chrised*!" Blake yells. He tries to scramble away and to catch the blood dribbling from his nose from dripping onto his shirt.

"This meeting," Simon says, "is over."

Karen stands first. The others are slower to react, but then, one by one, they rise, pushing back their damp, sweaty chairs, and grope toward the doorway. They mill there a second, then they hug. Helen's eyes fill with tears. They emerge from the darkness, squinting against the unexpected fluorescent light.

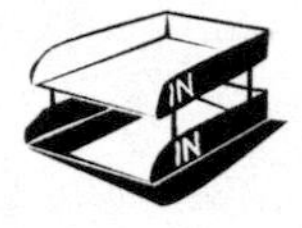

Jones shoves his hands into his pockets and inhales deeply. It's a bright, crisp Monday morning, the kind that gives you a little taste of the Seattle winter on the way, laced with an echo of the fading summer already passed. Jones stamps his feet on the plaza tiles. He's out in back of the Zephyr building. Around him are four or five loose groups of smokers, sucking down their first workplace cigarette of the day. He is here to watch them.

Ten minutes past ten: almost to the minute, that's when they turn up en masse each day. It took Jones a while to figure out why: that's when the morning snacks used to arrive, before Catering was outsourced. Now they're delivered anytime between nine thirty and eleven (the cookies either brittle or soggy, the fruit as cold and hard as blocks of ice), but the smokers have a tradition and they're not changing. Now he's aware of it, Jones finds it amazing. He has positioned himself in various strategic locations around the building and it happens the same way everywhere: it's as if there is a silent siren, inaudible to all but the smokers, who suddenly and simultaneously get restless. They shift in their chairs. They drift out of conversations. Their hands, not quite consciously, probe their pockets for lighters and packets of cigarettes. And by ones and twos, they detach from their departments and flow down the elevators to pool here, outside the rear doors. Then their mood improves: they greet each other and smile and talk about things not related to work at all. While they are here, they are the happiest people in the company.

Jones finds this fascinating. Is it just the nicotine hit, or could all employees benefit from regular short breaks? This should be a project, he thinks. He could try it with a group of nonsmokers. If he's right, it could end up in *The Omega Management System.* It could end up in companies around the world.

He has loitered here for about as long as he can without attracting suspicion, so he turns and heads back into the building, feeling excited. He pulls open the door and it leaps toward him, revealing that Freddy is on the other side of it, pushing. "Jones! What are you doing here?"

"Just getting some fresh air. What about you?"

Freddy checks that they're out of earshot. "She's not at

the desk this morning. Thought I'd come hang out with the regular Joes."

"Ah, good, good." Jones steps aside to let him pass.

Freddy squints at him. "You're not still poking around, are you?"

"What? Oh, no, no. I'm over that."

"Why, did you find something out?"

With heroic effort, Jones restrains himself from saying, *Why do you say that?* "No, not really. I just decided... you know, it doesn't really matter what the company does. I have my own job to do."

"Oh-oh. They got to you, didn't they? Let me check your belly button."

"What?"

Freddy laughs. "I'm just messing with you, Jones. It's good you're settling down."

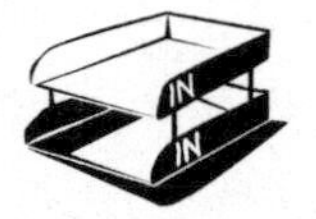

He intends to go directly back to Training Sales, but when the elevator doors open and there's nobody else inside, he decides to duck into level 13 and make some notes about his ideas. He swipes his ID card, presses 12 and 14 together, and watches the screen with his thumb resting on DOOR OPEN. The more he does this, the more fun it is. He jams the button at the right time: *ding!* Level 13!

The monitoring room contains four computers for agent use, so Jones logs in among the banks of TV monitors and opens up a new project file. Ten minutes later he is so lost in his thoughts that when Eve Jantiss breathes in his ear, "Interesting," he jumps about a foot out of his chair.

"Whoa." He laughs. "Don't do that."

"Look at you," Eve says. "All full of ideas. Daniel was right about you."

"Thanks." A grin surfaces on his face, which he is powerless to suppress.

She slides her butt onto the desk. Eve is dressed relatively formally today, wearing a gray skirt that goes below the knee. "Hey, let me ask you something. Are you free Thursday night?"

"For what?"

"We have a corporate suite at Safeco Field. Do you like baseball?" She smiles. "From that expression, I will assume yes."

"Are we having a function?"

"No. I just thought you might want to go."

"Okay. Sure. That'd be awesome."

"I'll pick you up at six thirty. Barker Street?"

"You know where I live?"

"Jones," she chides. "We know everything." She stands and begins to walk away. Jones resists the urge to watch. Then she says, "Oh, Jones, one thing..."

He turns.

"Now you're working for Alpha, you can't intervene in Zephyr. You're an observer. That's it."

"Yeah. I understand that."

"You understand the concept. You don't understand the implications. When you realize the difference... don't do anything stupid, okay?"

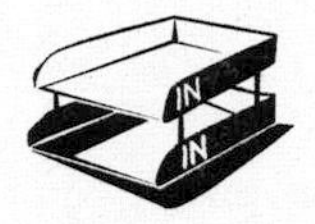

On Wednesday Jones, Freddy, and Holly head to the café across the road, Donovan's, for lunch. This is Jones's third month at Zephyr and he's eaten here almost every day; so, too, it seems, has most of Zephyr. Beginning at noon each day a steady stream of suits gushes from the elevators and bubbles across the lobby; it momentarily pools at the sliding doors then bursts across the road, where it stands in line for bagels and sandwiches, and discusses corporate politics. Jones looks around at them, these workers from Communications and Finance and Compliance and Travel Services and Corporate Supplies, who are not exactly his co-workers so much as his test subjects.

"Did you guys notice Megan?" Holly says. "When we left, she was staring at Jones."

Jones looks at her, unsure if she's joking. Freddy says, "Megan, really? That's weird." He turns his attention to a row of sandwiches under glass.

"I saw her in the gym again this morning. She's really doing well."

"You know, ever since they outsourced the morning snacks," Freddy complains, "I'm hungrier at lunchtime. I think they must be less nutritious."

"They'd better not be," Holly says. "I'm on a controlled intake plan."

"They cut out donuts," Jones points out. "That's not less nutritious."

Freddy says, "Oh God, can we not talk about donuts anymore? I get enough of this from Roger."

"Roger can't still be obsessing over that donut," Holly says uneasily. Freddy looks at her incredulously. "Anyway, that's done with. Wendell took Roger's donut, Wendell's gone."

"Roger doesn't think Wendell took it," Jones says, looking around for a table. "Now he thinks Elizabeth did. Hey, do you guys ever sit with people from other departments?"

Freddy and Holly look at him blankly. Freddy says, "That's not really how it works, Jones."

"Says who?"

"It's just... new chimp, Jones, new chimp." They are at the front of the line. Freddy slaps down five bucks and smiles at the man behind the counter. "The usual, thanks."

Alone in West Berlin, Roger stretches out at his desk. He folds his hands behind his head. His eyes lose focus. His mind is filled with Elizabeth and donuts.

It is obvious to him that this was a setup from the very beginning. Elizabeth knew he would leap to the wrong conclusion and accuse Wendell. She played him. Now it's too late to point the finger of blame where it belongs, because Wendell has been sacked—not, technically, for stealing Roger's donut, but that's not the point; the point is he's an ex-employee, and thus will be blamed for all departmental problems. Roger is better aware of this than most, since he secured his transfer to Training Sales by off-loading several particularly heinous accounting disasters onto ex-colleagues. No one has ever left Zephyr Holdings without being subsequently unmasked as a liar, thief, and fool. Ex-employees are revealed to be responsible for approving horrific cost overruns, for fraudulent orders and dubious expense claims. They are posthumously assigned leadership of doomed projects. No one will want to hear that Elizabeth is responsible for a crime that can be blamed on Wendell, because Wendell is gone and Elizabeth is still here.

She has backed him into a corner. A part of him admires her political skill. But a different, much larger part churns with worry. It would be one thing if Elizabeth was acting out of hurt and anger that he never called her after that time they slept together. That Roger could deal with; he would be *pleased* if that was the case. Roger has no problem with people hating him. What bothers him, what really unsettles his guts, is the idea that she is disrespecting him. Roger is a powerful, confident, good-looking man kept awake at nights by the heart-gripping fear that other people don't think he is powerful, confident, and good-looking. As part of the Zephyr Holdings interview process, he filled out a questionnaire that asked, "Which is better: to be successful or respected?" Roger wrote the now-legendary answer: TRICK QUESTION!!

Lately he has noticed Elizabeth throwing him surreptitious glances. At one point she simply stared at him, her expression blank, for several seconds. He felt a stab of fear: there could be no doubt that she was mocking him.

He doesn't know what he will do. Not yet. But a response is demanded. His honor requires it. His integrity requires it. Oh yes. Elizabeth will regret that she ever laid eyes on his donut.

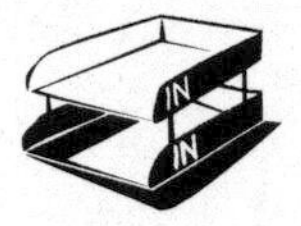

At four thirty on Thursday, Megan is summoned to Sydney's office for her six-month performance evaluation. Megan isn't worried; for her, these have always been casual and perfunctory. The only reason she has them at all, she suspects, is because Zephyr doesn't want to come right out and admit that PAs aren't real employees. So her reviews are mandatory but unimportant, which means they are usually conducted at the last minute, when something else has been canceled, in the elevator on the way to somewhere else.

She adjusts her bear ensemble—the Gone Fishin' bears work better on the far left of her desk, she decides, where their little ceramic rods can dangle off the edge of her desk—and knocks on Sydney's door. There is a pause, which Megan knows is Sydney waiting for Megan to deal with whoever it is knocking. After ten seconds, she knocks again.

"Who is it?"

"It's me."

"Come in."

Megan swings open the door. Sydney is sitting behind her desk. The desk is open-backed and Megan can see Sydney's little legs dangling down from her chair. She can't see Sydney's head or upper body: they are hidden behind her enormous computer monitor. Megan wouldn't want to suggest that Sydney is compensating, but she has the biggest monitor Megan has ever seen. "Is it time?"

"Yes."

She takes a seat in front of the desk and crosses her legs. Now she can see Sydney. She can also see the expanse of Sydney's desk, which is a snowstorm of papers. There is a shocking lack of knickknacks. Megan feels Sydney could do with a few bears.

"Okay." Sydney shifts a few papers around on the desk, apparently at random. Then she looks up. "You may not like what I have to say."

"Oh. Why not?"

"Because I'm managing you out."

"Out where?" Megan says, but realizes this is stupid.

"Out of the company." Sydney's eyes hold hers. "I'm sacking you."

She is too stunned to process this properly. "But... why?"

"Well, frankly, your performance. I had to give you the lowest rating: 'Needs Improvement.' " Her eyes flick around Megan's face. But Megan still has no reaction. Sydney seems to lose interest. She collects a few papers and begins searching for a stapler. "It's company policy to lay off any employee in that category. I have to follow the policy."

"Why do I need improvement?" Megan says. Her throat is closing up; only thin, strained sounds make it out.

"You know performance evaluations... there are criteria, I score you on them." Sydney locates her stapler. She positions it on her papers, then snaps it closed. She peers at the result. "Damn it all."

Megan has never heard of these criteria. "Last time you said we didn't need to do a formal review."

"The company's cracked down on that." Sydney frowns, as if Megan has gotten them into trouble. "They want me to do proper evaluations. And you failed in a number of key areas. First, tidy desk. Your desk is always covered in bears."

Megan's mouth drops open. "What's wrong with my bears?"

"Desks should be free of clutter. That's what the criteria say. Here, look." She passes across the papers. A staple hangs from the top-left corner.

"You never complained about my bears!"

"Megan, it's not me, it's the criteria. Listen to what I'm telling you. Second, you don't show any teamwork."

"But I work alone! I'll work with people if you want! I'd love to work with people! I'm stuck by myself!"

Sydney folds her hands on the desk. "Well, there's no point in complaining now."

"Then . . . why are you telling me these things?"

"It's part of the feedback process. I'm showing you what you need to work on to improve."

"So if I improve—"

"Not *here.* You can't improve here. You're being fired, Megan. This is just the process we go through. It's really for your benefit. A little gratitude wouldn't be out of place."

Megan's mouth works. What finally comes out is: "Thank you."

"You're welcome," Sydney says. "Anyway, those two categories hurt your score. But the clincher was your failure to achieve any goals."

"What goals?"

"Well, you didn't have any." Sydney picks up a silver pen and waggles it. Little daggers of reflected sunlight flash into Megan's eyes. "During your last evaluation, we were meant to agree on goals for you, but we never did. So where it says 'Goals Accomplished,' I had to tick 'None.' "

"I would have accomplished goals if you'd set some!"

"Well, you might have. It's hard to say."

"How can you sack me for not accomplishing goals I never had?"

"You don't want me to say you accomplished goals when you didn't, do you?"

"But this is wrong!" Megan's shock is wearing off. Her body begins to react properly: she starts to cry. "I do a good job! I do!" She covers her face with her hands.

Sydney is silent. Megan cries into her hands, her body shaking. She is ashamed at doing this in the boss's office, but can't stop herself. Then an awful idea grips her: that Sydney is smiling at her across the desk, not embarrassed by Megan's shame but amused. This is such a terrible thought that her head jerks up. It takes Sydney by surprise. The smirk drops from her face too late. Her lips tighten. "If you're going to argue, there's no point in wasting my time. The decision's been made. It's out of my hands." She crosses her arms. "Security's waiting for you."

Megan floats from the chair. She drifts to the door and sure enough, there are two blue-uniformed men by her desk. The rest of Training Sales, including Jones, is peering over cubicle walls. "Megan Jackson?" one of the Security men says.

They stand beside her as she puts her bears into her bag one by one. When she reaches out to close a letter she was writing on the computer, a blue-sleeved Security hand seizes hers. "Please don't attempt to operate the computer."

When her corporate-worldly possessions are stowed, Security escorts her through East Berlin. Megan can feel them all looking at her, these people from Training Sales she has worked alongside and never got to know. Even through her humiliation, she almost laughs: it is the first time they have really noticed her. She looks at Jones as she is marched by his cubicle: gangling, beautiful Jones, whom she will never see again. His face is pale and shocked. And his eyes are locked onto hers: he is finally, truly seeing her.

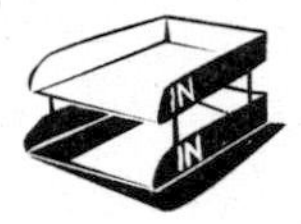

It's different than in August, with Wendell. He was gone by the time they left the meeting room. Today, Security arrived and plucked a person out. They feel like a herd of impala after the lions have finished their chase and are dragging away a limp carcass. They unconsciously huddle together, their ears twitching and their nostrils flaring, as Security returns and begins to remove her computer, piece by piece. They wipe down her desk. They spray something on her chair and tuck it in. Jones cannot look away.

"Why did they sack Megan?" he finally bursts out. "What's the point? Why?"

"It's okay, Jones," Holly says awkwardly. "It just happens. There's nothing you can do about it."

Roger's head appears around the Berlin Partition. "Hey. Freddy. Freddy."

Freddy knows what's coming. He hunches his shoulders. "What?"

"The pool. Who had Megan? Who won the pool?"

"Nobody."

"Oh." Roger's eyebrows rise hopefully. "So we're all still in it?"

"Yes," Freddy says. "We're all still in it."

Eve knocks on Jones's apartment door for five minutes straight. "Come on," she says, her voice muffled. "This is ridiculous. I know you're in there."

Jones doesn't even know how she got in the building. There is an intercom, which he studiously ignored when Eve buzzed it ten minutes ago, and no way to enter without a key.

"You hardly even knew her. You've been at Zephyr three months and you spoke to her about four times. People get fired, Jones. It's part of the great business cycle."

Jones digs into the bag of potato chips on his lap and pulls out a handful. He is sitting on his ragged brown sofa in front of a muted TV, which he zapped when Eve started rapping on the door. But apparently he's fooling nobody, so he stuffs the chips into his mouth and crunches down on them.

"You know what this is? It's petulant. I asked you three days ago if you understood your position. You said you did."

"If they're working for *no reason,*" Jones shouts, "why do

we need to *fire* them?" This sends a lot of wet chip fragments flying across the room.

"Because it's part of the study, Jones. We watch how people are recruited, how they adapt, how they work, and how they exit. We're not there to provide a corporate fantasy land where everybody gets a job for life. We're modeling the real thing." She pauses. "Let me in and I'll explain it to you."

"I *understand,*" Jones says irritably.

"Then come to the baseball game."

This annoys him so much that he stands up. "Megan had *friends* at Zephyr. It was part of her *life.*" Jones is actually not sure about this; he is making a few assumptions. "She was a *nice person.* What happens to her now? Do you even know?"

"She receives a redundancy payout and looks for another job. And we spread it around that she was hired by a competitor."

"Assiduous."

"Right. It's better if there's no contact between former and present employees. So we invented a bogeyman."

"You're not even going to tell her, are you? These people who work for you for however many years, they never even find out."

"Of course not. God, can you imagine what they'd do? Think about it, Jones: how soul-destroying would it be to discover that everything you've done over the last few years was *fictional*? All the late nights, the missed dinners, the stress, the deadlines, the grind—the only thing keeping these people sane is the belief that their work *means something.* You want to take that away?"

Jones stands in the middle of his living room with a bag of half-eaten chips dangling from one hand and says nothing.

"Look," she says, her voice softening. "I'm sympathetic to your position. Firing people sucks, no doubt about it. But what are you going to accomplish by throwing a hissy fit? Jones, if this concerns you, you're in exactly the right place. Right now a thousand middle managers are driving home listening to an Omega Management System audiobook, and if we tell them something works, they all try it. So don't complain about it, improve it. Find a better way."

Jones strides to the door and wrenches it open, drawing in a breath to expel a few caustic observations about the ethics of changing corrupt systems from the inside, possibly drawing on examples from the Nazis. Then he sees her and this bubble of air pops right out again. Eve is wearing—*wearing,* in the sense that delicate pieces of gossamer fabric have coincidentally drifted together to cover key parts of her body—a jet-black satin dress. Diamond earrings glitter at him; a necklace sparkles. The honey-brown skin of her chest tries to lure his eyes lower and her calves sing an idyll. She doesn't look like a Nazi. Not even a little.

Eve says, "And come to the baseball game, because I've already dressed up." She spreads her palms.

Eventually, he says, "This doesn't mean I agree with you. I'm still not happy."

"Okay." She smiles. Then her eyes wobble down to his Budweiser T-shirt and stained tracksuit pants. "Are you going to . . ."

"I'll get changed," he says.

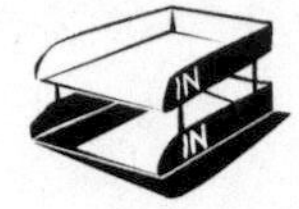

Jones wasn't a baseball fan in high school. He didn't play it well, didn't enjoy watching it, and didn't like the way girls sat in a tight clump to the left of the field, watching boys take practice swings. But something happened in college, something to do with the rec room's big-screen TV and the groups that would cluster around it. It didn't happen all at once; he just became increasingly engrossed by the ebb and flow of the game, the glory and the tragedy and the split-second difference that separated them, until one day he realized he loved it. Jones has been to Safeco Field more times than he can remember, but on none of those occasions did he drive down a ramp to an underground valet and find himself escorted to a set of private elevators; never before has he trod the gentle cream carpet that leads down a corridor marked simply: CORPORATE.

The—concierge?—leads them to a door marked ALPHA and holds it open for them. Inside it is all leather sofas and shadows and tall, glowing fridges. The far wall is lightly smoked glass and offers a view across the field so astonishing that Jones stops to soak it in. He realizes he will never be able to enjoy a baseball game from cheap seats again.

"Ah, a fan." Eve drapes her shawl over the coat stand. "I wondered why you went quiet. First time in a suite?"

Jones can't tear his eyes away. "Yes."

"I hate baseball. But I like the suite. Peaceful, isn't it?"

"I can't believe it's just us. Didn't anyone else want to use it?"

"Nah. In fact, most of the time it sits empty." Jones turns around, too outraged to speak. "Aw, what, you think we should open it up to the public? Maybe find some kids with cancer, loan it to them?"

"Well," he says. "Why the hell not?"

She snickers. "Jones, what makes this place special is not the leather furniture, or the catering, or the view. What makes it special is that *we* are in here while *they*—" she gestures to the crowd "—are *out there.*"

Jones grimaces. "Didn't your parents teach you to share?"

"Oh, they did." Eve walks to the bar area and studies the rows of bottles. Jones can see her face reflected in the mirror behind them. "In fact, Mom forbid my sisters and I to have individual possessions. Everything was everyone's." She reaches up to grab a dark, squat bottle of something Jones doesn't recognize and two delicate, bulbous glasses. "What do you think, is my whole life a rebellion against hippie parents?"

"That would explain a lot."

"The thing is," she says, sliding onto the sofa and patting the space beside her, "possessions are fun. For example, I'm not into cars. I have no idea how many cylinders my Audi has, or, now that I think about it, what a cylinder is. No idea. But when I look at it, Jones, I love it. I *love* it. Because it's mine and it's nicer than everybody else's."

Jones says, "That's one of the worst things I've ever heard."

She holds out a glass of brown liquid over ice and he takes it. "There's nothing wrong with enjoying life. In the end, what else can you do?" She raises her glass and takes a gulp.

He sits beside her. "Well, I don't want to get too radical,

but what about helping other people? Leaving the world a better place?"

Eve coughs explosively. She puts her glass on the table, which takes two attempts, and digs in her bag for a tissue. She dabs at her eyes. "Jesus, you nearly killed me." She takes a deep breath. "Whoo. Okay. Tell me how you justify buying a new pair of shoes."

"What?"

"When there are starving people in Africa, what kind of person spends two hundred bucks on shoes? See, once you buy into that paradigm, it's a bottomless pit. You can never feel good about yourself while there's anybody in the world poor or hungry, which there always is, Jones, and has been since the dawn of time, so you feel guilty and hypocritical all the time. *I'm* consistent. I admit I don't care. You want me to reassure you that Alpha is ethical, but I'm not going to do it, because ethics is bullshit. It's the spin we put on our lives to justify what we do. I say, be big enough to live without rationalizations."

Jones sips at his drink. It's Scotch, and heats him all the way down. "Just because I believe in ethics doesn't mean I have to be Mother Teresa. There's a middle ground."

"Ah, the famous *middle ground.*" He gets the feeling that Eve is enjoying this, but then, if he's honest, so is he. "Jones, you're one of those people who's never had to make a decision between ethics and results. You went to college and learned that companies with satisfied employees tend to be more profitable, and you went, 'Oh good.' Because that let you off the hook; you didn't have to decide what you'd do if it was a choice between one or the other. You won't work for a tobacco or gun manufacturer because those are bad companies; you'll only work for good ones, helping them to improve customer satisfaction and produce better products and—oh hey!—just by coincidence, those things increase company profits and get you promoted. Well, you're in the real world now, and soon enough you'll realize that sometimes you do have to choose between morals and results, that companies do it every day, even the ones you thought were good—and it's the managers who choose results who get the promotions. You'll fret about this for a few days or months or maybe even years until finally, one day, you'll decide you need to make the tough decisions because this is business, and that's what everyone else is doing. But because you feel guilty about having a six-figure salary and a current-year car, you'll sponsor a child in the Sudan and give ten bucks a year to the United Way and you're still being ethical most of the time—that is, when it doesn't get in the way of doing your job—and just because you lied a little or stole a little or took a job at a company that makes money off the backs of fourteen-year-old factory workers in Indonesia doesn't mean you're not a good person. But you'll stop bringing up the subject of ethics. *That,* Jones, is the middle ground."

There's a knock at the door.

"Come!" Eve calls. She looks back at Jones. "You should thank me. I just saved you years of wrestling with your conscience."

"You are unbelievable. It's like you're *evil.*"

A man enters wheeling a mobile hanging rack of plastic-encased clothes. She rises from the sofa, inspects the rack, and seems pleased with what she sees. The porter is dismissed, looking happy and dazed, but Jones can't tell whether this is because of Eve's tip or just Eve. Or maybe the porter is not dazed at all; maybe that's Jones projecting. "Come here," she says.

He gets up and looks at the rack. "You said to ignore Blake."

"Then. In the meeting. But he has a point." She pulls out a jacket and holds it in front of him. Even through the plastic, Jones can tell it's expensive. "For your eyes, I'm thinking something in charcoal."

"I can't afford a new suit."

"Suits. You need more than one. Don't worry, you'll pay me back." She holds it out to him.

He doesn't move.

A smile tugs at her lips. "I'm only offering you clothes. You don't have to take my morals."

"Look, I'm not an idiot. I understand that business is about making money. I just want to know that we treat our employees properly. That we, you know, care about them."

"Honestly? We don't. But maybe that's what you can change." She lets go of the suit.

Jones grabs it out of reflex. "Okay. Maybe I will."

She smiles, turns, and walks to the smoked glass. "Try it on."

He hesitates, unsure how revealing his reflection will be in that glass. Then he starts undressing. As he peels back the plastic, he gets a whiff of the suit's fresh, confident scent.

Eve says, "They're *dusting* the mound. Why do they need to dust? It's made of *dirt*." She shakes her head. "You know, you and I are working on similar projects at Alpha."

Jones threads his belt through his pants. "Really? What's yours?"

"Pregnancy." She turns around. "Are you done?"

Jones zips. "Pregnancy?"

She walks over and looks him up and down. Then she starts fixing him: correcting the folds of his jacket, straightening his tie, tugging his shirt into place. "It's a major cost. Maternity leave is just the tip of the iceberg. The more pregnant a worker gets, the less she works. She's drawing the same paycheck, but taking more breaks, leaving earlier, concentrating less, making more personal calls, and chatting longer to other co-workers, mostly about what it's like to be pregnant. Which, incidentally, results in a small but significant increase in the desire of her co-workers to also get pregnant, so she's effectively contagious. Then there's maternity leave, paternity leave, increased absenteeism to look after sick kids, decreased willingness to work overtime... Management needs to take note of effects like that. They'd be negligent not to." She reaches around him and yanks up his trousers. "What are you doing here? These aren't hipsters."

"You can't discriminate against employees because they're *pregnant*," Jones says. "Jesus, that's illegal."

"Same as it's illegal to discriminate against smokers. Like I say, we're working on similar projects. We're trying to discourage workers from activities that cost the company money." Her hands slip down Jones's butt, in a way that he suspects is not strictly necessary to adjust his pants. "Although, on a personal note, I don't see why I have to effectively subsidize every woman on the payroll whose life is so dull that she needs to inject *children* into it."

"I'm not really comfortable discussing pregnancy while you're squeezing my butt."

"I'm not squeezing. *This* is squeezing."

"Doesn't Zephyr have a policy on inter-employee relationships?"

"Of course. But we're not in Zephyr. We're in Alpha."

"Does Alpha?"

"We're surprisingly open-minded."

"You're still holding my ass."

"Is that a bad thing?"

He suddenly realizes he could kiss her. In fact, given that she's currently groping him, it's probably what she's expecting. But Jones still has a bad taste in his mouth from the pregnancy thing, and he reaches back and removes her hands from his butt.

"Oh, come on." Her eyebrows jump. "Really?" She looks bewildered. She turns, walks to the sofa, and drops onto it.

Jones says, "Sorry. I think that would be a bad idea."

"You're right. You'd get the wrong impression of me; it'd be awkward at work... we should keep things professional."

"Right."

"More Scotch?"

"Sure." He walks over to the sofa.

Eve refills their glasses. He can actually see her regaining her composure. By the time she hands him his glass, she is smiling. She looks so beautiful that he starts to wonder whether he made the right decision. "Well!" she says. "I can tell it's going to be interesting to have you around."

He smiles. "I hope so." They clink glasses.

Eve nudges the Audi over to the side of the road and takes her hands off the wheel. "Damn. I think you were right. I *am* too drunk to drive."

Jones looks around. He has some trouble focusing, but manages to conclude that they have arrived back at his apartment. "Want me to call you a cab?"

"Maybe I should sleep it off." She doesn't lean so much as slump in his direction. "At your place." Her lips form a rubbery smile. Jones studies it for a second.

"Okay."

"That's it? No 'We have to keep things professional'? No 'It's better if we're just friends'?" She gestures extravagantly, and whacks the rearview mirror off-kilter. "Ow."

"*You* said those things."

"I did?"

"And I just said you could stay. I didn't invite you to get naked."

Eve finds the door latch and spills onto the road. "Ha." She drags herself back into Jones's field of vision. "I don't believe for a second that you don't want to sleep with me."

Jones levers his body out of the Audi. This sends a rush of blood to his head, where he feels there is far too much of the stuff already. He comes around the car and helps Eve to her feet.

"Everybody does," she confides. "Every one of them. I don't see why you should be any different." She pokes him in the chest with her finger.

Jones fumbles to connect his keys with the apartment building's door lock. "*Everybody* wants to sleep with you? How do you know this?"

"When you do some investigating," she leans on him heavily as they negotiate the doorway, "you discover the minimum standard of what a man will sleep with is very low."

"So it's not that you're irresistible. It's just that men are sluts."

"It's both." They are in the stairwell now, and Eve abruptly stops. Jones has one arm around her waist, so this requires him to stop, too. "Kiss me, Jones."

Jones's mind says: *It's a trap!* The message races out to his lips, which pay no attention because they are in the process of kissing Eve. Her lips are soft and delightful and then they curve under his and she starts giggling. Jones pulls back. Eve starts up the stairs, and Jones has to catch her. "That's not fair. I wasn't ready."

"Said the slut."

"Aren't you trying to seduce me? How am I the slut?"

They reach Jones's apartment. He managed to put his keys in the wrong pocket downstairs, so now he has to release Eve to fish them out again. She slumps against the corridor wall. "Because you are lowering yourself. Whereas I," she begins to slide down the wall, "am already . . . lowered." Jones catches her. She looks up at him and smiles. But her head keeps moving, gathering pace, and then it flops back, so Jones is blinking at her neck and holding her limp body.

For a few seconds he doesn't move. "Eve?" he whispers, and when that doesn't work, tries it again. He gets one hand under her head and lifts it up. Her mouth hangs open. Her eyes are thin zombielike slits under dark, heavy lids. Eve is out. And, furthermore, this is not the kind of position Jones wants to strike in front of the neighbors, all of whom have peepholes and several of whom are not shy about using them. He struggles to get his door open, then Eve inside without banging some part of her against a wall, which is harder than it sounds because she has gone completely boneless, her arms swinging in big circles. He drags her through his living room and drops her onto his bed. Then he sits down heavily next to her and breathes deeply.

She doesn't move. It suddenly occurs to Jones that she has dropped dead, and he leans forward anxiously. She makes a little snoring sound. Jones carefully arranges her head into a better position. She stops snoring and smacks her lips. A tiny pool of saliva has formed at the corner of her mouth and Jones dabs this away.

He comes back ten minutes later, once he's closed the apartment door, changed out of his suit, and brushed his teeth. Eve is in exactly the same position. Jones hangs in the doorway. He is not sure which items of her clothing it would be a good idea to remove and which would be terrible. In the end, he decides he can deduct her shoes, watch, bracelet, and necklace without hitting any potential legal or (if it matters) moral pitfalls.

Eve is on top of the blankets and Jones doesn't like his chances of maneuvering her underneath them, so he pulls a new blanket down from a cupboard, throws it over her, and crawls underneath. "Mmm." He feels her buttocks press against his hip. "Bfff ett."

"What?"

"Mmm." She doesn't say anything for a minute. "Jones?"

"Yes?"

"Wake me in time for work?"

"Yeah, of course. I've set the alarm."

"Mmm. Good." She snuggles down into the covers. "Can't... miss tomorrow. We're... con-sol-i-dat-ing."

Jones waits, in case there's more. "Consolidating?"

"Mmm."

"Consolidating what?"

"Everything!" She makes a soft sound like a laugh. Her leg finds his and curves around it. "I love you, Jones."

Her breathing slows. Jones lies there, listening to it, until the alarm clock pops into life and two crackly DJs tell him it's six thirty in the morning.

"This is Sydney. I hope this works... I'm trying to forward a message from... um... Daniel Klausman. Hang on... I think I have to... no, that's not it. Maybe—click. Morning everyone, it's Janice. It's another all-staffer... you know what to do. Click. Janice, please distribute the following message from Daniel Klausman to the department heads. Thanks. Click. Good morning all, Meredith here... I have an all-staffer from Daniel Klausman for distribution. Thank you. Click.

"This is Daniel Klausman. Meredith, send this on to my department heads for distribution to all headcounts.

"Good morning, everyone. I'd like to thank you all for the goodwill and enthusiasm with which you embraced the necessary belt-tightening over the last few months. It wasn't easy, but we've made some very important changes.

"Unfortunately, our share price was hurt by a market overreaction to unrelated events, and we lost another 14 percent. This is obviously of concern, but it's worth noting that the drop is less than the 18 percent fall of the previous quarter, so in relative terms, we've gained 4 percent.

"We've made some great strides, but the work isn't over yet. Now more than ever, we need to show the world that Zephyr Holdings is the industry leader. We must prove our commitment to our strategic vision. Thus, most departments will be consolidated over the next few weeks.

"That's it from me. Have a great day. Click."

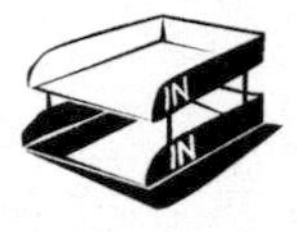

This is the first voice mail everyone gets Friday morning. They arrive, shrug off their jackets, and stow their purses; they pick up their handsets and enter their access codes; this is what they hear.

Except for Jones. Jones drags himself to his desk like one of the undead. He puts his elbows on his desk and rests his head on his hands. His voice-mail light flashes, throwing red spears into his eyes once every two and a half seconds. He can't find the enthusiasm to make it stop.

"Consolidated!" Freddy yelps. *"Most departments!"* He and

Holly rise as one. "You ask Elizabeth. I'll talk to Megan. She—" Freddy snaps his fingers. "Ah, crap! I keep forgetting she's gone." But Holly has already left. Freddy hurries after her, passing Jones, who looks as if he has just returned from a four-hour meeting with Human Resources. Freddy hesitates. "Don't worry, Jones. We shouldn't panic until we know something." His eyes widen. "Or do you already know?" He grabs Jones's shoulders. *"Are we being consolidated?"*

Jones says, "Oh God. Don't shake me."

Freddy doesn't know what is the matter with Jones. But it's clearly not the consolidation. And that's the issue now: who is about to lose their job. Holly is already in West Berlin, talking to Elizabeth, probably finding out who's going and who could stay if only the right word was whispered in the right ear; she is probably securing a new position right now, *right now*, while Freddy is messing around with Jones. "Not now!" Freddy yells. He scurries into West Berlin.

Elizabeth is nowhere to be seen, so Holly has jumped on to Roger and is haranguing him for information. Freddy barges into the conversation. "What? What did you say?"

Roger raises an eyebrow. "I was saying that in a consolidation, the department with the strongest manager comes out on top. We have Sydney. So stop panicking."

"Right! Sydney. Sydney will save us."

"Unless..." Roger hesitates. "Well, unless she's asked to choose between saving the department or her own position."

Holly claps a hand over her mouth.

"But I'm sure that won't happen," Roger says.

Freddy is not sure. Neither is Holly. She spies Elizabeth,

pale and unsteady, tottering back from the bathroom. Elizabeth has been using the bathroom a lot lately. Every time Holly goes looking for her, she's in the bathroom. "Elizabeth! What have you heard? Are we going to be consolidated?"

Elizabeth looks blank. "Consolidated?"

"The voice mail. Do you know if..." Holly trails off. She's staring at Elizabeth's blinking voice-mail light. Elizabeth hasn't heard the announcement. Holly is shocked. Elizabeth always knows what's happening before everyone else. But not, apparently, today. While everyone was listening to the voice mail, Elizabeth was in the bathroom.

Elizabeth says, "What's this about consolidations?"

"Um..." Holly shifts her feet. "Well..."

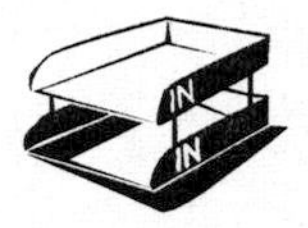

Zephyr Holdings has just gotten back to work after the network outage, but now that there's a consolidation looming, no one has the time for it. Throughout the building, work stalls. The wheels of industry crash to a halt and the rumor mill starts turning. Within minutes, Zephyr is manufacturing rumors at world-class levels. If rumors could be sold, this kind of productivity would be cause for special announcements and award ceremonies—but they can't, and even Senior Management knows this. When it realizes what is going on, Senior Management places a conference call to the departmental heads. All staff are forbidden to speculate about the consolidations, it instructs. They should know better; here Senior Management is trying to save everyone's job, and all they care about is whether they still have a job. Get back to work!

The departmental managers could not agree more. Their heads bob up and down, even though this is a phone call. Their voices drip earnestness. They are behind Senior Management 110 percent. Or more! The bids rise quickly.

But once they're off the phone their level of support drops, first to realistic levels, then lower. "Senior Management hasn't decided which departments will be consolidated," the managers say in response to their staff's nervous, sweaty questions. "Or maybe they have but they're not telling. Your guess is as good as mine. I don't know what the hell they're doing." Frightened employees huddle around coffee machines. Rumor production heads underground and flourishes there. The out-trays of laser printers grow thick with updated résumés.

Meanwhile, Senior Management gathers in the sun-drenched boardroom. Things get off to an awkward start when it is suggested, in not quite so many words, that perhaps it was unwise of Daniel Klausman to announce there would be consolidations before anyone had decided what, exactly, was going to be consolidated. Perhaps it would have been a good idea for Klausman to clue in Senior Management to his big plan. Maybe, just possibly, it would have been better for Senior Management to find out about the consolidations before everybody else.

Senior Management buttocks shift uncomfortably. Klausman does not attend these meetings, but it is widely accepted that he knows what happens in them. Some suspect the room is bugged: microphones in the flowers, cameras in the eyes of portraits, that sort of thing. Others wonder about moles. A few are developing the theory that someone in Senior Management *is* Daniel Klausman, but they keep this quiet because admitting you've never met the CEO face-to-face is tantamount to announcing your political irrelevance. Whichever it is, Senior Management is very keen to appear loyal. It's impeccably fair of Klausman to keep the whole workforce in the loop, they argue. They thump the table for the benefit of the hidden microphones, or the moles, or Klausman himself. "I've suspected this was coming for some time," says the VP of Business Management and Forecasting and Auditing. "My people are about to complete an analysis that shows almost 80 percent of our costs are attributable to just 20 percent of our business units."

This causes alarmed murmurs. "How can that be?" protests the man to his right. "That's what it was like before the *last* consolidation. We *cut* most of that 80 percent!"

"Oh, it's an all-new 80 percent," the VP reassures him.

That clinches it: clearly the company must continue to cut until those percentages come down. A motion is proposed expressing support for Klausman's decision, and unanimously passed. If there's one thing Senior Management knows, it's how to pass a motion.

That accomplished, Senior Management takes a break. Phew! They take the opportunity to check their voice mail or order coffees from their PAs. And as they do, they quietly and almost unconsciously coalesce into separate camps. Just in confidence, each camp whispers, these consolidations are only going to work if their own departments absorb several others. Heads nod. They sketch a quick strategic vision of the new company, in which most departments are trimmed down or eliminated, except their own, which grow huge and bloated. Yes! Heartbeats quicken. Understandings are forged. Each camp glows with warm, united purpose.

But as Senior Management resumes its seats in the boardroom, each camp realizes the others have formed camps, too. Brows lower. Everyone sees what is going on: certain members are trying to take advantage of the reorganization to inflate their own responsibilities. This accusation—at first concealed, then not so concealed, finally completely naked—lands with a slap on the rich oak table. The camps passionately deny it. It's not as if they get a pay raise for looking after more people! (Which is true. It was once the case, but not after what has become known as the Seven Secretaries Incident.) A larger department only means more work!

And this is true, too. To the non-manager, it might actually seem that Senior Management is prepared to selflessly take on more work for the good of the company. But this is why non-managers are not managers. You don't reach the upper echelons of Zephyr Holdings by shirking responsibility. You get there by grabbing as much of it as you can, forcing it down, and screaming for more. Senior Management craves responsibility in the same way that blind, bedraggled birds stretch open their beaks for regurgitated worms: from instinct. It is what they do. It is who they are. So, Senior Management realizes, as it looks around the table and sees nothing but hard, hungry stares, it is going to be a long day.

Elizabeth pushes her way out the bathroom door. It is ten o'clock and her third visit today. She has vomited once, quietly, and, if the pattern holds, a second incident will present itself in roughly twenty minutes. In the meantime she weaves her way back to West Berlin. Elizabeth can't spend the whole day on the bathroom tiles, hugging the toilet bowl. (Nor can she spend the day, somewhat more demurely, bent over a sink. What if Sydney saw her? Or Holly? Holly already suspects too much. Holly probably already knows, without quite realizing it. Elizabeth is not showing, not yet, but her breasts are ballooning and she is falling-down tired. The other day she actually fell asleep for a few seconds in a Training Sales meeting and when she opened her eyes Holly was watching her.)

She has started dreaming of ribbons. Blue, green, red; the kind little girls use to tie back their hair. Or, more precisely, the kind that mothers use to tie back the hair of their daughters. For some reason Elizabeth cannot get this image out of her head: herself and a little girl, and Elizabeth doing her hair. Since the network went down, this is what Elizabeth has been doing instead of work. It is a foolish and dangerous daydream, but she cannot shake it.

Her voice-mail light is blinking. It's not the all-staffer: she's listened to that one already. It was as frightening as Holly's and Freddy's reactions implied, and Elizabeth has already made half a dozen phone calls seeking more information. This voice mail, she figures, is a reply to one of those. Elizabeth may be a little slower, and take more frequent trips to the bathroom, but she is not out of the loop yet. She lowers herself into her chair and dials voice mail.

It is a male voice, rich and smooth. "Good morning.

This is Human Resources. We have noticed an irregularity in your work patterns. We have some questions. Please report to level 3."

Her first instinct is *Roger.* But he is on the phone, saying, "Look, I can probably get you a place in Training Delivery if Personnel Services gets consolidated. But what can you offer me if they cut Training?" If Roger was behind this, he would be watching her: she is sure of that.

So it's not Roger. It's just Human Resources. Her bowels tighten. That is much, much worse.

She turns and walks out of West Berlin.

A few minutes later she steps out of the elevator on level 3. In all the time Elizabeth has worked at Zephyr Holdings, she's never been to Human Resources, so her eyes widen at the dark blue walls and nonfluorescent lighting. She makes her way down the corridor, with its carpet so thick it feels as if it's snagging her shoes, and stops at the bare reception desk. She looks at the two doors, and as she does, the one on the right clicks open.

"Hello?"

Nobody answers. Elizabeth is not impressed. She has always found Human Resources difficult to get hold of, but this is ridiculous. She enters the corridor, her lips forming a hard line.

She notices it is getting warmer. Or is that her? It's hard to tell, these days. She feels a wetness growing at the small of her back, the shirt sticking there, and gets irritated. *"Hello?"*

A door to her left clicks open.

It is a small room, and the only furniture is a plastic chair. The chair faces a mirror. Elizabeth looks around. "Oh, come on."

There is no response. She walks in, puts her hands on her hips, and looks at the mirror. "Is somebody going to talk to me face-to-face? Or are you going to hide back there?"

Silence.

"Fine." She strides to the chair. Her nausea has subsided; she feels as if she could arm-wrestle alligators. She sits down and crosses her legs. "So?"

The voice comes as if from nowhere.

"Your name," it says. "State your name."

"Elizabeth Miller. Who are you?"

"State your employee number."

"It's 4148839."

"State your department."

"You know my department," Elizabeth says. "You called me there ten minutes ago."

"State your department."

Her lips tighten. She may be prone to falling in love with customers, but she can fight with the bare-knuckled passion of an aggrieved lover. "I'm not going to have a discussion like this. If you want to talk, come out and do it to my face."

"State your department."

Elizabeth keeps her mouth shut. Seconds tick by.

"State your department."

"Unless I see a human being in the next ten seconds," Elizabeth says, "this meeting is over."

She waits. Sweat trickles down her back.

"State your department."

Elizabeth stands up and walks to the door. She didn't even hear it close, but now it's locked. She turns to the mirror, hands on hips. "Open the door."

"State your department."

"It's Training Sales, you know it's Training Sales! *Now open the door!*" She knows as soon as the words emerge that this is a tactical mistake: she has given in without getting anything.

"Irregularities have been detected in your work patterns. Your bathroom breaks have sharply increased in frequency and duration."

Elizabeth inhales. There have been rumors that Human Resources monitors employee bathroom breaks. Elizabeth hadn't believed them. She walks back to the middle of the room and faces the mirror. "I don't see how that's any of your business."

"Perhaps you have a problem. A personal problem. You could share it with us. Human Resources is here to help. Human Resources is only concerned for your welfare."

"Just the same."

"Analysis suggests several possible explanations for your bathroom breaks. One is low-grade food poisoning. Another is recreational drug use. A third is pregnancy."

Elizabeth says nothing. But in her stomach, something flips.

"You are aware that Human Resources complies with

state and federal law requirements for maternity leave. You know that Zephyr Holdings is an equal opportunity employer."

"What has this got to do with me?"

"Are you pregnant, Elizabeth?" the voice lilts. "It's all right. You can tell me. You've got a friend in Human Resources."

"I'm not pregnant," Elizabeth lies. She does it with her chin up and her back straight. Watching herself in the mirror, she is convincing. The only giveaway is the color in her cheeks—but surely they won't notice that. Unless they have monitors. Could they have monitors?

"You know Human Resources has never discriminated against a pregnant employee."

"I don't see them getting promoted."

"We discriminate against employees who are late for work. We discriminate against employees who take excessive breaks. We discriminate against employees who are unable to give a long-term commitment to their jobs. But we do not discriminate against pregnancy."

"I ate a bad hot dog, all right? There. So now you know."

"Human Resources is only concerned for your job performance. That you may have chosen to place personal concerns ahead of your job, after everything we have done for you, is not relevant. Do you anticipate a falling off in your productivity, Elizabeth?"

"No."

"You are aware that if you do anticipate a falling off and conceal it, this is breach of contract."

"Breach of contract? How is it a breach?"

"You have made an agreement with Human Resources for salary in exchange for work. To knowingly reduce your ability to perform that work is bad faith."

"Look, if I *did* get pregnant, which I am not, it would *not* be a breach of contract."

No response.

"I mean, it couldn't be," she says.

"You are aware that breach of contract results in immediate termination."

She swallows, then says, very carefully, "I am not pregnant, to the best of my knowledge."

There is a long pause. It feels smug and self-satisfied to Elizabeth. But perhaps she is imagining that. She is hot and sweaty and needs to go to the bathroom.

"Human Resources has no interest in whether you are pregnant."

She starts. "What?"

"Human Resources would rather not know one way or the other."

"But you just—"

"Human Resources does not interfere in the personal lives of employees."

Elizabeth waits.

"Our only interest is ensuring your job performance does not decline from agreed-upon levels."

She sits rigid for a long time. Finally, her jaw clenched, she says, "You had better not be implying what I think you're implying."

There is a click, and the door swings open.

"Thanks for coming in," the voice says.

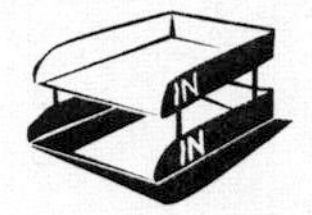

"Jones," Freddy says. "Jones. *Jones.*"

"What?"

Freddy studies him from the cubicle entrance. "What's the matter with you?"

With some effort, Jones sits up straighter. "I didn't get much sleep, that's all."

"Well, it's time for lunch." He looks at his watch. "Where's Holly?"

"I have no idea."

"Meeting room in the lobby," Roger says, walking past. "At least, she was ten minutes ago."

"A meeting room? Who's she meeting?"

Roger shrugs and walks out of sight.

"Hmm," Freddy says.

Holly turns up ten minutes later, carrying her bag. "Sorry, sorry. I got held up."

"By who?"

"Just customers. You know how Elizabeth's a sales rep, and I'm her assistant? Well, she has customers."

"Which ones?"

"Which ones was I meeting?"

"Yeah."

"What do you care?"

"I don't," Freddy says. "I just think it's incredibly devoted of you to hold meetings with Elizabeth's customers when everyone else is running around trying to save their job from the consolidation."

"Geez, you sound like Roger." She lowers her voice for the last word, since Roger is only a partition or two away. "Don't you think, Jones? Jones?"

"What?"

"Boy," Holly says, "what's the matter with you?"

"Well, so far I've found out squat," Freddy says in the elevator. "Nobody knows when the consolidation is happening, or who's getting consolidated, or why it's happening in the first place."

Holly sighs. "Same."

"But I did hear that Simon from Training Delivery clocked Blake Seddon. Right in the face."

"You're kidding! Blake Seddon from Senior Management?"

"And—get this—now he's wearing an eye patch. Like a pirate." He looks from Holly to Jones. But Jones doesn't smile. Jones has already seen Blake's eye patch: he was introduced to it on Monday at 7:30 A.M., during Project Alpha's morning meeting. Jones wasn't especially unhappy to discover that someone had assaulted Blake, but this was tempered by the fact that Blake now looked even more like he just stepped from a daytime TV soap. "Needless to say," Freddy continues, "Simon is now an ex-employee. And, of course, Assiduous snapped him up. I bet they loved the idea of getting their hands on someone who punched a Zephyr executive. They're probably getting him to run training drills."

"Hey, that reminds me," Holly says. "I called Human Resources to find out Megan's contact details, so we could send her a card—"

"That's a good idea," Jones says.

"—and they wouldn't tell me. They said she'd been hired by Assiduous." She throws a fearful look at Jones. "It's like you said." Jones doesn't react, so she adds, "Isn't that creepy?"

"I don't know. Not really."

"Not really? Before you were saying there was a conspiracy."

"Well, I thought about it some more." The elevator arrives at the lobby and Jones squints against the bright light. "I realized that in a market with only two major players, it's perfectly natural for there to be cross-pollination of employees." This is, word for word, a line from an Alpha training manual Klausman gave him last week.

Holly says, "But—" Then she stops, because waiting to step into the elevator is Eve Jantiss.

"Oh. Hello." Eve smiles. "Hello, Jones."

"Hi." And then he has to do it. "Do you know Freddy and Holly?"

"We've probably spoken on the phone. But I can never put faces to names." She laughs. She looks fresh and alert, and why shouldn't she? Eve had six hours of unbroken sleep last night. Jones, who was awake for every minute of it, knows this for a fact.

"It's nice to meet you," Holly says.

"Ymmrr," says Freddy.

"It's funny, isn't it?" Eve says. "We spend so much time here, but we don't even know what one another are really like." She puts a slight emphasis on *really*.

Nobody responds to this. To avoid any further mind games, which Jones is not in good shape to handle, he says, "Well, nice to see you," and begins to cross the lobby.

Freddy and Holly catch up halfway across. Freddy says, "Did you see me back there? She'll think I'm *retarded*."

They exit into sunshine and head up the sidewalk. "It's like you're two people," Holly says suddenly.

"What?" Jones says, startled.

"What Eve said. It's true. You come to work every day but you hardly get to know anyone. I don't even know the names of half the people I see in the elevators. They say the company is a big family, but I don't *know* them. And even the people I do, like you two, and Elizabeth, and Roger—do I really? I mean, I like you guys, but we only ever talk about work. When I'm out with friends, or at home, I never talk about work. The other day I tried to explain to my sister why it's such a huge deal that Elizabeth ate Roger's donut, and she thought I was insane. And you know what, I agreed with her. At home I couldn't even think why it mattered. Because I'm a different person at home. When I leave this place at night, I can feel myself changing. Like shifting gears in my head. And you guys don't know that; you just know what I'm like here, which is terrible, because I think I'm *better* away from work. I don't even *like* who I am here. Is that just me? Or is everyone different when they come to work? If they are, then what are they really like? How can we ever know? All we know are the *Work People*."

"Oh my God," Freddy says. "*Elizabeth* ate Roger's donut?"

Holly freezes. "No, I meant, Roger *thought* Elizabeth ate his donut."

"That's not what you said."

"It came out wrong." A strained edge enters Holly's voice. "You're jumping to conclusions, that's not what I was talking about!"

Jones says, "Why did she take his donut?"

"Look, please, if you tell, Elizabeth will know it came from me."

"Okay, okay," Freddy says. "It's just between us."

"It was a spur-of-the-moment thing. She was hungry, that's all. It wasn't anything personal. *Please,* promise me you'll keep this secret." Her voice wavers. Her face is pinched and anxious, her frown line a sharp tilde. "This is exactly what I was talking about!"

"Of course we won't tell," Jones says. "Right?"

"Right, right." Freddy licks his lips. Knowledge is power, and Freddy has a big, doughy chunk.

Holly still looks nervous. Jones says, "About that being two people thing. I know what you mean."

"You do?" She looks at him hopefully. "Do you think everyone does?"

They look at Freddy, who is lost in thought. "What?" he says. "I'm not going to tell Roger about the donut."

Rumor production slackens toward the end of October. Without any new information on the consolidations, the rumors turn in on themselves, becoming ever more fanciful. When someone claims that Senior Management is cutting Human Resources, that's the end; nobody can believe that. The atmosphere of desperate, ignorant terror essential to healthy rumors seeps away, replaced by a silent, wary paranoia. People bunker down, jealously keeping what they know, which is nothing, to themselves. As hands reach for jackets each night and briefcases are snapped closed, employees exchange suspicious farewells, each wondering if the other is concealing something. They conjecture what might await them the next day, and who might not. As they ride the elevator down, they eye the button panel and wonder how many holes it will soon have.

Jones loiters in the lobby, near the mission statement. This is becoming a habit: he keeps hoping he'll bump into Eve after work, but never does. Eve is supposedly a receptionist, but he has discovered she is practically never at the desk: all the actual reception work is done by Gretel. He sees Eve at the Alpha morning meetings, and occasionally in the monitoring room, but on those occasions there are other people around, like Blake Seddon. Jones wants to get Eve alone. He wants to follow up certain issues that were raised the night of the baseball game.

He is about to give up when a *clack-clack* of heels turns his head. "Jones!" Eve says. "I thought that was you." She smiles as she draws close. "I saw you on the monitors. What are you doing?"

"Waiting for you," Jones says, which is shockingly direct, but he is emboldened by the way Eve is smiling. "I thought maybe you'd like to grab a drink."

"That sounds like an excellent idea."

"Good." Now he is grinning like a goon, but can't help it. "Good, then."

"Give me one minute to freshen up. I'll be right back." She strides off in the direction of the bathroom.

Jones shoves his hands in his pockets and bounces on his toes. *Go Jones!* he thinks.

"Night," Freddy says, startling him.

"Bye! See you next week." He watches Freddy exit the sliding doors. Just before he moves out of sight, Freddy throws a glance at the empty reception desk, and in a pure flash of clarity Jones realizes there is a catastrophic scene looming in his near future when Freddy finds out there is something going on between him and Eve. The idea freezes his spine.

"Okay!" Eve says, taking his arm. She flashes him a bright, happy smile. "Let's go. I know a place."

She drives him to a low, ambiguous building by the bay that Jones has driven past a thousand times and never thought much about. It turns out to be a bar so stylish that it has dispensed with anything as obvious as trying to look like a bar, and at six o'clock on a Friday evening it is chock-full of deep orange sunshine and more pairs of expensive shoes than Jones has ever seen in one place. Eve threads her way through the crowd, a cocktail in hand, smiling and greeting people. He follows her to a balcony, where it is so packed that it's a fine line between conversation and slow dancing. "Sex on the Beach," she says.

"Pardon?"

Eve holds up her cocktail, flips her sunglasses over her eyes, and grins at him.

"Oh." Jones smiles. He has a Scotch and the quiet hope that Eve will continue to drink Sex on the Beach, or any kind of alcoholic beverage, really, until he has acquired enough courage to confront her about what she said to him that night in bed.

"Klausman loves what you're doing on the smokers," Eve says. "We were talking about it just today. You've impressed him. And impressed *me*, which is more important in the long run. What do you think: Will I make a good CEO one day?" She smiles.

"It might be difficult to explain to six hundred employees how you made the jump from receptionist."

"Well," she says, "there won't be six hundred employees for much longer."

"Right. So, look, I still don't get this. Why is Zephyr consolidating?"

She shrugs. "Companies reorganize. It's part of the business cycle: growth then contraction. We're interested in finding better ways to do it. We make sure Zephyr consolidates at least once a year."

"And then it grows?"

"Mmm. Not so much. Zephyr's been shrinking for as long as I've worked here. The trend toward more with less. You know."

"How many people are going to lose their job?"

"Depends on Senior Management. Alpha doesn't micromanage—we just tug a string here and there and see what happens. Klausman sent out an all-staff voice mail saying we had to consolidate. Now we watch how the company reacts."

He looks out over the water. "So an unknown quantity of people are about to become unemployed for no reason other than we want to see what happens."

She cocks her head. "Is that a tone?"

"It's a question."

"Aw, Jones, every time I start to think you might actually make it in this place, you go weak at the knees over how terrible it is to sack someone!" A few heads turn in their direction, which Eve ignores. "I thought you were past this."

"Are you?"

"What? Of course I am. What are you talking about?"

"How much of the other night do you remember?"

She freezes. "What did I do?"

"You . . . didn't seem happy with who you were." At the last moment, he shies away from: *You said you loved me.*

She laughs. "Well, clearly, I was drunk."

"And honest."

"Ah, crap, Jones. Crap. I was probably just trying to sleep with you."

"Why can't you admit you're lonely?"

There's a half second, then Eve laughs disbelievingly. "Oh, shit, you're serious."

"You have a lot of nice *stuff.* I get that. What else do you have?"

This comes out more critical than he intends, and Eve's dark eyes widen. "I get drunk and say a few stupid things and suddenly you have a window into my soul? No, Jones. I have a great life and a great job and if it means firing a hundred people on Monday, I'll do it without blinking. I have everything I want. Not happy with who I am? God, I'm not just happy, I'm *proud.*"

"You—"

"And there's nothing wrong with my stuff!"

"There's more to you than that. Eve, you feel bad about what Alpha does, I know you do. At least sometimes." She doesn't react to this the way Jones is hoping—doesn't react at all, in fact—so he presses ahead. "Freddy. You met him in the elevator today. He's the one who's been sending you flowers every week. Did you know that?"

Eve stares at him. "You moron, *of course I know that.* We *monitor* the whole company!"

Jones feels himself reddening. "Well, he's—"

"You know what it says in Freddy's file? 'Do not promote no matter what.' That's why he's been a sales assistant for five years; he's a project. They're *all* projects. Want to know something else? Holly, that girl you work with, she books meeting rooms for no meetings. She just goes and sits in them. Sometimes she takes a magazine, but mostly not.

She's the loneliest person I've ever seen. That PA your department had, the fat one—she kept a record of your movements. She was so infatuated with you she couldn't *breathe*, and *you didn't notice.* Do I try to fix these people's lives? No. I don't worry about them, I don't care about them. They're mice in a maze to me."

Jones walks away. This is not as impressive as it sounds, because the crowd is a crush: he feels not so much like the steely-jawed hero as the teary heroine. Still, he gets all the way down the stairs, out the door, and into the back of a cab conveniently waiting by the curb before Eve catches up. Then she raps on the window with her knuckles.

"Just go," Jones tells the driver. But Eve is a beautiful woman in a figure-hugging dress, and apparently this carries more weight with the cabbie than Jones's opinion. When he realizes the car isn't going anywhere, he rolls down the window.

"Ask Klausman to tell you about Harvey Millpacker. They started Project Alpha together way back when. Just the two of them and twenty ignorant employees, until Harvey got an attack of the guilts. One day, out of the blue, he comes in to work and announces it's all a sham. An experiment. Klausman had no idea it was coming, no chance to stop him, so that's it, experiment over. The company folds and everyone's laid off. The workers went nuts. There were death threats. But you know what? They were angriest at Harvey. Klausman had lied to them, but he'd given them jobs. Harvey got them sacked."

"Is this a morality tale?" Jones says. "Because coming from you, it's a little hard to take."

"The business manager was Cliff Raleigh. Fifty-eight,

divorced, not much in the way of friends or family. But at work he was a living legend. It's a disgrace how hard it is for older workers to find decent work these days. It's something Alpha wants to address." She shrugs. "Three months after he lost his job, Cliff shot himself."

Jones clenches his fists. He has always considered himself to be a peaceful person, so he is unprepared for the violence of his reaction. He wants to get out of the car and hit her so badly that he can taste it in the back of his throat.

"You," Eve says, "should think *really carefully* about whether you want to be another Harvey Millpacker."

"Go," Jones says to the driver, and when this elicits no action, he roars: *"Drive!"* But the cab doesn't move until Eve takes her hand off the door and steps away. Jones doesn't even get to *leave* until she approves, and, bottom line, he guesses that's about right.

On level 2 of the Zephyr building, Senior Management sits around the board table. It's been a long day for Senior Management. There's no rest for the executive. With darkness outside the floor-to-ceiling windows and a thunderstorm brewing, Senior Management puts the final touches on the consolidation plan.

There are two ways to look at Senior Management. One is that it's a tightly integrated team tirelessly pulling together in the service of whatever's best for the company.

The other is that it's a dog pack of power-hungry egomaniacs who occasionally assist Zephyr as a side effect of their individual campaigns for wealth and status. Nobody believes the tightly knit team theory anymore. Once, a long time ago, it may have been true, but the instant a dog-pack person made it into Senior Management, it was all over. It's like a fox getting into the chicken house; pretty soon there are only foxes and feathers. If Senior Management was ever made up of selfless individuals who put teamwork ahead of self-interest—and this is a big if—they were long ago torn to pieces.

It's important to understand this, because it's a prerequisite to making sense of Senior Management decisions, like the consolidation. The initial goal was to streamline Zephyr's business operations. But that was a week ago. Since then, it has been about empire expansion. Senior Management camps have waged fierce and bloody war. Departments were lost, claimed, and lost again. Many fine, decent ideas were lost in the mayhem; many innocent, hardworking employees, none of whom know it yet, were caught in the cross fire. It has been a week of senseless tragedy and mindless destruction, and now even Senior Management is a little tired of it.

But at last it's over. The final plan, which gives every employee something to be happy about, so long as they work in Senior Management, reduces the number of Zephyr departments by a whopping 70 percent. Many departments are out entirely, but most were rolled together, creating new departments with all of the responsibilities and some of the resources of two. Or three. Or, in one case, five. The plan is passed around the table, and as each Senior Management signature is added, hideous new creatures are formed from the stitching together of departmental organs. With the slash of a pen, Security is grafted onto Human Resources. Large, flapping sections of Legal are sewn into place. For reasons that have nothing to do with operating efficiency and everything to do with hardball bargaining between executives, the sole remaining Credit employee is stapled on. Lightning crashes outside the boardroom window as Senior Management finally, exhaustedly, attaches a departmental head. And there it is: a new department. Senior Management has given birth, right there in the boardroom. Its progeny lies on the table, a cruel abomination of nature, sucking in its first foul breath. Its yellow eyes glint balefully. Its limbs curl and flop on the polished oak. It throws back its ill-fitting head and roars with life, or something similar.

Below, the scattered few employees still at work pause and look up. Their bowels tighten. They exchange frightened looks. No one puts it into words, but everyone feels it. Something evil has come into the world.

Q4/2: NOVEMBER

GRETEL MONADNOCK carefully slides her Kia hatchback into a space right beside the elevators. She turns off the engine, gathers her jacket and bag, and closes the door behind her. The sound rolls up the length of the Zephyr Holdings underground parking lot and back. Usually Gretel drives right through this sublevel, passing car after car; she only keeps half an eye out for a space, and if she finds one it's a real thrill. But today a mere half a dozen or so cars occupy spaces. It feels strange. It is 7:25 A.M.

She is inside the elevator and pushing for the lobby when her cell phone trills. She digs it out of her bag. "Hello?"

"Hi Gretel, it's Pat again. Is everything still on track?"

"I've just arrived this second."

"Oh, *great.* Thanks so much, Gretel. You'll call me if you have any questions?"

"I will. Bye." Gretel turns off her phone. The elevator doors open and suddenly Gretel is looking at a young man in a blue Security uniform. He is standing directly in front

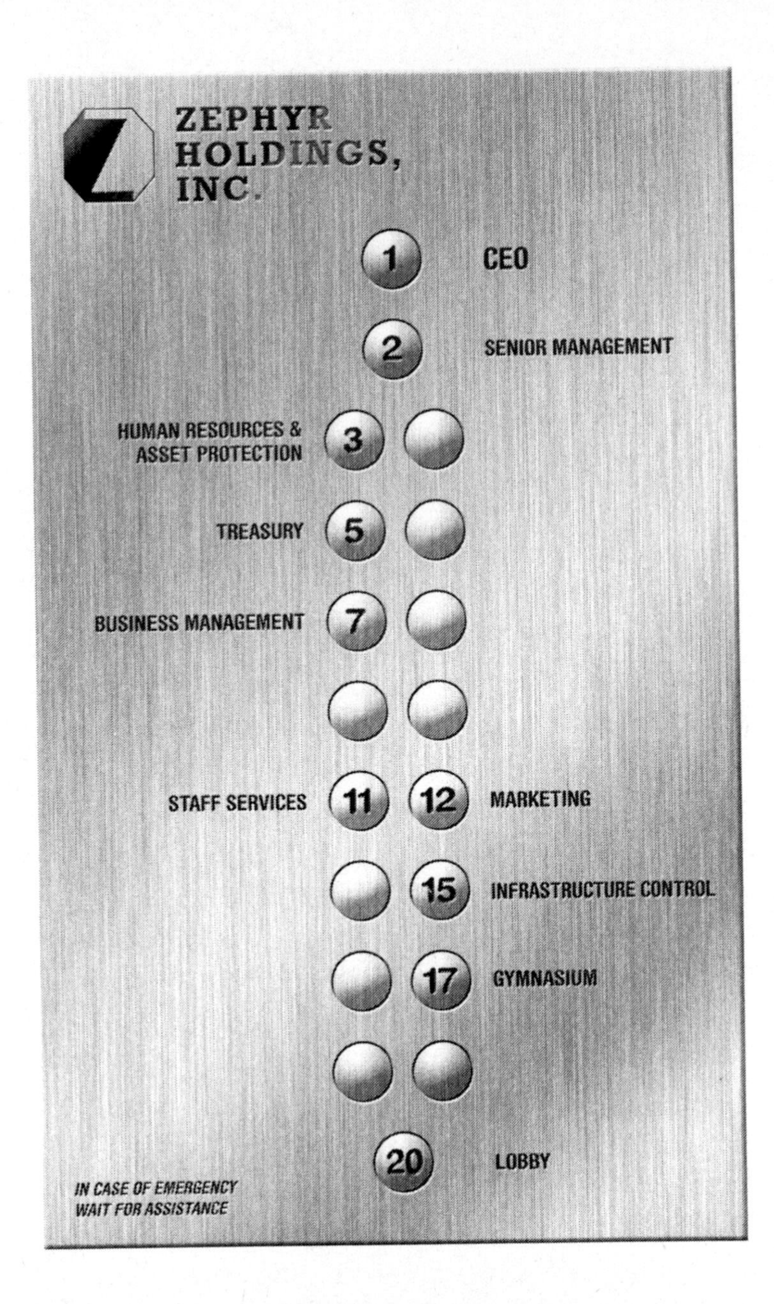
ZEPHYR
HOLDINGS,
INC.
1
CEO
2
SENIOR MANAGEMENT
HUMAN RESOURCES &
ASSET PROTECTION
3
TREASURY
5
BUSINESS MANAGEMENT
7
STAFF SERVICES
11
12
MARKETING
15
INFRASTRUCTURE CONTROL
17
GYMNASIUM
20
LOBBY
IN CASE OF EMERGENCY
WAIT FOR ASSISTANCE

of her, blocking her exit from the elevator. Behind him are two more uniformed men.

The man's eyes drop to her chest, in a way that Gretel always finds disconcerting, to read her ID tag. "You're the receptionist?"

"Yes."

"Right on time." He smiles, which is clearly meant to be reassuring, but his lips are wet and shiny and Gretel feels a brush of irrational fear. "There are complete instructions in your voice mail, I'm told."

He steps aside. This allows her to see that there are three more Security personnel by the lobby's front doors and a further six encircle the reception desk.

She puts her head down and walks to her desk. The *clack*ing of her heels echoes crazily. Nobody else makes a sound; they simply follow her with their eyes. When she reaches her desk, she realizes she is holding her breath.

Six stapled pages are waiting for her and her voice-mail light is blinking. She picks up the handset.

"Hi, Gretel. This is Pat from upstairs. I've got a message from Senior Management following. Someone should have called you at home over the weekend about this, but if you have any questions, I'll be in early Monday, too. Just give me a call. Thanks. *Click.* Pat, forward this on to that woman in reception—sorry, I forget her name. Not Eve Jantiss, the other one. HR has told her to come in early Monday morning, but can you make sure she does? Just keep calling her. Harrumph. All right. To reception: We have completed our consolidation plan, and as a result many employees have been reassigned to new departments. Other employees are no longer required. For security purposes, those people cannot be allowed to go to their desks. Security will disable direct elevator access from the parking lot to the upper floors, so everyone will come in via the lobby. As people arrive, you need to check them against the new employee list, and if they've been terminated, explain to them that . . . well, just explain it. You can say that HR will be in contact to forward their severance pay, personal belongings, et cetera et cetera. Then ask them to leave the building. Security will be on hand to provide assistance. Any kind of assistance. Thanks."

Gretel puts down the phone. While she was listening, the Security guard with the wet lips came over to stand beside her. He smiles. "So, everything clear?"

The first arrives just before eight: a middle-aged man in a suit with shiny knees and a baggy backside. He comes in through the front doors and begins to cross the lobby floor, glancing curiously at Security. Gretel freezes: she thought the guards were going to stop people, but apparently they expect her to. By the time she has unstuck her throat, the man is stepping into an open elevator and reaching for the button panel. Then his face blanches. He throws the nearest Security guard an anxious look. "Where's my floor?"

The guard jerks his head toward Gretel. For a moment the man's expression doesn't change. Then his shoulders sag. It's a moment or two before he can bring himself to leave the elevator and cross the lobby floor, and when he does, his shoes drag. He doesn't walk so much as slide to the reception desk, and when he reaches it, his eyes don't meet Gretel's; instead, they fix on a random point on the desk's orange surface. "I'm from Central Accounting. Is... Central Accounting still here?"

Gretel scans her pages. "Central Accounting has been consolidated into Treasury. The new department will operate from level 8." She looks up. "Many Central Accounting staff have been terminated."

The man tries to say it offhand, but it doesn't come out that way. "Have I been terminated?"

"Are you Frank Posterman?"

His eyes jump to her face. "No! Frank's the manager."

"Then yes."

His head rocks back. Gretel bleeds for him. But she keeps her face emotionless.

"I'm sorry." Already two Security guards are moving forward. Gretel reaches across the expanse of the desk and offers him her hand. "You need to leave the building now. Thank you for your service to Zephyr Holdings, and goodbye."

"She's good," Klausman says, watching the monitor. "Compassionate, but professional. She won't do anything to help you, but you feel like she cares. That's exactly the kind of attitude that dampens emotional outbursts. Mona, make a note."

The entire Project Alpha team is clustered behind him. This is today's morning meeting, relocated to the monitoring room so they can watch the action. Occasionally a tech in jeans and a T-shirt squeezes between them to fool with a keyboard, but otherwise the room's atmosphere is highly compressed Calvin Klein and Chanel No. 5. Blake stands behind Klausman's right shoulder and Eve his left; Jones is behind her. So far their conversation has consisted of "Good morning," "Big day today," and "Yes," but from the way her eyes keep flicking to him, Eve couldn't be any more aware of Jones if he was carrying a meat cleaver. Blake has picked up on this; during his and Eve's frigid exchange, Jones felt his steely blue gaze—or, at least, the half of it that isn't hidden beneath a black matte patch adorned with tiny letters that spell out Armani.

"Look at level 2," someone murmurs. All eyes leap to the monitor in the top corner. There Senior Management sits around a board table, their hands folded, their expressions somber. A speakerphone sits in the center of the table.

"They're getting updates from Security in the lobby," Eve says. She is wearing a strappy green dress. Her brown shoulders gleam at Jones.

"Well, thus far, I have to say I'm impressed." Klausman turns around for a second to see if anyone disagrees. The agents nod and murmur assent, except for Jones, who doesn't do anything at all. "They've followed the Omega recommendations protocol to the letter. Maybe a little overkill on the number of security guards, but better safe than sorry, eh? I remember a few years ago when Zephyr outsourced IT—not for the first or last time, of course"—chuckles from the agents; Eve's bare shoulders jiggle—"but the department manager, idiot that he was, told staff ahead of time. He actually called a meeting, announced it was everyone's last week, offered counseling, et cetera, et cetera, then sent them back to their desks. An hour later the phone system was down, company confidential files were on the public Web site, and when you tried to log on to your PC, you got a picture of a man doing something with a stapler that haunts me to this day. It took weeks to straighten out."

"The thing that concerns me," Blake says, when everyone has finished enjoying this little story, "is not the execution, but the strategy. Senior Management knows what it's doing, but it's hardly given any thought to why. Basically, they just jumped at the chance to reorganize."

Klausman sighs and turns back to study the monitor. "True. Eve?"

"Ah... well, it's a Drifting Goals systems archetype. Same problem we always have with Senior Management."

"Jones!" Klausman barks over his shoulder. "Do you know what she's talking about?"

"I can guess."

"Go ahead."

"The primary benefits of a position in Senior Management are increased status and increased salary. The disadvantages are decreased free time and increased stress. So, logically, the sort of people who end up working in Senior Management are those who are most motivated by money and status, and care least about missing time with friends and family."

Klausman chuckles. "A somewhat unsympathetic view, Mr. Jones, but yes, you have the general idea."

"We seem to be taking a fairly unsympathetic view toward employees currently being fired," Jones says. "I thought that's what we were doing."

Klausman, Eve, and Blake all turn around.

Into the awkward silence, Eve says, "Well, he's got a point. Senior Management is no different from any other department, for our purposes. I know we all feel a connection to the top execs—and hell, Blake's *in* Senior Management—but we shouldn't be identifying with anybody. We're objective researchers."

Klausman nods slowly. "Indeed. Indeed. Fair point, both of you. And note, everyone, how valuable a fresh perspective is in identifying areas of potential groupthink."

He turns back. After a second, so do Blake and Eve. Everyone around Jones looks thoughtful. Jones feels thoughtful, too, but not about Senior Management. He wonders why all of a sudden Eve is crawling up his butt.

Freddy arrives at Zephyr at eight thirty and his heart just about stops. A mass of people is milling inside the lobby. More alarmingly, a large group is gathered *outside* on the plaza, and blue-uniformed Security guards are progressively transferring people from the former to the latter. Freddy realizes it has happened. Zephyr Holdings has consolidated.

He forges blindly through the crowd toward the reception desk. Dozens of employees are trying to do the same thing, and it's hot with the press of anxious bodies. When he gets one hand on the smooth surface of the desk, he hangs on to it with all his strength.

Security, arranged around the desk, eyes the crowd with silent hostility. A guard looks at Freddy as if he is not positive that Freddy has been fired, but it wouldn't surprise him. Freddy feels terror bubble in his gut. On his left, a willowy female graduate trembles uncontrollably. A middle-aged man sweats into overalls on his right. One by one, they come before Gretel—not Eve; Eve is nowhere to be seen, which Freddy finds alarming all by itself—and are told they are no longer employed. There is no break, no respite: it is an uninterrupted stream of firings. With each one, the crowd groans as a single animal. By the time it's Freddy's turn, he has to fight the urge to flee before they can sack him.

Gretel's eyes move onto him. Freddy is shocked to see compassion in them. Sympathy in this cattle yard is so unexpected that it gets under his guard, unmans him. He sucks in a shuddering breath. He's glad Eve isn't here to see this.

"Which department?"

"Training Sales."

"Training Sales..." Gretel flips through her papers. "Training Sales has been consolidated into Staff Services. The new department is on level 11." She looks up. "All Training Sales staff have been retained."

Freddy's vision washes white. His fingers gouge the desk. *Saved! Saved!* The crowd gasps. Freddy lets out a whoop. He wants to kiss Gretel. He wants to kiss Security. He starts to laugh.

"Marketing Research," the willowy graduate says hoarsely, and Gretel runs her finger down the paper. Freddy comes to his senses and pushes his way through the crowd. He elbows, he shoulders; still, he is not quite far enough away to avoid hearing Gretel's response, or the ache of empathy that fills her voice.

An hour of this and even Alpha gets bored. Attention wanders from the monitors. Agents begin to discuss other projects, and the excellence of the BMW X5, and how terrific Blake's eye patch looks and where did he get it. Jones picks up his briefcase and begins to walk away. Klausman calls, "Going somewhere, Jones?" and Jones says, "To work," without stopping.

Eve catches him by the elevators. She leans against the wall, tilting her head so her dark hair splashes on her shoulder. "Can we talk?"

He shrugs.

"I wasn't sure you'd show up today. You didn't answer any of my messages." When Jones doesn't respond to this, she continues carefully. "Not that I blame you. I'm sorry about Friday. I really am. I kind of lost it."

He looks at her.

"You're so new, Jones. I forgot that. I expected you to take on too much too fast. This is a tough business, a really tough business, and I want you to succeed. You have such an opportunity here. I don't want you to lose it. But I didn't go about it the right way on Friday. I got mad and... I didn't mean to do that."

She looks so sincere; it's unsettling. When Jones drove down the parking-lot ramp this morning, he gripped his steering wheel as if he was trying to choke it to death. He spent the weekend mining out a deep, thick reservoir of bitterness toward Eve and Alpha—toward business in general, really—and the result of this was the resolution that while he might be powerless to change Alpha, he could at least hate them. This was, admittedly, not the most insightful or productive decision—but it was a decision nonetheless, one that allowed him to determine a kind of way forward. Now even this is under threat, because with Eve looking at him with earnestness swimming in her big bedroom eyes it's hard to cast her as the personification of corporate heartlessness.

He shrugs. "You told me the truth. I guess I needed to hear it."

She puts her hand on his arm. "Jones, you have this amazing empathy for the Zephyr staff. It's... unusual in Alpha. It's not especially helpful, doing what we do. But I shouldn't have told you it's wrong. I realize now it's that empathy that makes you special. I don't want you to lose it."

Jones is lost for words.

"Now," she says, "don't tell anyone in Alpha I said that. This is our little secret." She smiles, as if this is a joke, but there's no trace of humor in her eyes. "All right?"

Another agent, Tom Mandrake, comes out of the monitoring room and walks toward them, whistling. Eve removes her hand from Jones's arm and steps back. "By the way, I bought this dress for you. Do you like?"

"Um," Jones says. "Yes, it's very nice."

She smiles, genuinely, and does a little half curtsy. "Actually, to be honest, I bought it a month ago. But I wore it for the first time today."

Tom stops beside them. "You own dresses you've never worn?"

"Oh yeah. Lots." The elevator arrives. Before Jones steps into it, Eve says to him, "We'll talk later, okay?"

Elizabeth exits the elevator on level 11, her new home, with a certain wariness. But it is, of course, an exact replica of level 14. The carpet is the same retina-scraping orange. The sign on the frosted glass door says STAFF SERVICES instead of TRAINING SALES, but it's in the same position and the same HR-approved company font. In the actual department, the fluorescent lighting is just as cheap and there is even a single flickering fixture *(bink! bink bink!)*, although it's in a different position. There's the bathroom on the left, the manager's office and meeting room straight ahead (their glass walls shrouded by vertical blinds), and between them and her is the grand open pasture of the cubicle farm.

Here, at least, is a major difference: no Berlin Partition. Instead there's an ugly mess of two dozen cubicles jammed up against each other, as if the large ones of East and West Berlin had given birth to a litter. There's no sense in the arrangement, as far as Elizabeth can tell, which suggests there is no seating plan, and a land grab is in progress. She should have arrived an hour ago; by now she is probably stuck next to the xerox machine.

But before she can tackle that issue, she has a personal matter to attend to. She enters the bathroom, which is indistinguishable from the one on level 14 right down to the little black-and-orange tiles and pools of water around the basins left by careless hand-washers. She smiles at a woman she's never seen before, enters a stall, and closes the door. She sits on the closed seat, pulls out a nail file, and begins to trim. She does her left hand, then the right. She spreads her fingers and inspects them. Only then does she realize something important: she isn't nauseous.

She freezes. She has followed this routine long enough to know how it goes. Right now she should be flipping up the seat and retching. She stands and begins to pull up her skirt, which first requires unbuttoning a jacket because these days her work outfits are elaborately crafted to conceal a growing belly. She struggles out of her tights and checks her underwear. Nothing. Relief hits her like a gust of wind. She claps a hand over her mouth to suppress a burst of laughter.

She rearranges her skirt, sits back down, and rubs her abdomen through the fabric. She cannot stop smiling. If her morning sickness is over, then maybe her body is getting used to her new arrival. Maybe she and it are beginning to get along. It is both obvious and unbelievable: she is going to have a baby. The idea fills her with silent joy.

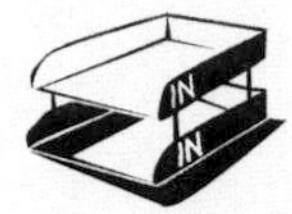

Jones presses 11 for Staff Services, his new home, and looks expectantly at Tom Mandrake. "Seven," Tom says. "Compliance is part of Business Management now."

Jones presses for level 7. "Compliance was on 6, wasn't it? You guys have gone down a floor."

Tom smirks. "No doubt that will be the subject of intense discussion today."

"So people really do care about their floor number."

"Absolutely. Anytime you rank people, they care. Doesn't matter what you rank them on. And you know what, they believe it, too. At least a little." The elevator stops at 11, and Jones steps out. "Have fun," Tom says. He winks as the doors slide closed.

Jones looks down the corridor at the frosted glass doors. Vague, person-sized shapes move about beyond them. These are the people Alpha is interested in, of course: the survivors. The rest are of no apparent concern. Jones wonders how this can be: How can you excise a human being from the company's tiny but fully developed society so easily? How can you excise hundreds? In Alpha it is common to compare Zephyr Holdings to a tribe, since both are self-contained social structures with hierarchies, etiquette, and norms—indeed, this is the basis for many amusing sidebars in Omega Management System books, describing (for example) how departments fight to protect resources in terms of warriors, meat, and feathers. But if this analogy is true, then this morning a rockfall left two hundred tribespeople trapped in a cave, and nobody gives a crap about them.

Jones can understand, at least a little, the behavior of the survivors: creating a lot of noise might trigger more rockfalls, and trap them, too. On top of this, their social order has mutated, and they are trying to grab a fingerhold in the new hierarchies. But why are the victims so accepting of their fate? This is beyond him.

He looks at the elevator button. Then he presses: DOWN.

On the screens in the level-13 monitoring room, the tiny figures of the recently redundant looked blurred and meaningless, cartoonish. So as he exits the lobby doors, Jones is surprised by their sheer presence. There are a lot of people crowded onto the plaza outside the building, talking and shuffling their feet and fogging the chill air with their breath. Jones looks from face to face as a fresh bay wind whips up Madison Street and ruffles everyone's hair.

"Hey," a man says. At first Jones doesn't recognize him. "They got you too, huh?"

It's a smoker. Jones has seen him out in back of the building. Once again, Jones realizes, he's an impostor. "Ah, no. I just came to see what was going on."

"Oh," the man says.

"Sorry. You don't deserve this."

The man looks at him quizzically. "Why do you say that?"

Jones is surprised by the question. He realizes Tom Mandrake was right. And this is why they are fatalistic; this is why Alpha can safely ignore them. They think they deserve it.

Jones says, "Because you don't."

The man considers this. Then, unexpectedly, he laughs. "Well," he says. "Maybe we don't."

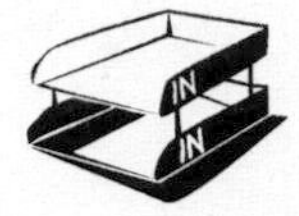

Freddy surveys the new Staff Services department with horror. He hurries into the farm, hoping someone (anyone!) from Training Sales arrived early and reserved a bunch of good desks. He pauses at the coat stand to shrug off his jacket, then realizes his usual hook is taken. Of course, it's not his hook: his hook is (or was) two floors down. But Freddy is peeved anyway. He has so little; now they want to take away his *hook*? He flings his jacket over the top of the one already there.

"Ah, Freddy. Just who I wanted to see." It's Sydney, in a sharp business suit so black it's like a hole in reality. "Tell me, is that dead pool still going?"

"Yeah, I guess. Why?"

"Oh, no reason."

"I thought everyone in Training Sales was retained," Freddy says, alarmed.

"Well, you never know," Sydney says. "You never know what might be necessary in this new environment."

"Not Holly. Please, Sydney, not Holly—"

"Who said Holly?" Sydney says, irritated. "I didn't say I was sacking Holly."

"You asked about the dead pool—"

"Look, forget I mentioned it. I might not sack anybody." She checks her watch, a glittering gold thing that dangles from her tiny wrist. "If you don't mind, I have an important meeting to get to."

Freddy stands aside. He watches her wend her way

through the crammed cubicles to reach the meeting room, knock once, and step inside without waiting for a response. Then he cups his hands around his mouth and calls, *"Holly?"*

Holly pops her head over a cubicle only a few desks away. "Hey, there you are."

Freddy scurries over. The entire remaining Training Sales department bar Jones—that is, Holly, Elizabeth, and Roger—is squeezed into a single cubicle, leaning against desks or sitting in chairs with their knees touching. Freddy looks around in dismay. "Is this all the space we get? We should call Relocation Services."

"We *are* Relocation Services." Elizabeth points at a memo that Holly, her brow furrowed, is now reading. "Or, at least, they're one of the departments we've been consolidated with. They arrived an hour ago and took all the best spaces."

Holly gasps, her fingers tightening on the memo. "We've merged with Gymnasium Management!"

" 'Merged' is one way of putting it," Roger says. "We're much more important than them."

Freddy says, "Um, I just ran into Sydney . . . and I kind of got the impression she was thinking of sacking someone."

Everyone falls silent. Then Elizabeth and Roger speak at the same time. Elizabeth says, "Why?" and Roger says, "Who?"

"She didn't say. But she asked if the dead pool was still on."

"Oh, God." Holly's eyes widen. "Oh, God!"

"Why would she sack someone now?" Elizabeth says.

"I have no idea."

Roger rubs his chin. "I understand that Senior Management hasn't appointed a manager for Staff Services yet. Maybe the managers of the old departments have decided to elect an interim leader."

"Oh boy," Elizabeth says.

"What?" Freddy's eyes flick between Elizabeth and Roger. "Is that bad? What does that mean?"

"Well, it'll essentially be an arm-wrestle," Roger says. "If Sydney wants the job badly enough, she might offer to sack one of us as a trade-off." Holly moans. "Or two of us. Maybe all of us, who knows."

They look at each other. "Well," Elizabeth says finally. "We can't have that."

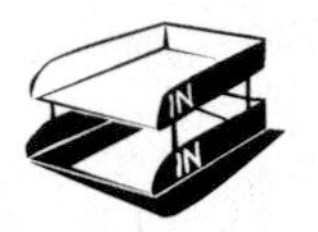

Outside, something is happening to the newly unemployed. At first they were shocked and miserable; they milled around without purpose. Then Jones said *You don't deserve this* and this strange, oddball idea jumped from person to person, spreading through the crowd. Soon naked anger is visible on several faces. An accountant pulls a logo-stamped Zephyr Holdings binder from his briefcase, drops it to the concrete, and stomps on it. People cheer. An engineer has a Q3 High Achiever coffee mug; he smashes it on the concrete. A graphic designer tugs off his shoe and throws it as high as he can. It bounces off a tinted window.

A pale, worried face appears at the window, then quickly retreats. The crowd roars.

It is a dull day, but overhead the clouds are darkening; the air is thickening. Jones backs away toward the safety of the lobby. He feels as if he just rubbed a lamp and now a genie is coalescing out of blue smoke: a big one, with rippling biceps and violence in his eyes. He tastes a mixture of joy and terror.

The lobby doors slide apart before he reaches them and Security escorts out a woman with a neat blue scarf and a leather clutch bag. Jones stands aside to watch it in amazement: the mob hurling its fury against the twenty-floor colossus of Zephyr Holdings even as the company delivers a steady stream of new recruits.

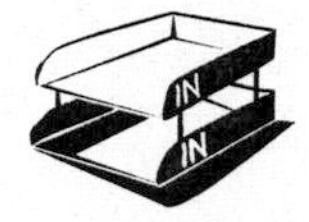

On level 11 Elizabeth produces a plan to save Training Sales that is so breathtaking in its audacity and so ferocious in its wrath against Sydney that everyone immediately endorses it. Then Roger says, "Very well, I'll play the main role, then."

Elizabeth says, "Well . . . I assumed *I'd* play the main part, Roger. Since it's my plan."

"Oh. I see. Well, if you want to pull rank, that's fine. I was just offering. If it's that important to you, do it."

"I'm not *pulling rank.* It's just *my plan.*"

Roger holds up his hands. "Forget it. I'm just trying to be

helpful. I didn't mean to get between you and your ambition."

Elizabeth's cheeks darken. "Roger, if it's important to *you,* then come out and *say* that. Just *say* it. Because I really don't care one way or the other."

"Well, if you *want* me to, I'm happy to do it. But it's no big deal, I don't mind either way."

"If neither of us care, *why are we having this conversation?*"

"Elizabeth. Please. Can we just make a decision?"

Elizabeth's face flushes. Little beads of sweat stand out on her hairline. She begins to breathe deeply and her hands rhythmically clench and open. Jones arrives at the cubicle just in time to see this and he stops in shock, thinking he's watching a heart attack. "Elizabeth?" Holly says, alarmed.

"Fine. Fine. You do it."

"So . . . let me get this straight," Roger says. "You *want* me to do it?"

"Yes." This is so strangled it is barely decipherable as a word.

"Well, all right, then." Roger's eyes flick to the sales assistants to make sure they all caught this. "I'm glad we got that settled."

It's quiet in the lobby, for by now every employee has been either accepted into the Zephyr fold or manhandled outside. The Security guards stand in a line along the glass wall with their hands folded behind their backs, watching. Gretel sits at the reception desk. She feels exhausted and tainted. She feels as if she has executed two hundred people and still has their blood on her hands.

There is a rising commotion from outside, so she gets up and walks over to one of the guards. She peers out the green-tinted glass wall. "Looks nasty out there."

The guard doesn't respond. His eyes are fixed on the mob.

"Maybe they'll storm the building," she suggests. "Maybe they'll smash the glass."

"You're perfectly safe, ma'am." He still doesn't look at her.

"Maybe the company shouldn't have fired so many people," Gretel says. She is surprised by the bitterness in her own voice. "Maybe we brought it on ourselves."

The guard blinks once, slowly.

" 'First they came for the Communists. And I didn't speak out, because I wasn't a Communist.' You know how that ends?"

The guard turns to look at her. Gretel takes a step backward, because the guard's eyes are hollow.

"Please, ma'am. I'm just doing my job."

"Sorry." It comes out as a whimper. She hurries back to her desk, feeling the guard's empty stare on the back of her neck. She takes her seat and hugs her arms across her chest.

A few minutes later, Roger knocks on the Staff Services meeting-room door. There's no response. He glances at the others. "Well, here goes." He turns the handle.

Inside, five managers including Sydney are arranged around a circular table. There's a piece of paper in the center of the table, and when she sees Roger, Elizabeth, and Holly, Sydney reaches out and flips it over. "Excuse me. We're busy."

Roger frowns at her. Elizabeth has to credit him; he's very convincing. "Sydney, wait outside, please."

Sydney blinks. "What did you say?"

"Out." He jerks his head toward the door. "We'll discuss this later."

Sydney looks lost for words. One of the other managers, a woman with thin, natty glasses, says, "This meeting is for department heads only."

"Right," Roger says. "I'm manager of Training Sales."

Sydney says, *"Pardon me?"*

"Sydney is... ah... ambitious." Roger winks at the woman. "You'll have to forgive her."

"*I'm* the head of Training Sales," Sydney says.

"No, I am," Roger says. "Have been for months."

The other managers look at Elizabeth and Holly. They point at Roger.

Sydney's cheeks flush a deep, angry red. "It's on file. Check the files!"

"Well, the network is down, so you know we can't do that." Roger doesn't even glance at her. He smiles engagingly at the other managers. "I'm sorry for this. But you can't blame Syd for trying, I suppose."

The managers look at each other. Two have no idea

whether Roger or Sydney is head of Training Sales: There are a lot of departments and a lot of turnover and who can keep track? It does seem plausible that the manager is the tall man with good hair rather than the five-foot-one woman. One of the other managers knows very well that Sydney is the Training Sales manager, because she once sent an e-mail, copied to Senior Management, that accused him of incompetence, laziness, and, memorably, alcoholism. He reacts first. "I'm sorry—Roger, is it? We didn't realize."

"Not a problem." Roger smiles. Then he looks down at Sydney. "What are you hanging around for?"

Sydney opens her mouth, then shuts it. She looks from one face to another and finds no sympathy on any of them. She stands and walks out.

Elizabeth and Holly step back to let her pass. Elizabeth looks back at the managers. "We'll leave you to it," she says and gently closes the door.

At first they hang around, in case a bloodied hand paws against the glass, or a body is slammed against the blinds. But when it becomes apparent that this battle will go the distance, Elizabeth heads off to call on some customers and the sales assistants go to lunch. Or, rather, they attempt to go to lunch, because the mass of angry ex-employees in front of the building has gotten everyone nervous, and Security won't let them out of the building. By one o'clock, hunger is increasing the possibility of a riot inside the building, too, so Human Resources makes some calls and manages to get a truckload of sandwiches delivered to a back entrance. These are cold and rubbery and make everyone feel guilty, because as they pick them up from the reception desk, the unemployed stare at them through the tinted glass.

"Ahhh," Freddy says. Jones follows his gaze to see Eve stepping out of the elevator with a man in a gray suit from Alpha. Neither looks happy. Jones's heart starts thumping.

Holly smirks. "Thought she'd been canned?"

"She wasn't at the desk this morning, I thought maybe she had been." Freddy sucks in a breath. "I'm so high on adrenaline, I could ask her out right now. You know how people who survive a life-threatening experience form a bond? That could work in my favor."

They watch Eve walk to the reception desk. "I don't get it," Holly says. "What *is* it about her? She's not that fit, you know. One time I saw her at the gym, she looked like she was about to pass out."

"You're right," Freddy says. "You don't get it."

Jones says, "That's true, though. You don't really know her. She could be an ax murderer for all you know."

"With those spindly little arms?" Holly says.

"*Before* you were telling me to ask her out. Now what are you saying?"

"Just... maybe she's not right for you."

"Jones likes her," Holly teases.

"No, that's not it. Don't be stupid." Jones forces himself to stop before: *Why do you say that?* "I'm just saying, maybe Freddy could do better."

Freddy snorts. "No I couldn't."

"He's right," Holly says. "Look at him. Short, glasses, working in the same crappy job for five years... if Eve Jantiss agreed to date *him,* I'd buy lottery tickets."

"Have you been going easy on the bicep crunches lately?" Freddy asks. "Under your arms there, it looks a bit flabby."

Holly's mouth falls open in outrage. "My body fat percentage is *fourteen.*"

"Well, if you think that's good enough." He pats his pockets. "I'm going for a smoke. I'll see you back upstairs."

In the elevator, Jones catches Holly pinching the undersides of her arm. She drops her hands to her sides. "God, he pisses me off sometimes."

When Freddy returns to Staff Services, he is bristling with indignation. "Do you know what they're doing?"

"Who?" Jones says.

"They made me go out back because of all the people, and I saw this new wooden fenced-in area going up next to the generator. The sign says SMOKERS' CORRAL. They're building a designated smoking area!"

Holly blows air in disgust. "I don't know why the company wants to waste money on smokers."

"It has pictures of cows on it! Cows with cigarettes in their mouths!"

She smirks. "Oh. That's funny."

"What gets me is they think this is *helping,*" Freddy complains. "Management is so out of touch, they think we'll *appreciate* this!" He looks to Jones for support, but Jones keeps his mouth shut. "Morons!" Freddy exclaims.

Holly says, "In the gym this morning, I heard nonsmokers will be getting an extra vacation day. Now that's a good idea."

Freddy's mouth drops open. "What?"

"Well, *I* don't take five breaks a day to go stand in the sun," Holly says. "Why shouldn't I get an extra day?"

"I make that time up! I work overtime!"

"What, I don't?"

"Bah. This is discrimination!"

"If you ask me, it's discrimination that *you* get time off to smoke while Jones and I don't."

"Leave me out of this," Jones says, before realizing how hypocritical this is.

"Besides," Holly says, "why should you get upset about me getting a day off? It doesn't affect you."

"You were *just* being a bitch about me taking five minutes for a smoke!"

"Are you calling me a bitch?" Holly yells.

Jones stands up. "Hey. Guys. Stop it, please. This is a stressful time. We need to stick together."

Freddy takes a deep breath. "I'm sorry. You're not a bitch, Holly. But I am *not* going to stand in a *corral* with pictures of *cows*."

After a moment, Holly says, "Yes you are."

Freddy sits down with a sigh. "I hate this company so much. I wish I had been laid off."

"No you don't."

He laughs softly. "No, I don't. At least here I'm in good company."

"What?" Jones says.

"I said at least here I'm in good company."

"Oh. I thought you said you were in *a* good company."

Freddy and Holly stare at him.

Jones says, "What if we could make the company better?

If we could change things . . . make it a better place to work. I mean, there are so many things we could do."

Holly looks at him blankly. Freddy says, "Jones . . . you're still new here. People suggest ways to improve the company every day. Their ideas go into the suggestion box in the cafeteria—where the cafeteria *was,* I mean—and they're never heard from again, except during all-staff meetings when Senior Management picks out the most useless one and announces a cross-functional team to look into it. A year or two later, when everyone's forgotten about it, we get an e-mail announcing the implementation of something that bears no resemblance to the initial idea and usually has the opposite effect, and in the annual reports this is used as evidence that the company listens and reacts to its workers. That's what happens when you try to make Zephyr a better place to work."

There's a click. Just a small sound, but Freddy, Holly, and Jones stand up at the same time. They peer over their cubicle wall, as, all around, other Staff Services employees do the same thing. The meeting-room door swings open.

Roger emerges first. His smile is brilliant.

The queen is dead; long live the king! The workers jostle for a glimpse of Roger, for a touch of his hand. He moves among them, greeting the people, shaking hands, thumping backs, kissing cheeks. "I will govern for all the people," Roger declares, and the workers cheer. "This is a new beginning. I promise you hard work—but also respect. Recognition. And reward!" The employees' faces brighten. Relocation Services and Gymnasium Management employees grin at each other. Workers from Social Club and Business Card Design clink coffee mugs. They are survivors. It is four thirty in the afternoon; it is the dawn of a new day.

The sales assistants are awestruck. Holly says, "Did you know Roger was so . . ."

"No," Freddy says.

Roger draws closer. The assistants give him big smiles and thumbs-up. Freddy grabs Roger's hand and pumps it enthusiastically. "Good for you, Roger. Well done!"

"I appreciate your support." His eyes jump from one to the other. "Things are going to be different from now on. Things are going to get done. We're going to find out who really took that donut."

It's spattering rain outside, but none of the outcasts go home. Droplets speckle their faces. Their makeup runs. Their hair frizzes. But their anger is not diluted. Promises are being made to set up a permanent picket line; a roster is circulating. They are not completely sure what they will demand, but one thing is for sure: *they don't deserve this.*

In the lobby, now deserted except for herself and Security, Gretel hears the elevator *ding*. She twists in her chair. The doors slide apart to reveal Eve and a man from Senior Management: Blake Seddon. All the girls swoon over Blake because he's young and good-looking and has more money than he knows what to do with. He's also currently wearing a black eye patch, which Gretel heard is because of an injury he received saving a little girl from being run over in the street right outside the Zephyr building. He smiles as he and Eve approach the reception desk, and Gretel feels her own mouth curve upward almost involuntarily.

Eve takes her seat behind the desk. Blake keeps walking up to the line of Security guards facing out the glass. "Hoo," Eve says. "What a day. What a day."

Gretel isn't sure exactly what about today has been so draining for Eve, given she has been largely absent for it, but she has learned not to ask questions. "Yeah."

"When this is all over, I'm going out and getting really, really drunk."

Gretel smiles. Another thing she's learned is that when Eve says something like this, it's not an invitation.

A Security guard comes up to the reception desk. "Umbrella," he says. "Do we have an umbrella for Mr. Seddon?"

Gretel reaches under the desk and retrieves a natty black number. The guard takes this to Blake Seddon, who flashes a smile in Gretel's direction, even as his eyes slide over to Eve. Then he walks out to meet the horde.

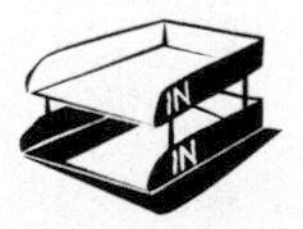

They see him coming and yell their disapproval. By the time Blake stops and raises one placatory hand, they are a seething, shouting mass. If he can feel their fury, he gives no sign. He simply waits underneath his black umbrella for them to quiet.

"My friends," he says. "My dear, dear friends."

For a second it seems the mob will actually run at him. But they are not so far gone. Slowly their outrage subsides again, and this time Blake is able to speak without interruption.

"These are difficult economic times." The rain spatters on his umbrella. "You don't need me to tell you that. It's a tough market and we face strong international competition. If we're to succeed as a business—indeed, if we're to survive—we need to make tough decisions. Zephyr Holdings isn't a charity; we either make a profit or investors take their money elsewhere. Simply put, if the company is making money, we can afford to hire people, and if it's not, we have to shed staff. It's nothing personal. These are economic decisions. You understand that. It's the duty of Senior Management to keep the company in the black, for the benefit of all stakeholders. We'd love to be able to keep every one of you on the payroll. But we are bound to do what's best for the company. If that means externally redeploying some employees, then, you'll agree, that is both logical and reasonable. Again, it's nothing personal. It's a standardized process of comparing the value of any given part of the company against the associated cost. It applies to product lines, to departments, and to employees. The simple fact of the matter, and I wish it could be otherwise but it can't, is that we must ruthlessly eliminate loss-making parts of the company to protect the profit-making parts. Now, as it happened, when we ran the numbers, you were loss-making parts. It's nothing personal. But I want you to understand that it's not arbitrary, either. We're not doing it out of vindictiveness. It's not because we enjoy it. We're simply trying to keep the company afloat. If things had been different—if you had been more productive, or were earning lower wages—then perhaps I wouldn't be talking to you right now. But, unfortunately, you weren't adding value. So while you may be feeling aggrieved, you need to realize that this is simply the logical consequence of your own cost-to-benefit ratio. You were pulling the company down. I don't want to come off as overly critical, but you do deserve this."

The crowd is silent. His words unearth their darkest suspicions. There are a few pockets of outrage and resistance, people urging others to keep the faith, but the horde's collective back has been broken. They knew it in their hearts, the unemployed; they knew it. Their eyes drop. There is more talking, even some arguing, but it is all irrelevant from this moment, when, in ones and twos, people begin to drift away.

Jones is walking to his car, his footsteps echoing in the underground parking lot, when he becomes aware that the vehicle behind him is not just looking for a space but actually stalking him. He turns around and the smoked window of a black Porsche 911 whirs down, releasing a cascade of classical music and revealing the one-eyed figure of Blake Seddon. "Are you allowed to drive with an eye patch?" Jones says. "I'd have thought that was some kind of license violation."

Blake grins. "It probably is. Hey, is that your car there? Boy. Time for an upgrade, Jones." He checks his mirror. "I have a question for you: When you left Alpha this morning, why did it take you so long to get to your desk?"

"What, you were watching me?"

"You could say I kept an eye on you."

"Ha ha," Jones says. "Eve came after me. She wanted to talk."

"Then what?"

He hesitates. "Then I went out to the front of the building to see what was going on."

"Hmm," Blake says. "I thought you'd lie about that."

"You probably have me on tape."

"I do."

"So why ask me about it?"

"They were angry today. I've seen a few mass layoffs, but none like this. We've never had to step in personally. It's practically a violation of the Alpha charter. Klausman didn't make the decision lightly."

"Maybe we should have stayed out of it. It could have been an excellent learning experience. That's what Alpha does, isn't it? Watch and learn?"

"Something I'm interested in learning," Blake says, "is what made today different."

Jones shrugs.

"You told them something."

"I wished them well for the future."

"Bullshit."

"Do you have audio?"

Blake laughs. "No, Jones, we don't have outdoor audio."

"Okay, then."

"You weren't this cocky before. Something's changed. I want to know what. I want to know if it's *you* or *her*."

"Who?"

"Please," Blake says.

"I'm serious. I don't know what you're talking about."

Blake purses his lips. Then he leans closer, hanging his arm out the window. "The thing to know about Eve, Jones, is she's bloodless. Whatever happened to that girl, she wasn't there the day they were handing out consciences. She shouldn't be here; her ideal job would be giving lethal injections in San Quentin. Maybe you've seen a glimpse of that, but you don't know the half of it. She doesn't have feelings like you and me. She knows she *should* have them. But she doesn't. I'm telling you this, Jones, so the next time you think you're being clever and sophisticated around Eve, you might instead realize that to her you are nothing more than a big, gangling puppet."

"I didn't realize you were so insightful," Jones says. "Do you want me to lie back and talk about my mother?"

Blake snorts. "Look, I don't blame you for being interested in her. She's a terrific lay. One of those girls who acts like she's never done it before. You wouldn't pick it, would you?" He sees something on Jones's face that satisfies him. The Porsche's window begins to whir upward. "Take care, Jones."

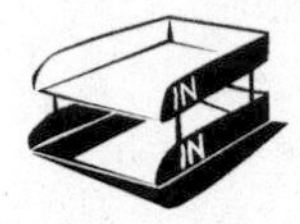

"So let me get this straight," says Penny. She and Jones are clearing plates in the kitchen of their parents' suburban home; above Penny's head, a clock in the shape of a cat swings its pendulum tail to mark each second, its eyes swiveling from side to side. "This Blake guy thinks you're working with Eve."

"I guess so."

"Aren't you Alpha people all on the same side?"

"We're meant to be. But there are politics. When Klausman retires, they'll probably kill each other for his job."

"He's retiring?"

"Um . . . no, I don't think so."

Penny fixes her hair, a few strands of which have escaped from her ponytail. "Okay. Back up. *You're* working for Alpha."

"Right."

"And that's why you can afford things like these nice suits."

"Well, actually, I still owe Eve for those."

"Fine. Then she gave them to you. Because you're her flunky."

"Protégé."

"Whatever."

"I'm not a flunky."

"What's the difference?"

"Um," Jones says.

"You know, you talk about her a lot," Penny says suspiciously. "This Eve."

"Well..."

"What?"

"I'm very attracted to her. Didn't I mention that?"

"No! I thought you hated her!"

"I do. But also... I don't know. I'm confused. When Blake said he used to be with her... I felt jealous."

"Oh boy."

"I'm not defending it. I'm just being honest. Eve and I did spend a night together."

"*You* spent a night together. *She* was passed out."

"Before that, though, I saw something. And since that time at the bar, she's... been less evil."

"Wow," Penny says. "What a recommendation."

"Also, I don't want to be crass, but she is incredibly hot."

"Ste-phen."

"*You* were obsessed with that guy at the gym, you didn't even know his *name*."

"Hmm."

"But you're right, the things Eve does, you have to hate her. She leaves you no alternative. That's the problem."

"Putting aside your weird feelings for evil women, and regardless of what's between Eve and Blake, everyone in Alpha is united in wanting to squeeze blood out of the Zephyr staff, am I right?"

"Right."

"And you want to stop this."

"You haven't seen this place. It's brutal. And remember, it's not just Zephyr. The techniques they invent end up in thousands of companies. They're probably applied to millions of workers."

"And rather than quit, you're going to work undercover, as a kind of saboteur."

"Yes."

"Even though you have no real authority in Alpha. And in Zephyr you're a desk jockey."

"Uh . . . yes."

"And if you *do* sabotage Alpha—if, say, you tell everyone in Zephyr what's going on—they'll just fire everyone, close the company, and start again. Right?"

Jones sighs. "Yes."

"And then there's the fact that one of the people you'd be sabotaging is this woman you're quote very attracted to unquote."

"Exactly."

"Well. That's some pickle."

"I thought you might have a solution."

"Sorry, Stevie. I don't see a way out of this one."

"Damn it."

"Maybe you should just quit."

"Then they'd hire somebody else to do my job. I need to find a way to *force* Alpha to make Zephyr better."

"Well," Penny says finally, "good luck with that."

From the living room: "Do you two need any help in there?"

"No, Mom," Jones calls. He scrapes off his dinner plate.

Penny says, "How much of this are we telling Mom and Dad?"

"Um," Jones says. "Tell them I got some new suits."

According to *The Omega Management System,* every corporate reorganization goes through three stages. Stage one is Planning: a giddy, euphoric state Senior Management enters as it contemplates how much stronger the company could be with a strategic realigning of its business units; also, by odd coincidence, how much more responsibility each member of Senior Management would gain. It's an exhilarating time, but only for Senior Management; for everyone else, it's often hard to see how the benefits promised by this reorganization are different from the benefits promised by the last reorganization, nine months ago.

Next comes Implementation, which is like musical chairs with exit interviews: chaos reigns and all anyone cares about is where they're going to sit. It is a mix of triumph and tragedy for the workers—triumph for the employee who has moved far away from a hated co-worker, tragedy for he whose computer screen is now visible to anyone entering the department—but a dark period of disillusionment for Senior Management, because now their pristine visions run aground on the rocks of reality. Their inverted paradigms tear open, spilling regular, right-way-up paradigms; their lateral thinking is longitudinalized and put back in the box. They dreamed of one cohesive superdepartment; now they have three ex-departments forced to sit together fighting a civil war. *Why can't people just get along?* Senior Management wonders. It is heartrending.

Last is what *The Omega Management System* officially calls Realignment but is privately referred to by Project Alpha agents as "Evacuation." This is when all the employees who are unhappy with their new role polish their résumés and start trying to find a better job somewhere else. If they're successful, they leave; otherwise they stay, along with those who were close enough to Senior Management to be tossed a political scrap. In essence, the company is quickly reduced to the incompetent and the corrupt. But it will struggle forward, laboring for as long as possible under the illusion that it is suffering from mere teething issues and not a deep, systemic sodomy of the entire corporate structure, until that becomes impossible and Senior Management does the only thing it can: announce a reorganization.

Alpha dreams of a future without reorganizations. Not that it has anything against them per se: on the contrary, it recognizes that business conditions change and businesses must react. Alpha's objection is that they don't change every fourteen months, which is the Fortune 500 average time between restructures. The typical reorganization, Alpha has found, costs three weeks of productivity, and 82 percent deliver no measurable benefit. That is, rather than reorganizing, a company could give every employee a couple of weeks' bonus vacation and still come out ahead. Or, more to the point, it could *not* give employees an extra vacation, and make more money.

The chief problem, Alpha suspects, is that reorganizations are fun. For Senior Management, that is; obviously not for anybody else. Given the choice between investigating why half a percent of revenue is being lost to inefficient inventory control and sketching out a bold new vision of the company's future structure, Senior Management invariably plumps for the latter. If Senior Management captained a ship, it would take twice as long to reach its destination and have been completely rebuilt en route. Alpha has nothing against vision, but it wishes Senior Management would keep its hands on the helm and stop dicking around with the architecture.

Until that day arrives, though, Alpha aims to find ways to make reorganizations less disruptive. It has tried a variety of techniques, up to and including the current "surprise" reorganization, which was Eve Jantiss's idea for eliminating the usual productivity loss involved in stage one. This appears to have been accomplished, for Zephyr has unequivocally skipped straight into the middle of stage two. Civil wars are brewing. Alliances are coalescing. Warlords, like Roger in Staff Services, are rising. On Wednesday at 8:50 A.M., the first sortie is launched. It comes from Infrastructure Control, in the form of a voice mail to all department heads. It regrets to announce that the costs charged to each department for floor space, cubicles, parking spaces, and phone lines must rise. The building is still the same size, Infrastructure Control points out, as is the parking lot, and there are just as many phone lines. But there are fewer employees to pick up the tab. Infrastructure Control has no option but to raise prices.

New superdepartmental managers listen to this with their faces turning purple. Cubicle partitions to cost nine hundred dollars! Five hundred per month for a computer! Six thousand a year per window! The managers seethe in their leather office chairs, which are now three times as expensive.

This is naked profiteering! The phone lines between departments (two hundred dollars per socket plus usage charges) run hot, as managers share their fury. Vows to involve Senior Management are made—although not carried out, not yet. Senior Management seems a little tetchy about the consolidation at the moment; has been ever since two hundred angry workers camped out in front of the building and started throwing things. Instead, a crisis meeting is called. In the lobby, Gretel watches in amazement as the elevators spit out manager after manager, each striding toward the meeting rooms with a firm tread and a dark brow.

Soon all the managers are there, even Roger. The only exception is Human Resources (or rather, Human Resources and Asset Protection, as the merged department is now known), whom nobody called. Even managers find HR creepy. It is led by a short man with wet lips and slickly parted hair that curls up at the ends; knowing he has your complete personnel file at his fingertips is enough to give anyone the heebie-jeebies. So it's everyone but him, and when Infrastructure Control arrives, the room's atmosphere is thick with anger.

The Infrastructure Control manager is a short, muscular man with a dark beard. He is an oddity in Zephyr Holdings: a person who started on the floor and was promoted through hard work. This makes other managers uncomfortable. The idea that you can get ahead through sheer competence, and not politicking, backstabbing, fleeing impending disasters, and clambering on board imminent successes, undermines everything they know. Infrastructure Control strides to the front of the room and folds his impressive forearms. "All right, what's the problem?"

Infrastructure Control is buffeted by a gale of invective and airborne spittle, as the managers let him know exactly what. But he doesn't step backward. His expression doesn't change. When the well of their anger runs dry, he shrugs. "Nothing I can do about it."

Whoa! A new gale howls through the room. Since Infrastructure Control has not reacted well to fury, the second assault is tinged with plaintiveness. Surely, the managers plead, he will not rob them to stuff his own coffers. Surely he can see the position they're in. He must understand they can't operate under these outrageous cost increases.

Infrastructure Control shrugs again. "All I know is what our total costs are and how many people we've got to split them across."

Goddamn it! The third gale is the most violent yet. They are not getting anywhere, the managers realize, so they just vent. The attacks get personal, referring to Infrastructure Control's blue-collar career and lack of formal education. Infrastructure Control meets every narrowed eye. Finally, this gale blows itself out, too. "If you want Zephyr to lower its total fixed expenses," he says, "why don't you take it up with Senior Management?" He walks out.

The managers *will* take it up with Senior Management. They would like nothing better, because now that Infrastructure Control suggested it, they can blame him if Senior Management gets crabby about being disturbed. The managers cluster around a speakerphone.

Senior Management is apoplectic. What in the hell does Infrastructure Control think it's doing? The whole point of the consolidation is to reduce costs, not jack them up! It's people like Infrastructure Control, Senior Management realizes, who are ruining its beautiful plans. By the time he reaches his desk on level 15, a voice mail is waiting for him. He is required on level 2. Immediately.

It is Infrastructure Control's first visit to level 2, and he is pleasantly surprised. It is all wide open spaces and deep, rich oak; there are freshly cut flowers and expensive oil paintings. There is some nice infrastructure here, all right. He is shown to the boardroom, where the entirety of Senior Management waits. They point him to a seat at one end of an enormous table and, after a suitably intimidating pause, ask him to explain himself.

"Well, it's simple enough. Our fixed costs haven't changed, only now there aren't as many departments. So I have to bill them each more."

Senior Management waits, but that appears to be it. They are stunned. Where are the PowerPoint slides? The bullet points? The references to shifting business paradigms and emerging market opportunities?

"But the departments are *smaller*," a woman says. "They're using *less* of the infrastructure. If anything, they should pay less."

"And who do I bill the empty floors to?"

"Why would you bill them to anybody?"

"Because they're still there."

Senior Management doesn't like his tone. It doesn't like his implications, either. Glances are exchanged. Senior Management would prefer an alternative explanation: that Infrastructure Control is a greedy little price gouger.

"What, then," Senior Management says, giving him one last chance, "can we do to keep departmental expenses the same as before?"

"Well, you could fill the floors. Hire more employees."

There is a collective intake of breath. *Hire more employees!* This is barefaced heresy. Senior Management looks at one another, stunned. Infrastructure Control is dismissed from the boardroom.

For long moments, the room is silent except for the quiet ticking of the bar fridge. Then a woman leans forward. "This idea of billing departments for fixed resources . . . it's just an accounting trick, isn't it? The infrastructure is already there. It's not going anywhere if we stop billing departments for it. So we could fix this problem in a second by simply eliminating the department of Infrastructure Control."

Slow smiles emerge around the board table. Finally, a solution! There is an appalled protest from a man whose main accomplishment in the consolidation was to gain responsibility for the department of Infrastructure Control, but he is quickly silenced. The announcement goes out; Human Resources is notified; by the time Infrastructure Control gets back to his desk, two Security guards are waiting for him.

Sydney, diminutive ex-manager of Training Sales, stands in an elevator, its doors open to the lobby, running her eyes up and down the panel of floor numbers. She has a dilemma: she doesn't know which button to press.

There's no way she's going to level 11. Working for Roger, until this week her subordinate, would be too humiliating to bear. Maybe some people would take a knife in the back and keep smiling; not Sydney. Since her ousting, she has gone from department to department, calling on old friends. Or people she thought were friends; apparently they were only acting sympathetic because she was a manager. That was a nasty surprise—but then, everyone has always been against Sydney; that's what she's been saying.

So here's her problem: she's out of alternatives. Of all the numbers on this button panel (and there aren't many), the only ones she hasn't tried are the upper echelon: Human Resources and Senior Management.

The idea is seductive. Sydney doesn't belong in the lower departments; she should be up top. Where else is there for a person with her sweeping, hostile vision, her passionate dislike of people, her willingness to make other people make sacrifices? Senior Management, Senior Management, Senior Management!

Only you don't just walk into a Senior Management position. You grease your path over a dozen well-catered dinner parties and games of golf. Sydney hasn't done that. And even in this desperate situation, she couldn't bear to start. She is too good for that.

A girl with large freckles arrives. "Going up?" she says brightly. Sydney stares at her until she retreats.

Senior Management, alas, is out. And that only leaves one number: 3. Human Resources.

Sydney feels an affinity with Human Resources. She likes the name, with its not-so-hidden implication that employees are an exploitable resource, like stock or real estate.

And not a particularly valuable one, despite that old chestnut about employees being the company's most important asset. Sydney knows the truth: give the company cash resources, give it strategic partnerships, give it inventory; give it anything but prickly, unreliable, idiosyncratic humans. People are the worst: you can't stack them, or (easily) relocate them, and you can't even just leave them alone to accumulate value. That's why the company requires HR: a department to transform humans into resources.

Sydney stretches onto her toes to push 3. The doors close. As the elevator rises, she hums a little tune to herself. She is nervous, but optimistic. She thinks she will fit right in.

Freddy enters the level-11 cubicle farm and stops at the coat stand. The jacket that took his hook on Monday is two hooks down today. Freddy smiles. He hangs his jacket in its rightful place and heads off to his own cubicle with a light heart and an energetic tread.

He's getting to know the other Staff Services workers. The people from Business Card Design are tall, pale, and elfin. Ex–Relocation Services employees are small, stocky, and humorless; they also have the best square-footage-to-employee ratio. Anyone large, boisterous, and fit-looking is from Gymnasium Management. Social Club employees have bright, darting eyes and strain toward you, seeking conversation. Then there is Training Sales. They, Freddy decides, are the rogues of the bunch. The sharply dressed assassins. Everyone is a little wary of Training Sales. So that's the all-new Staff Services department: a loose conglomeration of elves, giants, peacocks, gnomes, and organized criminals.

Freddy reaches his cubicle and sits. What the department doesn't include, he abruptly realizes, is Training *Delivery.* He goes cold. Was Training Delivery lost in the consolidation? And if so, what is Training Sales meant to sell?

Possibly there is a reasonable answer. Possibly Senior Management decided to leverage Training Sales' skills into a higher-value sector, one that doesn't involve training. But Freddy has worked at Zephyr for a long time. He's pretty confident it's a screwup.

Holly arrives at her desk to find a voice mail from Roger, summoning her to his (new) office at her earliest convenience. The voice-mail woman says, "Received . . . today! . . . at . . . five . . . fifty! . . . four," so clearly Roger's earliest convenience occurs long before hers. She finds the idea that Roger has been at work for almost three hours a little creepy. On the one hand, she can't imagine how Roger could be any worse a boss than Sydney. On the other, she fears he might demonstrate.

Halfway to Roger's office, she finds herself staring at a

TV monitor. It's bolted to the ceiling, but so large that it hangs down over the cubicle aisle, forcing taller employees to duck as they pass. Its screen is blank. Next to it is a steel anti-vandalism cage with a large bulb inside. Neither the light nor the screen serve any apparent purpose. A few employees stand below, looking up nervously, but Holly just squeezes past. She doesn't waste her time wondering about inexplicable things in Zephyr Holdings anymore.

There's a PA at a desk just outside Roger's door, just like Sydney had Megan on level 14. Roger's PA is a slim young man with rakish glasses and a tie with big yellow happy faces that Holly finds a little too confronting at nine in the morning. "Hi. I'm here to see Roger."

"You're Holly Vale?"

"Yes."

"He's expecting you, I'll take you right in."

The PA trots to Roger's door, opens it, and beckons for Holly to enter. But Holly just stands there, shocked. If you have an office, you close the door and make people knock on it before they come in; isn't that the whole point? When managers say they have an open-door policy, that means you can ask to see them without an appointment, it doesn't mean the door is actually *open.* It doesn't mean you don't *knock.*

She realizes that the PA is looking at her and jolts into motion. She can deal with a job that performs no identifiable function and a work environment prone to producing mystery TV screens; she supposes she can get used to a manager with a literal open door, too.

Roger's office is drenched with morning sunshine; outside the window it's a solid slab of blue. Roger sits at his broad, gleaming desk with his hands folded in front of him. "Hello, Holly. Have a seat."

The office is already well furnished. She sinks into a wingback chair and carefully places her arms on the rests. Then there's a pause, during which Roger continues to smile. Holly's own smile begins to feel fractured. She shifts in the chair and smooths down her skirt.

Roger says, "I have some good news."

"Oh!" Holly says, mostly out of relief at the commencement of dialogue.

"I've been doing some thinking about how to get this department up and running. I want Staff Services to be the most efficient, productive, and profitable department in Zephyr." He pauses. Holly nods encouragingly. "And I've decided that means redefining many job roles. In fact... everyone's role."

Silence. This time Holly can't wait it out. "I just saw Freddy, and he said there's no one here from Training Delivery. Are they in another department, or—"

"Gone. Didn't make it through the consolidation."

"Oh." She waits, but Roger seems disinclined to fill in the obvious blank. "So... what are we meant to do?"

"That's a good question. But not one that you, Holly, need consider. Like I said, I'm redefining job roles. Yours is now the gym. Someone needs to get that place in order. That's you."

Holly's fingers dig into the armrests. She feels as if she has just staggered off the treadmill. The endorphins! The endorphins!

"Happy?"

"Oh, *Roger!*" For an insane moment, Holly is on the

verge of throwing herself across the desk and hugging him. "Thank you! Thank you *so much.* I'll do a great job, I promise. The gym has always been good, but there are things we could do, simple things, to expand its reach and get more people using it, like classes for—"

"Great," Roger says. "That sounds great." He smiles. There's another pause.

"Thank you so much," Holly says again.

"I thought this would suit you."

"I really appreciate it."

"Because if it doesn't work out, it's easy enough to reassign you."

"It'll work out. I promise. *Definitely.*"

"Good. Good." Roger leans forward, resting his elbows on the desk. "While we're chatting... I want to ask you something."

Holly feels it coming before he even opens his mouth.

"Holly," he says, "who took my donut?"

Jones threads his way through the crowded cubicle farm of Staff Services, chewing his lip. It has been an unsettling morning for Jones. First, Eve wasn't at this morning's Alpha meeting. At first he thought she was late, then very late, then Klausman sat down and said, "Eve's off with a virus today, apparently," and Mona went *awww* and Blake blew air through his nose as if this was somehow amusing. Jones thought, *She'd better get a doctor's certificate,* but the idea of an Eve-less day was surprisingly shocking, disappointing, and that was bad: Jones shouldn't be feeling things like that about a person he wants to professionally destroy. Eve is like gambling, he realized: he knows that she's addictive, that she's bad for him, and that unless he gives her up there are going to be consequences, but still, he wants more. Maybe Jones should call someone. Maybe there's a support group he can join: Evaholics Anonymous. Maybe all this will end up with Jones in a bar somewhere with Blake Seddon, knocking glasses of beer together as they reminisce in alternately fond and bitter tones about Eve Jantiss, the bitch who screwed and scarred them both and ruined all their plans.

He snapped out of this fantasy to realize he was being assigned a new job: to restore the company network. He said, "Really? It seems people are actually happier without the network. They're moving around, talking... my feeling is this may actually be good for the company."

"Of course the *staff* like it," Blake said scornfully. "It means they can't do as much work. No doubt the *staff* think it's terrific. We're not here to entertain them, though, Jones."

"I'm not suggesting otherwise," Jones said, in the cool, measured tones of a man resisting the urge to clock Blake with his coffee mug. "I'm just wondering if this might not *increase* productivity. Have you heard of work-life balance? It's the crazy idea that employees work better when they're happy and motivated."

Blake leaned back and folded his arms, regarding Jones as if he had just heard something very stupid. From the head of the table, Klausman said, "Ah, Jones, we're not big fans of that whole work-life balance thing. It's not that it's not a great concept. It is. In theory."

"Like communism," Blake said, eliciting chuckles. There will be no drunken reminiscences, Jones decided.

"The problem is it's a myth. We've run the numbers; it doesn't check out. The amount you gain from reduced absenteeism and error rates is swamped by what you lose to reduced working hours and off-task behavior. Simply put, happy employees aren't more productive. They're less."

"In most situations," Mona interjected. "Remember?"

Klausman nodded. "Ah, yes. When it's expensive to replace an employee, it can be worth spending money to keep them happy. But that's the exception."

"So what you're saying," Jones said, "is there's no point spending money on employee welfare unless they're in Senior Management."

Blake said, "By Jove, he's got it."

"What I'm saying," Klausman said, "is that when it comes to work-life balance, we're fighting for the *work* side of that equation. *Capisce?*"

"Yes," Jones said.

"Good boy. This is one of those occasions where I don't want to wait for Zephyr to fix itself. Most of Senior Management doesn't even have a computer; it'll be months before they figure out something's wrong. No, the company needs a network, Jones, and you are going to give it one."

Jones opened his mouth to say, *How?,* but that wasn't very dynamic or Alpha-like. So instead he said, "All right," and everyone looked happier.

The third unsettling thing happened as the meeting was

wrapping up. Blake announced, "And keep an eye on Staff Services. The new manager there, Roger Jefferson, has a lot of fresh new ideas." This was apropos of something, but Jones had been packing up his briefcase and thinking about the network, so he missed what, exactly. But when he looked up, Blake was watching him with a small, patronizing smile, and Jones realized that for reasons he wasn't yet aware of, today was going to suck.

He finds out why when he reaches the cubicle. Freddy and Elizabeth are in an animated discussion, sitting with their knees almost touching in the cramped quarters. Freddy is shaking his head emphatically. "No, no, no. Jones! Come here, I need your support."

"Freddy, I understand what you're saying," Elizabeth says. "It's just there's nothing we can do about it. There are no other options."

"What's going on?"

Freddy waves a printed memo. "Look at this! Roger calls it an 'Accountability Program.' From now on, we have to pay for everything. Our desks, our computers—he's *billing* us for them. He's made us personally responsible for departmental expenses!"

"There's going to be a run on office chairs," Elizabeth muses. "We should stock up. Maybe we could sell them to other employees at a markup."

"When Staff Services work becomes available, we have to tender for it. The lowest tender gets the job. And we pay for all expenses ourselves! He's turned us into subcontractors!"

"Oh," Jones says. "That sounds bad."

Freddy grinds his forehead with the heel of his hand.

"All I ever wanted was a little job somewhere with no accountability. Somewhere I could do what they asked me, more or less, and not have to wonder if every day is going to be my last. Is that too much to ask? Is it?"

"What's going on?" Holly says, appearing beside Jones.

"Holly! Back me up here. Is this Accountability Program the worst idea you've ever heard or what?"

"Um... no, I think it's all right."

Freddy gapes. "All right? *All right?*"

"Why shouldn't we be responsible for our own expenses? You know Lianne? She always photocopies like a dozen pages before she gets it right. And that guy in Procurement, who used to do nothing but e-mail jokes all day. Why should I subsidize people like that?"

"*Subsidize?* When did you start talking like a manager?"

Holly shifts from one foot to the other.

Freddy says, "Oh, no."

"I'm running the gym now." She licks her lips. "I don't know if I'll still sit here or not, but... I'm running the gym."

Freddy sags in his chair. "This is a disaster."

"Boy," Holly says, nettled. "Thanks for the congratulations. Remind me to get excited when you tell me *your* new roles."

"Nobody's getting new roles," Elizabeth says dully. "Nobody but you."

"Oh," Holly says.

"Oh," Freddy says. "Oh yeah, gee, I wonder why Roger's handing out special favors to Holly. Let me think. Hmm."

Holly's eyes widen. "Yeah? Why?"

"It wouldn't be because you told him about a certain *donut,* would it?"

Elizabeth's eyes leap to Holly. Holly's cheeks flush.

"Oh, God," Elizabeth says.

"He was going to find out anyway," Holly says, her voice rising. "Look, I'm sorry, Elizabeth, but he was going to find out. He's obsessed."

Suddenly a Klaxon tears through the room. The bulb in the ceiling cage bursts into life, throwing swirling sheets of orange light over the cubicles. In an instant level 11 resembles the scene of major roadworks. Jones jumps. "What the hell?"

Everybody peers over the cubicle walls. In between stabbing flashes from the orange light, they see the TV screen:

TENDERS INVITED

JOB #0000001

TASK

Reallocation and auction of cubicle space

(level 11)

DETAILS AVAILABLE FROM STAFF SERVICES PA

"It's work." Freddy's voice trembles. *"Work."*

Cautiously, employees drift out of their cubicles to stare at the monitor. Then, one by one, glancing at each other warily, they head for Roger's PA.

"Look at them!" Freddy stares in disgust. "Everyone ready to beat each other out for a pay packet. You know what, I'm not going to tender. What happened to sticking together? What happened to teamwork?" He gives Holly a dirty look.

"Hey," Holly says. "You know what Roger told me? He

said there's no such thing as teamwork. It's a con. The company doesn't promote teams. If you want to get ahead, you have to screw everybody else and look after yourself. Co-workers are competitors. Roger told me the truth: there's no *I* in team, but there's no *U*, either!" There is silence. Holly's chest rises and falls. Her cheeks flush. "But... I really am sorry, Elizabeth."

"Maybe now he knows, he'll forget about it." She looks away.

"I bet he does," Holly says. "Honestly, you know, that wouldn't surprise me."

Freddy stares at her.

"I'm sure everything will be okay," Holly says. Her voice is so plaintive that Jones has to look away.

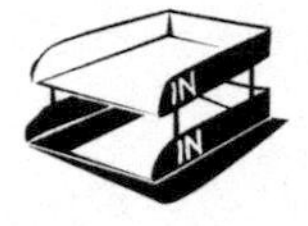

In the lobby, Gretel has a migraine from the flashing switchboard lights. She shouldn't even be here: this morning she called in sick, but a woman in Human Resources and Asset Protection sucked air through her teeth and said, "Oh, dear..."

"What?" said Gretel, but suddenly she was listening to a traffic report on the state of I-5. She closed her eyes, sitting on the edge of her bed in her pajamas. Her boyfriend slumbered beside her, one hand on her thigh. Then the voice came back. "Gretel, I'm going to transfer you. Okay?"

"I—" Gretel said, but then she was back to the radio station. She waited.

"Gretel?" A man's voice, loud and painfully cheerful. "Jim Davidson. What's this about you being under the weather?"

Jim was HR's personnel manager. "Yes, sorry, Jim. I'm feeling terrible."

"I'm sorry to hear that," he said, but his tone didn't change at all: he made it sound as if this was a joke they were sharing. "Unfortunately, that puts us in a bit of a pickle."

Gretel squeezed the phone. "I'm sure Eve won't mind covering me for one day." This was a lie: she was sure Eve *would* mind. However, it would not *kill* Eve, and after the horrors of Monday, when Gretel was under siege and Eve was nowhere to be seen, it might even be what Eve *deserves.*

"Yes, I'm sure—if Eve hadn't called in sick ten minutes ago."

Now Gretel is stabbing buttons on the switchboard while her head pounds and dampness collects under her arms. Exactly why Human Resources is unable to hire a temp is unclear to her, as is why this is *her* problem. Jim did explain; he spoke at length in that cheery, teeth-cracking voice about the upheaval following the consolidation and how difficult it would be to deal with a new crisis especially since all the people who might have been able to step into her role for the day had just been sacked. After two minutes of this, Gretel agreed to come in so he would stop talking.

She should have held out. As it was yesterday, and the day

before that, the switchboard is completely swamped, because half the company has just changed jobs and nobody knows anyone's new number. Human Resources and Asset Protection has promised to issue a new directory, but not for two to three weeks—which, Gretel knows, means it'll be a month and a half, contain numerous key errors, and there won't be enough copies. On top of this, there is no IT department to update the phones, so everyone's caller ID is wrong. You need to dial an additional number to reach employees outside your own department, so Gretel can't connect anybody until she knows where they're calling from. The employees don't understand this, so this morning Gretel has had two hundred conversations like this:

"Good morning, reception."

"Hi, can you give me Kevin Dawson's new number? He was in Corporate Marketing... I'm not sure what that's called now."

"Can I have your name and department, please?"

"Um... Kevin Dawson? In Corporate Marketing?"

"No, not the name of the person you're trying to reach. Your name."

"Oh! It's Geoff Silvio."

"In... ?"

"Well, I guess it's called Treasury now."

"Just a moment, Geoff."

During all this, the switchboard flashes a solid bank of yellow lights at her, informing her that there are twelve more identical conversations lined up and ready to go. At eleven o'clock she is so desperate for the bathroom that she literally runs across the lobby floor, and when she emerges, a man from Senior Management is walking past the reception desk, looking at all the flashing lights, and he frowns at her.

Gretel realizes around twelve thirty that once again she has no hope of lunch: the inflow of calls isn't slackening at all. She enters a numb, robotic state where her mouth and fingers move first and her brain catches up a second later. Over and over, she punches TRANSFER to end one call and activate the next. "Good afternoon, reception."

"It's me."

"Yes, hello," she snaps. "I need to know who you are and where you're calling from before I can connect you."

There's a surprised pause. "Gretel, it's Sam."

Sam is her boyfriend. Her mouth drops open. She covers her face with her hands and starts to cry.

Is Roger a bad person? It's a difficult question. Right now it is occupying center stage in Elizabeth's mind. He is petty, yes. He's scheming. He's arrogant *and* insecure, a terrible combination. He has never shown her any affection bar the physical, and that was brief and impersonal. Sometimes when she looks at him, she wants to tear out his neat brown hair and stuff it in his mouth.

She's heard of women craving odd foods while pregnant, repulsive combinations like ice cream and gherkins. Well, Elizabeth craves Roger. She aches for him to wrap her in his arms. Just thinking about it brings a whimper to her lips.

Elizabeth has been in love more times than she can count, but until now she never felt desire as a physical force. Right now, if Roger asked, Elizabeth would strip naked and make love to him on the orange-and-black carpet.

Sitting at her desk with her hands clenched into fists, she tries to talk her body around. There are many logical reasons why she should not desire Roger, and she silently argues each one of them. But none of them stick; all are washed away by the rich, red hormonal tide within her. The rational part of her, the part that sold training packages, bobs helplessly adrift on an emotional sea. *What do you know about anything?* the ocean says. *Look at your job. Look at your priorities. Thanks for the input, but I'll take it from here.*

She has to admit that her body makes a good point. But *Roger*! Why, why, why Roger? Does her body see hidden depths to him? She can't. She pleads with it to change her mind.

Getting the network back turns out to be easier than Jones expects. He starts by thinking about which department should logically control Information Technology, and decides it's his: Staff Services. So he knocks on Roger's door and pitches the idea. Roger listens in silence, then turns his chair to face the window for a while. Jones doesn't know whether Roger is thinking deeply or simply striking a pose, but he doesn't mind waiting. After a minute, Roger swivels back. "You're asking for a significant capital investment on the part of this department."

"I guess."

"You know I'm trying to make individual employees *more* accountable for expenses. This runs contrary to that paradigm." He presses his fingers together. "I'd need to basically loan you the money."

Jones blinks. "How would I pay that back? What, you mean I personally would bill other departments for network usage?"

Roger smiles. "Let's not get carried away. I'm externalizing expenses, not revenue."

"Then—"

"What I am prepared to do is pay you a royalty on network billings, up to a certain ceiling."

"So... I'm responsible for all the costs, but only get a percentage of the revenue?"

"We can negotiate the exact numbers," Roger says. "But frankly, if you don't like it, I have a department full of staff who would kill for a job like this."

"Hey," Jones says, bristling. "Setting up the network is *my* idea."

"That's why I'm giving you first bite at it."

Jones opens his mouth to argue, then realizes he's not here to earn a salary from Roger. He's here because Alpha wants a network. "Okay, okay."

"You'll need help. A big job like this. You should subcontract to other Staff Services employees."

"I will." Jones has no intention of fooling around with wires and computers.

"Don't just give the work to your friends," Roger warns.

"You'll get better value by making them bid for it. Just a word of advice."

"Thanks, Roger," Jones says.

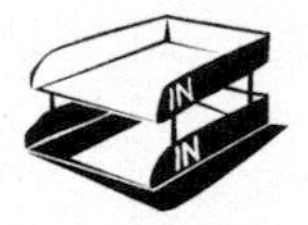

He gives Freddy the task of scouring Staff Services for anyone who knows anything about computers, and settles down at his desk to phone IT consultancy houses. After each call, he puts a line through their name if they tried to sell him something he didn't ask for or used the word "solutions" more than three times. An hour later he finds a guy called Alex Domini who, he suspects, heads a one-man shop, and makes an appointment to see him the next day.

His voice-mail light is blinking, so he dials in to find a message from Sydney. "Ah, Jones? Can you—*yes, I will get to you in one minute. Just—just stay there, all right?* Jones, come down to reception, there's a package for you. *Now look—*" The phone clicks.

Jones puts down the phone. Surely Sydney isn't working the phones in reception? But one elevator ride later, he discovers she is: almost lost behind the great orange desk, she is fending off half a dozen waiting employees and snarling into the headset. This is such a sight that Jones stops to gape at it.

"Gretel left," says a voice. He turns to see Klausman, standing there with a mop in one hand. Jones blinks. He has to give it to Klausman: in that janitor disguise, he is practically invisible. It's a psychological thing: you see the gray overalls in your peripheral vision and don't bother looking any closer. "She just walked out. Human Resources had to send down someone to fill in."

"Gretel *quit?* "

Klausman shrugs. "She didn't say. Not impressed, though, Jones. Not impressed. We're trying to run an efficient operation here. We don't have room for unreliable employees. It throws the whole system off."

Jones glances back at Sydney. It doesn't look as if he'll be getting near that reception desk in a hurry. "I guess that's what happens when there's no slack in the system."

Klausman considers. "Maybe so. Hmm. That would be worth measuring. It would certainly be ironic if after all this time it turned out that hyperefficiency was counterproductive."

"Indeed," Jones says.

Klausman watches Sydney struggle with the phones. "Breaks my heart to see the system fail like this. It actually hurts. You know the goal of any company, Jones? To externalize. An efficient company should be like a healthy human body: extracting nutrients from the environment and excreting waste into it. Sources of income are our nutrients, and sources of costs are our wastes."

"So . . ." Jones says, "Zephyr eats money and shits costs?"

Klausman laughs. "You're probably too young to remember, Jones, but there was a time when a man filled your gas tank for you. A boy carried your groceries to your car. There was a time when you hardly ever stood in line, not outside of a government office. But labor is a source of cost, so companies externalized it. They, as you say, shat it out. And those costs landed exactly where they belonged: on their customers."

"And on their remaining staff."

"Quite so. Quite so. Hence: 'Doing more with less.' You know, Jones, I wish I had more employees like you. Actually, I wish I had fewer employees *not* like you. You know what I mean. You're an exception: graduates are generally idiots. Enthusiastic idiots, yes, but that's no compensation. In fact, if anything, that exacerbates the problem." He scratches his nose. "I'm thinking of cutting the graduate program. People say it brings in new ideas, but they're mainly *stupid* ideas. A man's brain is no good to a company until he's at least forty, in my opinion. Or a woman's. Can't be sexist, now. Of course, the problem then is when they do have good ideas, they can't be bothered to do anything about them." Klausman falls silent, musing. "Anyway, my point is that you have a future here, Jones. I can see you running this place one day. Not soon." He winks. "But one day."

"Jones? *Jones?*" Sydney calls.

Klausman already has his back turned and is mopping the floor. Jones jolts into motion. "Hi."

"I had to sign for this." Sydney pushes a courier's bag across the counter, glaring at him—because of the package, her new duties, or just a general attitude, Jones can't tell.

"Sorry. Thanks." He tears open the bag. Inside is a shrink-wrapped box that says NOKIA 6225 and a plastic-encased SIM card. There's no note.

"Hey, new cell phone," says a man beside him. "Where'd you get that from?" Jones has no idea. The man looks at Sydney with a bemused expression. "Got one for me, too?"

"What?" Sydney snaps, having not followed this. Jones takes the opportunity to carry his package over to the visitors area and sit down. When he has successfully unpacked everything and put it together, he is rewarded with a little animation, a friendly tune, and: YOU HAVE 1 NEW TEXT MESSAGE.

A few button presses later, he has that, too. It says: IM SICK + BORED CALL ME

As he heads back to the elevator, Klausman and his mop veer in his direction. Jones's heart races. He is suddenly sure that Klausman is going to grill him about the phone, which, for some reason, he shouldn't have. His fingers tighten on the package. His brain vomits up a mass of inexplicable advice, like: *Don't tell him it's from Eve.* But then the elevator doors open on a packed elevator of loud, laughing suits, and as they walk by, Klausman's eyes remain glued to the floor. Jones steps into the empty car. When the doors slide closed, he remembers to breathe. He laughs shakily at his own reaction. He is clearly becoming either paranoid or insightful. He wishes he knew which.

"Hello?"

"It's me."

"Ah! Jo . . . one second . . . *choo!* Oh, God. Sorry. It's good to hear your voice."

"You sound like you're dead."

"Not yet. Just... very... phlegmy."

"Want me to come over?" He waits. He can't believe he just said this.

"Sorry, what?" There is a rustling noise. "Oh, God, that was my last tissue."

"I'll come visit you," Jones says. "With tissues."

"Oh... Jones. That's really sweet, but... I'm not exactly looking my best."

"I don't mind."

"My eyes are puffy, my skin is greasy, my nose is red—not to mention dribbling—"

"Well, that's why you need tissues."

A pause. "You seriously want to come over?"

"Yeah."

"Even though I look like someone just dug me up."

"Sure."

She starts to laugh, which turns into a coughing fit. "Jones, you are something else."

"Come on, give me your address."

"Well," she says, "so long as you know what you're in for."

He is not hugely surprised when Eve's address turns out to be a sleek, modern building fronting the bay, nor that her apartment is at the very top and has its own elevator. He presses the intercom button while a light breeze tugs at his shirt, and takes the opportunity to think about what he's doing.

What he needs are some ground rules. Yes, he is visiting Eve. And yes, he is attracted to her. That's fine, so long as he handles it properly. There will be no flirting. No touching. He will not discuss incidents from his past, particularly of the romantic variety. He will keep the conversation on task; that is, he will get Eve to talk about Alpha so that he can learn how to break it.

"Hello?" the intercom croaks.

"It's me."

The door in front of him goes *clack*. He pushes it open and rides the elevator to floor P, which Jones guesses stands for penthouse. It opens onto a six-foot corridor with a single door at the end, and as he approaches, this goes *clack*, too. He turns the handle and steps into Eve's apartment.

He is expecting a huge, light-filled room dotted with ultramodern furniture in coordinated colors. He is half right: it is enormous. And the sun does bounce off the bay beyond the floor-to-ceiling windows. But it is also practically empty. The only furniture is a single, lonely-looking table in the middle of the carpet and a few wooden chairs. There's a giant TV, but it's on the floor. Facing it is not a sofa but a spongy-looking mat.

He takes a guess and heads up a spiral staircase, past a gigantic stylized painting of the Seattle skyline—which, if Jones has his geography right, includes this building. Then the reflection of something colorful catches his eye, and he turns around to see a walk-in closet filled with clothes and shoes.

It is easily the size of Jones's bedroom. On each side are racks jammed with pants, skirts, dresses, and jackets. At least half still have tags attached, sporting names like Balenciaga,

Chloë, Prada, and Rodriguez—which mean very little to Jones, other than expensive. The far end of the closet is a solid wall of boxes, and as Jones draws closer he sees each one has stuck on it a Polaroid photo of a pair of shoes. He is dumbstruck. There are enough clothes in here for Eve to wear a completely different outfit each day for about two years.

"Jones?"

He leaves the closet and finds the bedroom next door. Inside, Eve is propped up on a king-size bed, looking pale and bleary in a thin nightdress. The curtains are closed and the lamps on—which, as this room actually has furniture, rest on bedside tables. A full-length mirror stands on the far side of the room, beside one of two large wooden chests of drawers. There are more cupboards. One corner of the carpet contains a mound of balled-up tissues, suggesting that Eve recently staggered out of bed and swept them all there.

"Sorry," she croaks. "Is this too gross?"

"In my job, I see a lot worse." He holds out the tissues—eight boxes' worth, because Eve was very specific about the brand, which turns out to be sold only in tiny, beautifully packaged boxes. He's a little relieved to see that Eve is genuinely ill, because it will make it easier to stick to his ground rules, and a little disappointed, for the same reason.

"I love you so much for coming." Her smile is unusually loose, almost goofy.

"Are you high?"

"I did take a number of anti-flu tablets, once I knew you were coming over."

"Was it a large number?"

"I wanted to perk up for you." The smile wobbles across

her face again. Her pupils are huge; at first he'd thought it was the low light. She slides down the pillows and clasps her hands above her head in a position Jones finds confrontational. "Come, sit with me."

"Uh... no, I'm okay."

"You can't just stand there."

"How much are all those clothes worth?" he says.

"I don't know. I never added it up."

"It must be..." He starts to do sums in his head, then realizes the figure is going to be ludicrous. "How are you going to wear all that?"

"It's not just the wearing. It's the acquiring, and the having. Come on, sit."

He stays on his feet. "Don't take this the wrong way, but have you considered therapy about this?"

"I do see a therapist. But I'm not allowed to tell you what we talk about."

"Oh. Okay. Wait, you're not allowed to tell *me* specifically?"

"Yeah."

"Why not?"

"I can't tell you."

Jones exhales.

"He said you won't understand."

"I'm trying to think why you're discussing me with your therapist."

"Because you're important to me, Jones." She blows her nose. "God, thank you so much for these tissues."

He eyes her. "If you don't want to tell me, that's—"

"He says you're a mother figure to me."

Jones sits on the bed.

"I know what you're thinking," Eve says. "*Mother* figure? But it's nothing to do with sex. It's about roles." She leaves a pause, in case Jones wants to say something. "My dad's a loser, not like you at all. Mom was the strict one."

"You think I'm strict?"

"Dr. Franks—that's my therapist—says you fill a need for moral guidance that's been missing since I left home."

"This is very disturbing."

"It's really a compliment. It speaks to how much I look up to you."

"I thought you didn't even like your mom."

"I don't."

"I'm confused."

"Maybe you should see Dr. Franks," Eve says. "He's very good."

Jones stands up again. "Did you give me that phone because you're sick and you wanted your mom to come take care of you?"

Eve laughs, then sneezes, then laughs again. "That's so funny. I have to tell that to Dr. Franks. Jones—hey, come on, sit. Sit down." She waits until he complies. Then her lips curve. "Kiss me."

"What?"

"Are you worried about the virus? Don't be a sissy."

"Eve, I'm not going to kiss you."

"Why not?"

"Because... it would be a bad idea."

"I want you to know I don't think of you as my mom."

"Fine. I accept that. But no."

"It's because I'm sick and ugly, isn't it." This isn't a question. Her face pinches.

"Eve, you're very attractive. Even with a bit of tissue stuck to your nose."

She rubs her nose and inspects her finger. "That's embarrassing."

"You're not ugly," Jones says firmly. "Trust me."

"How can I trust you? You're the new wiz kid at Alpha. That was *me,* a few years ago." She puts a hand on her chest. "That was me. And *you* won't even *kiss* me. How do I know you won't hurt me?"

Jones blinks. "I won't hurt you." As this comes out, he realizes he really means it. Exactly how this dovetails with his aim of sabotaging Alpha is not clear.

"Prove it."

"No."

She sneezes.

"Anyway," Jones says, paddling for calmer conversational waters, "illness is a major cause of corporate productivity loss. As an agent for Alpha, you should know better."

She wipes her nose. "You know with peacocks, only the males have colorful tails? The gene that causes that also lowers their immune system. That's why females find it sexy, not just because the colors are pretty, but because they're proof the male is strong enough to fight off infection even with a lowered immune system."

"Why does everyone around here use animal analogies?"

She grins. "Because it's a zoo. A big, corporate zoo."

"Well, I don't have feathers coming out of my butt. And I'm not going to kiss you just because you have a long list of practical reasons for it."

"I'm a practical girl." She nods. "A practical, practical girl."

"I noticed."

"But that doesn't mean I have no feelings, Jones. I also have a nonpractical reason."

"You do?"

"I do. Do you want to hear it?"

"I'm not sure."

"Yes or no?"

Jones hesitates. The correct answer here is clearly no. It is also probably to stand up and walk out of the apartment. But what he says is: "Yes."

She smiles. "Okay. I..." She looks down and laughs. "Now I'm embarrassed."

"Forget it," he says, already regretting his decision.

She puts her hand on his. "I want to be honest with you. But... this is new territory for me." She pushes herself up in the bed and adjusts the pillows behind her. When she arches her back, Jones's eyes drift helplessly down to where her breasts push out her nightgown. He tears his gaze away, but not before he realizes he is in serious, serious trouble.

"So," he says, "you slept with Blake."

Eve freezes. "What?"

In one sense, this is a terrific success: it plugs a lot of Jones's more alarming feelings and gets him back on task. But he can't believe he just used a line from *Days of Our Lives.* This is the noxious nature of Blake, Jones realizes: he brings you down to his level.

"You think I slept with Blake?"

"Did you?"

She looks stupefied. "God, I *wish.*"

Jones says, "I have to go now."

"Jones! No, I mean, years ago, I had a thing for him, it didn't work out. I don't want to sleep with him now. I couldn't; it'd be too competitive. We're Alpha's top two after Klausman. You can't date someone who's the same level as you. You have to go up or down."

"I'm pretty sure it's the other way around."

She frowns. "But then to get promoted, one of you has to climb over the other. No, no, it's much neater if you understand who's boss from the beginning."

This makes a kind of sense. Jones wonders if he is losing his grip on reality. Then he realizes he is being seduced by a woman with a throat infection on a bed dotted with used tissues, so the answer is probably yes.

"A while ago, Zephyr made everyone sign this thing called a Love Contract. It indemnified the company against issues arising out of people screwing their boss, or their secretary. I should say, issues that arose when they stopped screwing their secretary. But it wasn't enough. We had a sexual harassment complaint from an employee who wasn't harassed. She said she was discriminated against because her co-workers, who were dating, gave each other preferential treatment." Eve rolls her eyes. "I mean, that was probably true, but it's not like the company banned *her* from dating co-workers. If you ask me, the real culprit was her skin condition. But anyway, now nobody in Zephyr is allowed to date anybody else." She bites her lip. "Alpha, of course, is outside those rules."

"I'm pretty sure it's illegal for a company to say who its staff can and can't form relationships with."

"That's true. But Zephyr's policy doesn't ban relationships, it bans sexual harassment. And harassment is defined as making an unsolicited approach. You see, you can't ask anyone out unless they ask you to. Which they can't, because that would be sexual harassment." She smiles. "Alpha didn't invent this. Zephyr came up with it all by itself. That's the magic of Alpha, right there."

Jones doesn't say anything. This helps; it reminds him why he needs to sabotage Alpha. It also explains why so many Zephyr employees have chewed fingernails.

"Anyway," Eve says, "what else did Blake say?"

"He wasn't very complimentary about you."

"Yeah, that's a given. Ah, forget it. I don't care about Blake. I don't want to talk about him. I want to talk about you."

"It's okay, you don't—"

Eve leans forward and takes his hands. Jones's sentence terminates with a sound like *uck.* "Jones," she says. In the lamplight her eyes look enormous: huge and dark and unreadable. "I knew you were smart right from the beginning. The way you found out about Alpha so fast... that impressed me. Then we went for a ride in my car and I thought you were an idiot. You had to be, because whenever people raise ethics, it's a cover. They're worried what other people will think, or whether it's legal, or else they're just too scared to make a decision. But you're something else. And I finally worked out what. You're a good man." Jones feels his eyebrows bounce up. "You probably don't even know that that's rare. But it is. It is to me. Every man I know is either smart and selfish, or generous and stupid. And I don't like those people, Jones. Guys like Blake and Klausman, I respect them, but I don't like them. You... you're different. This is going to sound stupid, but I swear to God, I didn't even know there could be someone like you. I didn't think it was possible." To Jones's alarm, her eyes begin to glisten. "You make me feel like a piece of me is missing." She pulls a tissue from a box and wipes her nose. "I'm not saying I want to be exactly like you. That's probably impossible. But I don't want you to become like them, either. You are admirable, Jones. I feel it in my heart. You're good. I think . . . we could learn from each other. I think we need each other. I think . . ." She stops. "I *know.* I know I need you. I really need you."

"Oh. Boy," Jones says. In his mind, there are alarms going off everywhere. His hands are sweating. His chest is constricting. Violently different ideas about what to do next crash against each other in his head.

"If you laugh," she says, "I'm going to kill you."

"I'm not going to laugh."

"I haven't done this before."

"What?"

"I mean, said things like this."

"Oh," Jones says, with relief.

"I'm not saying I'm a virgin."

"Right. Sorry."

"Not since I was thirteen. But that wasn't exactly voluntary, and there was no one else until I was twenty. So you could say I'm a late bloomer." She smiles at his expression. "Ah, Jones, you are so cute when you're appalled."

All he can say is, "Oh, God."

"Kiss me. Please?"

He kisses her.

Her lips are dry and cracked; still, when they touch his, something hot and brilliant sparks behind his eyeballs. Maybe it's his ground rules. Jones has imagined this moment many times, sometimes idly, sometimes not so idly, and in none of those scenarios was Eve sick. This should, therefore, be one of those times when fantasy is deflated by the mundane prick of reality. Only it's not. Kissing her feels like the best thing he has ever done.

She gets her hands inside his shirt and tries to pull it open from the inside, but it's new and the buttons don't budge. Her lips curve beneath his; they both laugh. Eve doesn't remove her gown but eventually Jones works out that he should do it, which initially seems like a challenge but turns out to be an amazing voyage of discovery. He kisses her from navel to shoulder, and when he arrives, she grabs his face and gasps, "I love you!"

"I love you, too," Jones says, and the terrible thing about this is that it is true.

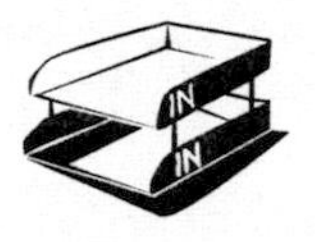

He almost makes it back to bed, but knocks the freestanding mirror with his hip in the darkness. The rotating section flips back and one end bangs against the wall while the other clocks him in the shin. *"Owwrg."*

"Jo-o-o-ones?"

"Sorry."

"What are you doing?"

"Bathroom." He climbs under the sheets.

"Oh. Mmm." Her arm snakes over his chest. Her head nestles into his shoulder. "I thought... you were trying to sneak off."

"No."

"Mmm." A happy sound. Her fingers tighten on his bicep, then relax. To Jones, who has been single for a year, it is beautiful. In this moment, there is no Zephyr. No Project Alpha. No corporate heartlessness or productivity maximization. There is just him and Eve. There's not a trace of cruelty in the dim lines of her face. No hint of selfishness in the sweep of her hair. The world is perfect.

Chapter 12 of *The Omega Management System* ("Meetings: The Good, the Bad, and the Unnecessary") devotes several pages to the advantages of breakfast meetings. *The earlier the better!* is the executive summary, because people are at their most mentally alert first thing in the morning. It is a particularly good time to tackle seemingly insurmountable problems: you will be amazed, the book says, at how frequently a morning meeting will deliver breakthrough solutions. Jones was skeptical on first reading, but now he realizes Omega is right. Because it's 5:30 A.M. and it has just occurred to him how to beat Alpha.

Q 4 / 3 : DECEMBER

PENNY COLLAPSES into the café chair and peers at him. "What are you doing?"

"What?" Jones says. "Nothing."

"You're smiling."

"Am I?"

"Did you bring down Alpha?"

"No. Well, I had an idea. But I haven't done anything yet."

"Oh. So you went the *other* way."

"What other way?" he says, but now even he can feel the smile.

"Pathetic," Penny says. "I'm disappointed in you, Stephen."

"And yet," Jones says, "I don't care." He laughs.

At ten o'clock on Tuesday an odd smell wafts through Staff Services. A warm, doughy scent, laced with sugar. People stand up in their cubicles and peer around. There, coming through the door—a trolley! And—they rub their eyes—it is piled high with steaming donuts.

Workers break from their cubicles. For a moment it looks like there might be carnage: torn pastry and cubicle dividers spattered with hot jam. But Roger is there with his PA plus two Staff Services employees—tender winners—and they stand firm. "Wait in your cubicles!" the PA orders. "Do not approach the donuts. The donuts will come to you."

The employees hurry back to their desks. They sit with growling stomachs and ears pricked for the trolley's squeaky-wheeled approach.

Freddy, Jones, Holly, and Elizabeth sit in their cubicle without speaking. They know what's coming. They listen to the growing sounds of chewing and sucking, until the trolley squeaks up to their cubicle entrance and nudges inside. Roger has a donut in his hand. His lips are speckled with sugar. The PA and the two employees are each finishing one off. On the trolley are three donuts.

"Last cubicle!" Roger says. "Go on, tuck in. Freddy, Jones."

They reach out and cautiously take a donut. Neither is brave enough to bite into it.

"Holly."

"That's okay. I don't want one."

"Of course you do. Go on."

"Really, I'm not hungry. And if there aren't enough to go around—"

"Take the donut."

Holly reluctantly reaches for it. She holds it in her lap

and ducks her head so that her hair hangs over her face in a blond sheet.

"Hmm," Roger says. "You know what, Holly, you're right. We're one short."

Elizabeth shrugs. "Fine. I don't mind."

"I could have sworn we had the right number." Roger puts his hands on his hips. "I'm sure we had exactly one for each employee."

Elizabeth abruptly stands up. Her thin gray coat, which these days she never takes off, billows down to the floor. She stares at the ceiling and begins breathing fast.

"I can only suppose," Roger says, "that someone must have taken two." He shakes his head, bewildered. "But who would do that? What sort of person would take an extra donut, knowing they'd be stealing from a co-worker?" He looks at his PA.

"I don't know, Roger."

"Jones? Freddy? Holly? Any ideas? No? No thoughts? What about you, Elizabeth?"

Her head snaps down. Her face is flushed a deep, angry red. *"I took your donut.* Is that what you want to hear? There. *I took your donut.* I was hungry, I ate it. My God! You are so petty! So *petty*!"

Roger folds his arms. "So you took my donut."

"Yes!"

"Wendell," he says, "was *fired* for that donut. Do you realize that?"

Elizabeth puts her hands to her face. "Oh my God."

"On the one hand, Elizabeth, I appreciate that you've finally confessed. But you need to understand the gravity of the situation. This isn't just about a donut. This is about teamwork. It's about respecting your co-workers. What is a person meant to think when you steal their donut? What does it say about your respect for them?"

"I can't resist you," Elizabeth says.

"It's a sad state of—" Roger stops. "What?"

"I think about you all the time. I don't mean to. I can't help it. It's making me crazy. I... I..." Her voice tightens, then she spits it out. *"I want you."*

Holly claps a hand over her mouth. Freddy's mouth sags open. Jones's eyes expand until they take up his entire face.

"I see." Roger's voice is a growl. "You're being funny."

"I'm desperate," Elizabeth whispers, "for... *you.*"

Roger's lips tighten until they are almost invisible. His jaw muscles work. Jones, Freddy, and Holly simultaneously push back in their office chairs, moving themselves out of the firing line. Then Roger turns on his heel and strides out. His three surprised lackeys are left to maneuver the trolley around and wheel it after him. The Training Sales team listen to its slow, squeaky progress.

Freddy says, "Oh. My. God."

Holly says, "Elizabeth, you kick *so much ass.*"

Elizabeth's face is drained of color. "I need to sit down." Holly leaps up. Elizabeth takes her hand until she can grip the chair's plastic armrests. She looks from one awestruck sales assistant face to another. "That... I was just joking, you know."

"Oh God, of *course,*" Holly says. "That's why it was so *funny.*"

"Right." She is starting to shake. "Exactly."

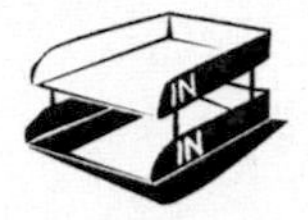

Roger slams his office door hard enough to make the glass wall shudder and the vertical blinds bang. He stalks to his desk and snatches up the phone. He gets as far as dialing the first three digits of Human Resources . . . then hesitates. If he completes this call, Elizabeth will be off the premises within ten minutes. But that will be the end of it: she will then be beyond his power. The story of this humiliation, however, will live on in corporate memory. It will be the punch line to Roger's entire career.

With a strangled growl, he slams the handset back down. He throws himself into his leather chair and puts his head in his hands.

A large yellow envelope of the sort used for internal mail sits on his desk in front of him; it must have been delivered while he was out. One end bulges oddly. Roger sits up, unseals the envelope, and tips its contents onto his desk. A plastic cup sealed with a yellow lid tries to roll away; he grabs it. It is empty. A sticker on the front says NAME and EMPLOYEE ID #, and has spaces for writing in both.

He checks the envelope and finds a memo stuck to the inside. It's from Human Resources and Asset Protection, to all department heads. In the interests of company productivity, it says, Zephyr Holdings has introduced a drug-testing policy. Every week, one employee will be randomly selected from each department to provide a urine sample. Employees who fail the test, or refuse to comply with it, will be terminated. This is covered by Section 38.2 of the standard employee work contract, a clause Roger recalls having queried when he first joined Zephyr. If he remembers right, Human Resources told him not to worry about it because the clause was just a standard industry thing and Zephyr didn't actually do drug tests.

The memo contains a list of all the employees randomly selected for the first round of testing, and advises departmental managers to keep this relatively quiet. There is no need to make this into a big deal, the memo says. Employees should not be made to feel they are being singled out.

Roger has an encyclopedic knowledge of Zephyr employees. So he notices that every one of the randomly selected employees is female and in her twenties or thirties. He notices that the employee selected from Staff Services is Elizabeth.

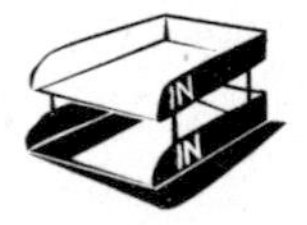

The other day Eve and Jones were in the underground parking lot and she was fiddling with his tie and giggling while he made jokes about Tom Mandrake's taste in shirts when Blake's Porsche cruised by. The windows were tinted too darkly for Jones to tell whether he and Eve had been spotted, but ever since Blake has seemed even more disgusted with him than he was previously. He has tried to be more discreet, but now it is eleven o'clock, Holly and

Freddy are out of the department, and Jones is having trouble thinking about anything but Eve. *Screw it,* he thinks. He is going to visit her.

He bounces out of his chair and walks to the elevators. He knows where she'll be, because yesterday afternoon Human Resources announced that reception could be adequately staffed by a single person, and thus there was no need to supply Eve with help while Gretel Monadnock is on stress leave. This caused much amusement when relayed in this morning's Alpha meeting, to everyone except Eve (and, for diplomatic reasons, Jones), and culminated in a bet from Blake that she wouldn't last the week. "Are you saying I don't usually work the phones?" Eve challenged, and Blake said, "That's exactly what I'm saying." Eve shook her head and said, "You have no idea," even though it seemed to Jones that Blake had a very good idea indeed. Eve will require some moral support in the days ahead, he suspects.

The elevator opens onto the lobby and Jones crosses to the reception desk with a brisk stride. Eve is hunched over, lines of strain on her face. She doesn't look at him. "Holy *God,*" she says to her handset. "How hard is it for you to understand? *I need to know your name before I can connect you.*" Then she sees Jones and tears off her headset. "This is insane. They just keep calling."

"Aw," Jones says.

"If Gretel isn't back tomorrow, I'm going to make sure she doesn't come back at all, I swear to God. How long has she been off, two weeks? It's pathetic." She shakes her head. "Want to go to lunch?"

He blinks. "Don't you have to stay here?"

"I'm done. I am done." She stands. "The company won't collapse if nobody answers their damn calls for an hour or two."

"You expect every other employee to do their job," Jones points out. He notices Freddy standing outside the tinted lobby glass. Freddy is staring in at Jones, a cigarette in one hand, and there is something wrong with his expression.

"Yes, well." She gathers her handbag. "You and I aren't like every other employee, are we?"

"Eve, is something wrong with Freddy?" She doesn't say anything. Jones turns back to her. "Eve?"

She puts her hands on her hips. "Oh. I told him."

For a second he is too flabbergasted to speak. He simply cannot conceive that she could have done this. "About *us*?"

"Look, he came up and started bugging me. I didn't have time to deal with him. I just told him." She comes around the desk. "He had to find out eventually, Jones. It was cruel to keep him in the dark like that."

"You didn't mind before! Jesus, you strung him along for six months before today!"

"Well, before now, he had a chance." She smiles and tilts her head, in a way Jones usually finds cute. "But now . . ." She reaches for his tie.

Jones pushes her hand away. It's like flicking a switch: Eve's face turns to stone. A second passes, then another. They stare at each other, mentally feeling out the shifting ground.

Eve says softly, "Don't ever touch me like that."

Jones looks to his right. Freddy is still watching them through the glass, but as Jones's gaze meets his, he turns away.

Jones says, "Apologize."

"For what? For not keeping that we're screwing each other a secret?" Jones winces. He is well aware of the security cameras, the hidden microphones, the snarl of wiring that connects them all to level 13. "For telling Freddy that his best friend in Zephyr is lying to him?"

"Don't you dare tell me this is a lesson."

Eve raises her eyebrows. "Why? Do you need one?"

"Fuck you."

"Done that," she says.

Freddy is already gone when Jones exits the lobby doors. He squints in the sunshine and catches a glimpse of Freddy's back disappearing around the corner of the building. Jones breaks into a run. Freddy is walking at a fast clip, but Jones catches him next to the new Smokers' Corral, under the big, painted eyes of cartoon cows. "Freddy!"

Freddy turns. There's a smile on his face, or, rather, a gruesome, twisted attempt at a smile. "Hey, Jones."

"Freddy, I am so sorry—"

"No, no, it's okay. Really. You don't have to say anything. I mean, it's not like she was ever going to go for me anyway. Holly was right. I'm not the kind of guy who gets girls like Eve. I'm the guy who hasn't been promoted once in five years." He lets out a short bark of a laugh. "So it's all good. You just saved me forty bucks a week in flowers."

"Freddy, you're not that guy. You're better than that.

You're better than this place deserves." This comes out with real venom, but he can tell from Freddy's expression that he thinks Jones is just being polite, which inflames him even more. "Freddy, this place is wrong. It has to change. It *has* to." And then the words just pop out: "And if Senior Management won't change it, we have to overthrow them."

Freddy says, "What?"

"We need a rebellion. A revolution. A resistance. To make Zephyr Holdings a good place to work again." Jones hesitates, unsure if Zephyr ever was a good place to work. "Why can't the company care about you? Why doesn't it give a shit? You're not a resource, you're a *person.* This company is hollowing itself out. It's mined too deep into its own employees. We need change, not just because that's what we deserve but because that's the only thing that will save Zephyr from eating itself."

"Jones, you sound a little crazy."

"Why can't the company be better? Only because Senior Management doesn't want it to be. That's the key: control of Senior Management. If the workers act together, we can get that. How could they stop us? We're the company. We just need to unite. We need to form a union."

Freddy blinks.

Jones says, "Or let's go back to 'resistance.' "

"Resistance is better."

"So are you in?"

Freddy holds up his hands. "Jones, I get what you're saying. And, yeah, it'd be nice if things were better. But it's not going to happen. First, it takes three weeks' notice in this place to organize a meeting. Second, as soon as Human

Resources finds out what you're doing, they'll toss you out of the building."

"I know." Jones licks his lips. "But I have a plan."

Freddy's gaze drifts to the Smokers' Corral. Two people are headed over there now; they walk inside and take seats at the wooden bench, feeling in their pockets for cigarettes. "Is this plan going to get me fired?"

"No."

He looks back at Jones. "You promise?"

"I swear it." And in this moment he really means it; he means it with all his heart.

"Okay," Freddy says. "Let's hear it."

Holly sits alone in a small meeting room off the lobby. There is an open folder and some scattered pages on the table in front of her, but these are just props in case someone peers through the little window in the door behind her. She's not actually meeting anyone.

She didn't expect to do this again. Not after Roger assigned her the gym—the gym!—the one place in Zephyr Holdings that makes any sense to her whatsoever. Forty-five minutes ago, she saw her red voice-mail light blinking, and dialed in to discover that Roger had called.

"Holly. After some further investigation, I've found we're unable to keep the gym. It turns out it's just not cost-effective. This news will come as a disappointment to you, I'm sure, but you know how these things are. I hope you understand it's nothing to do with you; you would have done a great job. Come see me if any of this is unclear."

So he didn't actually say, *You're a fool and I took advantage of your stupidity to find out who took my donut,* but Holly heard the message clearly enough. By the time she got the phone back in its cradle, everything was burning: her eyes, her ears, her heart. Elizabeth was sitting behind her in the cubicle, and Holly didn't dare turn around for fear that Elizabeth would see her and ask what was wrong. Instead she stayed rigid in the same position and swallowed over and over. But there was something thick and bitter rising in her throat, and it was, she realized, going to pop out of her in a completely humiliating sob, so she grabbed a random folder from her desk, hugged it to her chest, and stood up. Elizabeth glanced at her face—her red, sweaty, swelling face—and her lips parted in surprise, and behind them, Holly knew, was a question she couldn't face, so she ran out of the cubicle. The first three lobby meeting rooms were full, and she began to panic that she was about to have a wet, messy breakdown right there in the lobby, under the curious eyes of passing co-workers. But the last one was free, thank God, and she hauled open the door and threw herself inside. She sat with her back to the door so nobody could see her face and let herself go.

She supposes she must be an idiot. This is the kind of thing that Freddy would have seen coming a mile away. He probably did see it coming and that's why he was so hard on her. She can't bear to imagine Freddy's reaction. She doesn't want to see disappointment in his eyes.

There's a knock at the door. *"Busy!"* she calls, her voice shrill. But the door clicks open. *"Busy!* Do you mind?"

"It's me."

She freezes. "Freddy, I'm in the middle of something here."

"Sorry." There's a pause.

"So you heard."

"Yeah. Sorry, Holly. Roger's a dick."

"I'm actually meeting people." She straightens her folder. "They'll be here any minute."

She hears him shift his feet. "Holly, Jones and I are doing something... I can't explain it here. But can you come outside for a second? It's important."

"Sure. Just let me finish my meeting. Okay?"

There's silence. Then Freddy does something completely shocking, something she would never have expected and which could get him fired: he bends down and kisses her lightly on the cheek.

At 4:10 P.M., one-page questionnaires appear throughout the Zephyr building. They are on Zephyr Holdings stationery, titled STAFF SATISFACTION SURVEY. Most people

don't see where they come from. Others catch sight of one of three figures, flitting between the cubicles: a kid in a beautiful ash-gray suit, a short dark-haired man with glasses, and a young blond woman with incredibly toned calves. Nobody can put a name to them, but they're vaguely familiar, in the way that almost everyone in Zephyr Holdings is. The employees pick up their questionnaires and begin to read.

Thank you for participating in the Zephyr Holdings company-wide Staff Satisfaction Survey. Your feedback will be used to measure how effectively the company is providing a productive and rewarding workplace, and to improve working conditions for all employees.

Please do not write any identifying information on this questionnaire. Your responses are anonymous.

This elicits a few derisive snorts. The employees are familiar with Zephyr's version of "anonymous" feedback. They've provided anonymous feedback before, only to be contacted by their managers for further clarification. They've had confidential discussions that ended up in their permanent record. They scour the questionnaires for tiny ID numbers and hidden watermarks.

Q1: Do you feel that Zephyr Holdings is a good place to work?

Cynical laughter pops and crackles through the building. "Check out question one," they tell each other. The only thing more amazing than the catalog of brutal methods the company uses to demean its workers is that it thinks it's helping. Not that the employees are going to say this. Positive feedback is taken very seriously, often ending up in annual reports, but negative feedback leads to HR investigations into employee attitude problems. So the staff, or at least those who have been in the company more than five minutes, scribble down the expected responses, sprinkled with phrases such as "team-oriented environment" and "opportunities" and "productive." When they see interns writing honest opinions, like "I have worked here six months and haven't seen anyone from Senior Management yet," or "Nobody has explained what the consolidation was for yet or why," or "This survey is the first hint I've seen that Zephyr Holdings is actually aware of such a thing as staff satisfaction," they gently still their pens; they sit them down and educate them.

Q2: What could be done, in your opinion, to improve the working conditions at Zephyr Holdings?

This raises eyebrows. Men and women congregate in huddles. That's a trick question, right? Does the company really want them to say "Nothing?" That would be a bit much even for Zephyr Holdings. That would take obsequiousness to a new level. Debate rages. The old-timers, the hard nuts who entered survival mode a long time ago, say it is impossible to overestimate Senior Management's opinion of itself. They write "Nothing" in a firm, unwavering hand. The idealists—graduates, mainly—take the question at face value. There is a lot of space and they use it all, pouring out ideas. The remainder answer more cautiously. They start with "If I HAVE to suggest something," or "This is probably too expensive, but..." then they too begin to dream. What if instead of being berated for leaving early and getting nothing for staying late, one could balance out the other? What if you didn't have to fill out time sheets in ten-minute increments, but were trusted to find the best way to make yourself productive? What if Zephyr acknowledged that you have a life outside the company, that you don't spring into existence when you turn up in the morning and vanish when you leave? These are wild, crazy thoughts, but they pour out, one after the other.

Q3: Do you feel that you and your colleagues deserve these improved working conditions?

Whoa! Whoa! Alarm registers on their faces. The huddles draw tighter. They know for a fact that Senior Management doesn't think they deserve better, because if it did, things would *be* better. But it has always at least pretended it does. During all-staff meetings, executives in well-pressed suits preach about how employees are the company's greatest asset—and while it's hard to reconcile this with the never-ending rounds of layoffs and outsourcing, it's nice to hear. This survey question suggests a line is being crossed: if Senior Management thinks its employees will answer "No," it is no longer bothering to hide its contempt.

Q4: Do you have confidence that Zephyr Holdings Senior Management will implement improved conditions as a result of this survey?

Everyone falls silent. The answer is clearly "No"; you would have to be an idiot or an intern to believe otherwise. But that's why the company should never ask such a question. The point of a staff satisfaction survey, like a suggestion box, is to give employees the impression that the company cares without requiring it to actually care. So this question can mean only one of two things: either Senior Management has grown a heart, or the survey is not from Senior Management.

Q5: If you deserve improved working conditions but you don't believe Senior Management will implement them, do you agree that the only way to achieve a satisfactory work environment is to overthrow Senior Management and install new leadership, replacing the current regime of incompetence, greed, and corruption?

Ding! On level 2, this is the sound of revolution. The elevator doors slide open and Jones, Freddy, and Holly step out. Around the floor, PA heads slowly rise.

Level 2! What a place! It is offices, offices, as far as the eye can see, and not a cubicle in sight. Sunlight streams through huge, floor-to-ceiling glass walls. Interior foliage glows with health. The carpet! The carpet! It's thick enough to wrap yourself up in—there are no well-worn trails leading to the coffee machine and bathroom. Is that a waterfall? Oh. No. Just a watercooler. But a waterfall wouldn't seem out of place, not in this land of honey and clover. It is exactly what they expected: a luxurious Paradise in which the powerful relax and are fed grapes by their PAs—well, not grapes, but coffees—while workers below toil in barely conditioned drudgery. They have seen glimpses of this promised land in Zephyr Holdings annual reports, the background for many a picture of a smiling senior executive, but the reality is even more galling. Where are the cutbacks here? Where is the belt-tightening?

"Excuse me?" a PA says. Freddy recognizes her as a girl who disappeared from Training Delivery about a year ago. He thought she'd been sacked. "How did you get up here?"

The answer is *Jones has special clearance,* but Jones is not telling the PA that. He's not even telling Freddy and Holly; they think he got one of the network nerds to hack the system. "We're here to see Senior Management. All of them, please."

The PAs exchange glances. "You need an appointment. And even then, you're not supposed to come here. There are meeting rooms on level—"

"Get them out here," Jones says. "Right now."

The PAs look at each other again. They have apparently developed some kind of telepathic language, because once more they silently reach a decision. "I'll call Mr. Smithson. Would you like to take a seat?"

"No," Holly says.

Stanley Smithson, vice president of Staff Services, is piloting a leather chair in the cockpit of his level-2 office when his phone rings. VANESSA P, the screen says. Vanessa is Stanley's PA, and less than an hour ago Stanley told her in what he thought was a clear and direct manner that he was not to be disturbed. Stanley blows air through his teeth. He does not demand extraordinary efforts from Vanessa. She needs to bring him the occasional coffee. She needs to type up his Dictaphone tapes, on which he records his ideas, insights, and general outlines for memos (the actual text to be drafted by her, since she's the one with the degree in English). And, most important, she needs to make sure he is left alone when he needs time with his thoughts. It's not much of a challenge, is it? Is it too much for a vice president of a major corporation to ask? Apparently so, because here she is on the phone.

He puts down his frequent-flier-miles brochure. It's essential for executives to stay mentally fresh, and that's why when Stanley feels the pressures of the corporate world closing in, he takes time out to meditate: he tells Vanessa to hold his calls, he pulls out the brochure, and browses through all the places he can fly for free. It's deeply soothing. Sometimes Stanley gets the gnawing sensation that he is faking his way through his career—that he has risen through the corporate ranks due mainly to obsequiousness and good luck, and it could just as easily be, say, Jim from Security (sorry, Human Resources and Asset Protection) up here deciding whether to form a Process Improvement task force while Stanley wanders around the parking lot, making sure nobody is walking off with a laser printer. But the brochure assures him otherwise, massaging away doubts and reinflating his confidence. Stanley must be unusually talented and insightful, because he can fly to Berlin for free while Jim (apparently) can't afford a car manufactured this century.

He lets the phone ring a few more times—because Vanessa should know better—then punches for speakerphone. "Yes?"

"I'm very sorry to disturb you, but there are some people here to see you."

"You didn't tell me I had an appointment."

"Ah, you don't. But . . . I think you should come out here."

Stanley's brows descend. This is highly irregular. He sighs, loud enough for the speakerphone to pick it up. "All right. I'm coming."

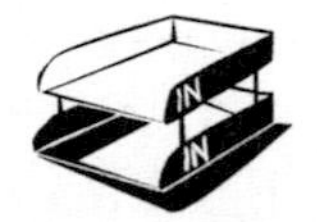

When Stanley emerges, he has a faint smile on his face. But this quickly fades at the sight of Jones, Freddy, and Holly, who are clearly not fellow executives or important investors or anyone else of consequence. His eyes flick between their ID tags. Stanley himself doesn't wear one; he considers it demeaning. "What do you want?"

The young man says, "We're here on behalf of the employees of Zephyr Holdings. We have a set of demands."

Stanley starts to smile. But none of the three people facing him joins in, so he turns it into a frown. "You're joking."

"No, we're not. It's very important. We need to see the whole of Senior Management."

"Well, you can't. How did you get up here?"

The other man, the short one, says, "We think the working conditions at Zephyr Holdings need to improve. And we want to talk to Senior Management about it."

"The company *has* a suggestion box," Stanley bristles. He has no idea who these people are, but nobody in scuffed shoes tells Stanley Smithson what to do. You need much more expensive shoes than that to give Stanley orders. "I really don't see what you're trying to achieve, barging up here—"

"You're not listening. These aren't suggestions."

"That's enough. You three are leaving, right now." Stanley starts forward, planning to physically bundle Jones, Freddy, and Holly into the elevator. But he has forgotten that people usually do what he tells them because they are paid to, not because he is a dynamo of hot, charismatic masculinity. None of the three budges, and when Stanley realizes they're not going to, he pulls up. He feels his face redden. "I'm calling Human Resources and Asset Protection. You only have yourselves to blame. I hope you realize that."

He strides to the closest PA's desk and picks up the phone. His hand is trembling. The last time Stanley was involved in such a physical confrontation, he was seventeen. Then the handset clicks in his ear. Stanley turns. The young woman has followed him to the desk and pulled out the phone cord. Stanley stares at her in disbelief.

"Nobody's calling HR," she says.

Daniel Klausman is wandering through Treasury, emptying trash baskets while keeping an eye on an interesting political tussle between three accountants, when his pocket starts shaking. It's his cell phone. He has it on vibrate because the idea of a janitor with a cell phone might alarm the Zephyr workers, might get them thinking about their own careers and the ratio of the work they put in to the rewards they get out. This is an idea Klausman has tried to impart to other Alpha agents, mostly successfully. The exception is Eve Jantiss, who parks a blue sports car in front of the building. Eve's argument is that Blake gets to drive a sports car to work so why shouldn't she, and the fact that Blake is in Senior Management while she answers phones hasn't swayed her. Klausman has a great deal of respect and admiration for Eve, but he is aware that she is driven by something like pure greed. For a long time now he has had the niggling feeling that one day Eve will, at least in a political sense, knock him down and clamber over his limp body.

He walks to a service closet, leaving behind the Treasury cubicle farm and its emerging political dynamic. As well as being out of the sight of curious Zephyr employees, the closets have the advantage of being one of very few places in the building that are not under electronic surveillance. This was not always the case, but Klausman once had an embarrassing incident wherein he said uncomplimentary things about an Alpha agent while that person was standing in the monitoring room. Also they kept catching employees having sex in the closets, and while everybody quite enjoyed getting those tapes out for the Alpha Christmas party, he worried that if the terrible day ever arrived where Zephyr's secret was blown, this would look very bad. It's one thing to simulate an entire company in order to secretly study its employees—if that ever becomes public knowledge, Klausman will still hold his head high in any gentleman's club in the nation—but another to build a collection of hidden-camera sex tapes. That could give people the wrong idea.

He closes the closet door and fishes his cell phone from his overalls. "Yes?"

"Mr. Klausman." It's Mona. But her voice is oddly tight. "May I ask—has Jones been assigned some kind of project with Senior Management?"

"No, of course not. That's Blake's area."

"Then I think you should come to 13. Right away."

"What's happening?"

"Um . . ." she says. "I don't know."

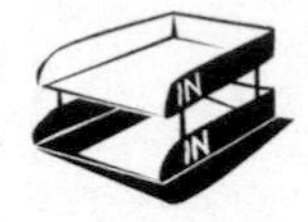

Stanley Smithson retreats, but only to gather reinforcements. He returns with the Phoenix. Freddy and Holly's eyes widen in recognition. To most Zephyr workers, Senior Management is a jury box of anonymous faces, but everyone knows the Phoenix. He's a thick-necked man with a red face, blue shirt, and graying hair. Currently his sleeves are rolled all the way up to his biceps, which, while not quite the gasp-inducing specimens they were when he was a storeman, are still highly impressive compared to the atrophied muscles of his fellow executives.

There is a well-known business principle that everyone rises to his or her level of incompetence, because employees who are good at their jobs are given promotions until they reach a role they're bad at, and then they stay there. The Phoenix is an exception: he has been incompetent at every job he's ever held, yet keeps getting promoted. When his job was to carry boxes from one part of the company to another, they would sit in reception for hours until, several reminder calls later, he ambled in to collect them. Then, via means that nobody ever quite worked out, they would vanish for up to two days before arriving at their destination, a few floors away. Also, employees soon realized they couldn't pass the Phoenix in a corridor without getting caught in a conversation. There was no escape: if you liked sports, you were in for a thirty-minute lecture about player wages, but if you didn't, he would try to educate you. If you were foolish enough to express a differing opinion, the Phoenix's voice would grow louder and more insistent as his thick eyebrows descended. If you still failed to concede, he would start poking his finger at you. People began feigning hearing problems, or waiting until some other poor soul had become ensnared before hurrying past, head down, breath held.

Then one day the warehouse was outsourced. There was quiet rejoicing: at last, workers could move between floors without a sermon on the declining skills of elite ballplayers! But, to everyone's horror and amazement, the Phoenix survived, being transferred to Inventory Control. Two years later, facing sky-rocketing employee turnover, that department was merged into Logistics. Twelve members of staff were laid off, but not the Phoenix. A decade and uncountable disasters later, he was assigned to head a Sigma Six task force, which was mission-critical for ten months, then crashed and burned and nobody ever mentioned it again. All task force members were let go or farmed out to distant fringes of the company, except for the Phoenix, who over the years had accumulated so much leave that he had become too expensive to fire. Human Resources forced him back into Logistics, despite that department's objections, until the vice president became so frustrated that he laid down a him-or-me ultimatum. This was unfortunately timed, as internal jockeying in Senior Management had left him on the outer edge of a new group of power brokers, who saw this as an excellent opportunity to replace him with someone more likely to share their views. The Phoenix thus became the new Logistics vice president. It is clear to the Zephyr workers that he is immortal.

Freddy and Jones exchange nervous glances at the

Phoenix's approach. Holly's eyes fix on the bulge of muscle where his arms disappear into his shirtsleeves. "What the hell do you think you're doing?" the Phoenix bawls. He comes at them like a bad-tempered bear. "This is Senior Management, not the goddamn cafeteria. Get the hell out."

Holly says, "We have a set of demands—"

"I don't care if you've got a gold medal." The Phoenix is always coming out with lines like this, which sound as if they should be witty but when you think about them make no sense. "Get your asses out of level 2."

The three shrink before his advance. Then, from behind, they hear it. *Ding!*

An elevator-load of Zephyr employees spills onto level 2. They have taken a while to arrive because there was an argument about the elevator's load-bearing capacity; a little metal sign declared a weight limit and an uncomfortable discussion ensued, with people eyeing one another's waistlines and buttocks. Also, to convince the elevator to go to level 2 they had to swipe Jones's ID card and toss it out to the others before the doors closed, and on the first attempt a woman who used to be in Business Card Design—so deft with a mouse, surprisingly deficient in gross motor skills—failed to clear the doors and they had to all jump out on level 5 and try again.

But now they're here! They number more than two

dozen: clerks, gnomes, elves, accountants, engineers—a Zephyr mixed bag. They pour out of the elevator like clowns from a tiny automobile: just when you think there couldn't possibly be any more, out come two more. Stanley's eyes widen. The Phoenix backs up a step.

"We didn't want to do it this way," Jones says. "But we're prepared to."

You carry out raids at dawn because that's when the enemy is at its most disoriented. It's like that on level 2 of Zephyr Holdings, except it's four thirty in the afternoon. Senior Management is weary from a long day of increasing shareholder value, the buzz from the wine over lunch has worn off, and it's been more than an hour since their last coffee. When Zephyr employees burst into their offices and tear the phones out of their hands, they are too befuddled to react. Every one of them, Blake Seddon included, is dragged from his or her leather office chair, hauled into the boardroom, and stuffed into a seat around the great oak table. They sit there in shock while a scruffy, angry throng coalesces around them. Every few minutes, above the growing din, they hear a *ding* and even more people crush into the boardroom. Soon they are pressed so tight that they are like a single animal, the zephyremployee, an enormous beast, normally docile and easily tamed, but (apparently) aggressive and unpredictable when provoked. The boardroom fills with their excited talk, the kaleidoscope of their shirts, blouses, and ties, and the hot, sweaty odor of their bodies.

Senior Management tries to protest, but the employees angrily shake their chairs. They try to communicate with one another via facial expressions. None has any idea what is happening, but as a young man clambers onto the boardroom table and holds up his hands for quiet, they all feel the same sickening feeling: the bulwark of the suggestion box has failed.

The noise drops away. Jones clears his throat. It is very important that Jones not betray weakness at this point, but knowing that and executing it are two different things. He feels his knees tremble. His eyes meet Blake Seddon's, and he sees rage in them. Jones swallows, then again. His throat constricts tighter and tighter.

Senior Management—not Blake, but an older man with outrageous eyebrows—grows tired of waiting. "Just what do you think—"

"I have something to read!" Jones shouts. The man falls silent. He swallows again. "It's an old speech, but we have adapted it for modern times. The important thing is that it still holds true today. So *you,*" Jones says, his voice rising, as Senior Management starts to interject again, "are going to *sit there* and *listen* to it."

He takes a breath. "*We hold these truths to be self-evident:* that all employees are created equal, that they are endowed with certain unalienable rights, that among these are dignity, respect, and the pursuit of a life outside of work.

"That whenever any company becomes destructive of these ends, it is the right of the employees to alter or to abolish it, and to institute new management, laying its foundation on such principles as to effect their safety and happiness.

"Prudence will dictate that management should not be changed for light or transient causes; and accordingly all experience hath shown that employees are more disposed to suffer, while evils are sufferable, than to right themselves by abolishing the management to which they are accustomed. But when a long train of abuses and degradations, pursuing invariably the same cost-cutting objectives, evinces a design to reduce them under absolute despotism, it is their right, it is their duty, to throw off such management.

"We, therefore, the employees of Zephyr Holdings, solemnly declare that we are, and of right ought to be, free and independent; that we are absolved from all allegiance to Senior Management, and that all authority of Senior Management over us is totally dissolved." There is a lot of shouting and executives trying to talk over the top of him by this point, so Jones decides to repeat it. *"Totally dissolved!"* he yells.

There is bedlam. Senior Management struggles to free itself from the grasping hands of the employees. It shouts about proper channels. The employees shout back. A lot of hostile feelings fly around the boardroom. Years' worth of anger pour out. "We're not human resources!" Freddy shouts, his face red. "We're *people*! You got that, now? Are you getting this?"

For a while, nobody in the monitoring room of level 13 speaks. Finally Mona breaks the silence, her voice small and hesitant. "What is he doing?"

Klausman doesn't answer. He doesn't feel outraged or shocked or even surprised; not yet. He watches Jones on the monitors and feels . . . dull.

"Doesn't he understand this company isn't *real*?" Mona says plaintively. "Senior Management doesn't run Zephyr. *We* do. What is he trying to accomplish?" She draws confidence from his silence; her voice rises. "We can sack half the people in that room if we want to."

"No, Mona," he says. "We can only sack all of them." He glances at her and sees confusion in her eyes. It's mirrored in the eyes of the other half-dozen agents present. They are so used to being on the inside, Klausman realizes. They no longer remember anything else. He looks back at the monitors. "If we intervene, we reveal Alpha. And Zephyr is over."

Tom Mandrake says, "There's practically no one from Human Resources and Asset Protection in that group. So long as we control them—"

"Jones knows how we work," Klausman cuts in, irritated.

He wishes Eve were here; he wouldn't have to explain the implications to her. "If he gains control of Senior Management, we can be sure other departments will follow."

There's silence for a few moments. Mona says bravely, "I can't see how this will work. You can't *abolish* Senior Management. Zephyr isn't a *democracy.* It's a corporation."

"I believe," Klausman says, "that Jones is advancing the theory that those two concepts are not mutually exclusive."

"Blake won't let it happen," Mona says stubbornly. "He'll stop this."

"Let us hope so," Klausman says. "I'm sixty-three. I don't feel like starting again."

Jones is beginning to think he's actually done it, that Senior Management has crumpled, when Blake's voice cuts through the tumult. He doesn't shout; he simply raises his chin, speaks clearly, and suddenly everyone listens. Jones has to admit it: Blake has presence. "Do you want the company to collapse? Because that's what I'm hearing. You want Zephyr to go bankrupt." He rises from his chair and no one tries to restrain him. He straightens the cuffs of his jacket. His blue eyes rake the crowd. "You're unhappy about staff conditions. You think we don't care about your welfare. Well, you're right. Zephyr is not here to care about you. It's a corporation. If you were expecting a theme park, resign. If you're prepared to do your job, stay. But don't demand that we care. Zephyr can't afford to care."

The workers grow hesitant. They are not totally sure how corporate finances work—from their perspective, it's easy to view Zephyr as an endless source of money, its existence neither threatened nor enhanced by how intelligently that money is spent—but Blake's words clearly contain some kind of truth.

"We did not hire you to fill your lives with happiness. *Your* welfare is not the goal here: Zephyr's is. You want to reverse that—put your own interests above the company's. Well, I'll tell you plainly: this would kill Zephyr stone dead. It would put every one of us out of a job."

The employees' shoulders slump. Someone says, "Still, things could be a *little* better..."

Fear steals into Jones's body. He is not here to make things "a little better." He's here to take control of Senior Management. Anything less will undo him.

Blake senses victory. His tone softens; he holds out his hands placatingly, palms up. "Look, it's been a long day." He is the epitome of rationality—especially compared to sweating, wild-eyed Jones, standing on the boardroom table. Blake is calm, firm leadership in a five-thousand-dollar suit. He is exactly the kind of person you would want to be making decisions that affect your ability to earn a living. "Obviously, we're all a little emotional. Perhaps we've said things we didn't mean. Of course Zephyr cares about you. Employees are our greatest asset. You were right to bring this to our attention. We *do* need to make changes. Not abolishing Senior Management, not bankrupting the company—but yes, changes." He nods thoughtfully. "And to prove it, I promise you this: first thing tomorrow, Senior Management will go through the suggestion box and read every submission *very, very carefully.*"

The employees murmur, raising their eyebrows and shrugging. Jones hears phrases like, "Well, it's an improvement," and "At least they're listening now," and he knows it's over. Because everybody would rather have a bad job than no job at all.

"No!" he shouts. He shakes his fist—this is no help to his argument, but he can't help himself. "You want to tell these people what's best for the company, Blake? You don't even know what Zephyr is! It's not the logo, or the bottom line, or the investors, or the *customers*—" Jones is leaking sarcasm by this point. "It's *us*! Look around, you see us? We're it. *We're Zephyr*! We spend half our waking lives here. We know it better than anyone. We care about it more than anyone. That's what people do, Blake, when you put them in a workplace: they get emotionally involved. We're not inputs. We're not machines. You can't outsource some of us and expect everything to be the same. Maybe you wish we were easier to manage, but bad luck: we're human and we're difficult. And we have lives outside of work, goddamn it, and you can't keep stealing pieces of that! You can't keep feeding the bottom line with *us*! If you do, if that's all you know how to do, then goddamm it, this company *deserves* to die!"

The workers roar with approval. It stuns him. Jones thought he was delivering a final, hopeless rant. Instead he has turned the crowd. He looks from one cheering face to another.

It's unclear who starts the chant. It's not Jones. It should be, but he is too dazed to press his advantage. The important thing is that it starts, and drowns out Blake's efforts to respond.

"Resign! Resign! Resign!"

It rolls around the boardroom like a boulder. One member of Senior Management after another tries futilely to raise his or her voice against it. Blake Seddon holds up his hands for quiet and is completely ignored. The Phoenix struggles against the workers holding him down.

Blake gives up any attempt at dignity. With the veins on his neck standing out, he shouts, "We will *not* resign! And you don't have the authority to make us!"

Most of the crowd doesn't even hear him. Jones does. "You're right. We can't force you to quit. But you can't force us to listen to you. Stay up here. Call yourselves Senior Management. But we won't be doing things your way. We'll be taking charge from now on."

The other members of Senior Management exchange looks. Jones knows the thought is wriggling into their brains: *What if this rebellion is for real?* Zephyr is already reeling from a catastrophic reorganization. If a bunch of PAs, clerks, and sales assistants start trying to run the company . . . well, surely the end is nigh. Each member of Senior Management possesses a hefty stockholding and a munificent termination clause: the kinds of things that can be difficult to extract from a deceased company. And not only that: if Zephyr goes under while they're on board, they would be unemployed with a bad CV.

An executive who resigns before a corporate collapse, on the other hand—and Jones sees the realization dawning on several Senior Management faces at the same time—is in a different position. This person receives his payout. He cashes in his shares. His CV positively glows, because he clearly disagreed with the direction of the company—a decision stunningly vindicated by its subsequent collapse. That person has a future. That person is a corporate genius.

Stanley Smithson pipes up. "Very well . . . as much as it saddens me, I will resign. I would like to say that—"

"I also resign!"

"I resign, too!"

A mighty cheer goes up from the employees. Jones looks at Blake, but that would be hoping for too much. Blake simply stands there with his arms folded and shakes his head. As the executives shuffle through the crowd, heading to their offices to collect their belongings and shred incriminating documents, Holly throws her arms around Freddy and kisses him in blatant disregard of the company's Employee Conduct and Anti–Sexual Harassment policy. Word ripples out of the boardroom to those pressed outside, unable to fit in. It reaches the PAs, who rise from their chairs in disbelief. They hit the phones, spreading the news throughout the building. Employees lined up outside elevators, still waiting to get to level 2, hear the unbelievable truth: *Senior Management has been sacked!*

Outside the building, a few smokers look up to see the lights on half a dozen floors happily flicking on and off. Even higher they can make out dozens of tiny figures crammed against the glass-walled level-2 boardroom—but they have to squint, because the sun is setting. The way its hot orange rays bend around the glass, it almost looks as if a group of golden parachutes are floating gently to the ground.

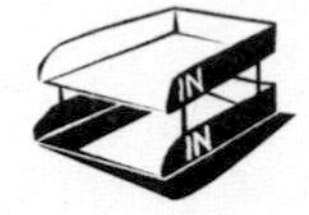

The party runs hot before Freddy discovers that the boardroom contains a stereo system and a bar fridge stocked with expensive champagne; afterward, it's anarchy. On level 2 there is dancing. In the lobby, employees congregate to excitedly review the day's events—there is nothing astonishing about this except that it is the first time in years that a group of employees from different departments have talked to each other without a written agenda and a prebooked meeting room. On level 12 a marketer screws up a memo on budget cuts and kicks it across the room, which blossoms into an impromptu soccer game that spans three floors, with bonus points scored for reaching key desks.

Nobody has any idea what will happen next. Most don't think about it—tonight is for celebrating, not strategic planning. But a few are worried. They retreat back to their cubicles and sit there nervously. They feel dread fill their bones. To them, this isn't a party—it's the collapse of natural order. Senior Management may have been incompetent; it may have been corrupt; it was certainly full of assholes—but they were *their* incompetent, corrupt assholes. Senior Management was Zephyr's parents, and even though they were remote and uncaring and tended to leave the kids locked in the car while they shot twelve rounds of golf, their absence makes these employees feel like orphans. They listlessly pick papers out of their inboxes and click through their task lists, futilely seeking something like a return to normal.

On level 11, Staff Services, the paper football bounces off Roger's glass office wall. Roger peeks through the vertical blinds, then lets them quickly fall closed again. Like most of the managers in Zephyr Holdings, he is hiding. When they rebelled in France, they beheaded dukes, didn't they? They decapitated the cousins of cousins of royalty.

There is a power vacuum in Zephyr Holdings now, one large enough to make Roger's saliva glands tingle. He can feel the company straining to suck managers like him upward to fill it. But it's too risky. The workers are volatile, their passions inflamed. He regrets that whole tender-for-work thing. He regrets the swirling light. If he leaves the sanctuary of his office, he is pretty sure his employees will hang him from it by his tie.

At 9:30 P.M. Jones is playing strip poker around the board table. He is down to his shoes, socks, boxer shorts, and tie, and is being eyed appreciatively by a young woman from Treasury. Freddy is doing much worse: he only has underpants left, and Holly, sitting beside him, keeps reaching down and snapping the elastic. Freddy yelps at this, but Jones gets the feeling he doesn't mind very much.

Everybody draws, and Jones ends up with three queens.

"Ho, ho," Elizabeth says, from the head of the table. "You guys are in for it now. I am loaded up."

The accountant lays down two pair with a certain hopeful glance in Jones's direction, but Holly creams everyone with a flush. "You wouldn't," Freddy says, and Holly grins wickedly. Jones finds it startling, then realizes why: he's only ever seen small smiles from Holly. He has never seen her really happy.

Freddy holds up his hands in surrender, makes like he's going to climb onto the boardroom table, then runs for the door. There are howls of outrage as his white underpants flash by. People leap up from the table, scattering cards. Holly is out of her chair in a second and bolts after him like a leopard. Jones doesn't think Freddy is going to get very far.

Suddenly he wants to go home. This has been an amazing day, but for Jones it's not finished. There is a reckoning to be had with Alpha; maybe not tonight, but Jones can't relax until he faces that. Until he severs his link to Alpha, he's not really a part of Zephyr.

It takes him half an hour to get out of the building, because when people see he's leaving, everyone wants to talk to him. But he finally makes it, and he's walking along the stained concrete floor of the level-2 subbasement parking lot, reaching for his car keys, when a voice he immediately recognizes as Eve's floats into earshot. He stops and looks around. Someone replies to Eve, then there's a third voice. They seem to be behind the elevator shaft, so Jones cautiously heads in that direction. He rounds a thick pillar and stops, because there everyone is: the whole of Project Alpha.

Nobody speaks. Jones hesitates, then decides he might as well get it over with. He takes a step and Klausman says, "Don't... you... dare." He speaks quietly, but there is rage in his voice, and something else, too: something like grief.

Jones stops. He looks from one Alpha agent's face to another and sees a mixture of anger, confusion, and shock. Eve's face is blank, as if he's not even there.

He nods and turns away. At first he feels cowardly, even embarrassed. But with each step, his mood rises. By the time he reaches his car, he has practically forgotten about Daniel Klausman and Alpha. He is thinking about Freddy's white underpants, and how Holly ran after them.

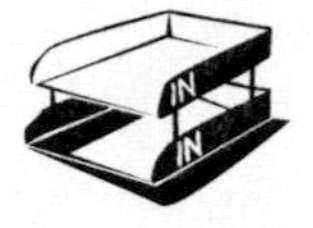

He is almost home when his cell phone rings. He fishes it out of his pocket and glances at the screen. Then he pulls the car over and parks outside a small clothing store.

"Where are you?" she says.

"In my car." This doesn't seem to answer her question, so he adds, "Alone."

"Okay. I can't talk for long, but I just wanted to tell you: you are *awesome*."

Jones thinks: *Crossed line?*

"Hello?"

"I'm here."

"I've been pissed at you all day, you know. But when I saw what you were doing... *damn,* Jones! You killed Senior Management. It's unbelievable."

"I thought you'd be... less enthusiastic."

"Well, it screws Alpha. We'll be digging our way out of

this for months. But who cares? You took on the company and kicked its ass. Look, I'll have to distance myself from you in front of Alpha—say I'm appalled at your behavior, you betrayed our trust, blah blah blah—but Jones, I am so attracted to you right now, you have no idea. Hello? You still there?"

"Yeah. My mouth is just hanging open."

"Yours and everyone else's. My God, when I saw Klausman, I thought he was having a heart attack. None of us are getting a weekend now. You should feel sorry for me; I'm about to have a twenty-hour meeting."

"You sound excited about it."

"Well . . . not about *that.* I'm just excited." There is a falseness in her tone. Jones thinks Eve just lied to him.

"You still there?"

"What's going to happen in the meeting?"

"Well, we figure out what the hell to do." She laughs in his ear. "Blake's already saying we should shut Zephyr down and start again. Klausman won't hear it. He's not going to let his baby die. Which you already knew, right? You're such a frickin' genius. You actually found a way to change Zephyr. And I don't think there's a thing we can do about it."

"Is that what you're going to tell them?"

"I'm not sure yet. There's a lot of politics involved. This is an earthquake moment for Alpha. Some people might get shaken right out, others will . . . well, come out better."

A sick feeling develops in Jones's stomach. "Are you excited because you think I've done a good thing for Zephyr?"

"Of course."

"Or because I've done a good thing for *you*?"

There's a pause, then she says, "Why do you say that?"

His body flushes cold.

"Jones? Hello? Jo-o-ones?"

"Yeah," he croaks.

"Is this a bad line? Hang on. I'll call you back."

The following Monday, Jones wakes at 6:14 A.M. He knows this without even opening his eyes, because he's one of those people who always wakes just before his alarm goes off. And Jones's alarm has been set for 6:15 A.M. every weekday for the last three months.

But not today. This morning, Jones's internal clock has been fooled. He rolls over and pulls up the sheet. He smiles without opening his eyes. This morning, Jones can sleep in, because he doesn't have an Alpha meeting.

Elizabeth arrives at Zephyr at 8:55 A.M., almost an hour late. She feels guilty for taking advantage of the lack of Senior Management to grab a little extra sleep—until, cruising through the parking lot, she passes empty space after empty space. Apparently she's not late at all. Relatively speaking, she's early.

She catches the elevator to Staff Services and wends her way between empty cubicles. A sudden burst of loud voices prompts her to turn and peer over the dividers: three people are by the coffee machine, sharing a joke. She keeps walking. Just before her cubicle, she finally sees someone at a desk: a young guy with spiky hair. He looks up, surprised, and she smiles at him. He quickly changes the screen on his computer. Belatedly, she realizes he was working on his CV.

The second she bends down to tuck her bag under her desk, her phone rings. She picks up. This is a big mistake. "Elizabeth," says Roger, his voice deep and utterly commanding. "We need to talk."

Wait! some part of her shrieks, but already the blood is rising in her head like a storm. Her fingers sing with pins and needles. Her toes freeze. Her body floods with the insane, unspeakable, insatiable craving: *Roger, Roger, Roger.*

Horrified, she watches her feet turn around and clump her blindly along the carpet. When she reaches Roger's door, her hand *(traitor!)* comes up and knocks. When Roger calls her in, her body trills in response.

Roger sits with his hands folded neatly on his desk. His brown hair is neatly parted. His suit jacket sits on him as easily and perfectly as a sculpture, the shoulders dusted in gold from the morning sun. For a second, Elizabeth thinks she is going to vomit.

"So?" To her relief, her voice comes out hard and sardonic. "What's the story?"

"Have a seat."

She shrugs, as if she doesn't care one way or the other—as if her heart isn't trying to break out of her chest and her brain not drowning in a dull roar of lust. She folds both hands firmly around the armrests, where they are less likely to do anything stupid.

"I'm not sure how to put this." He hasn't glanced away from her, even for a second, since she entered the room. "Last week, in your cubicle... you had some fun at my expense."

Yes! Elizabeth will die to defend this fiction. "I suppose so," she says nonchalantly. Her hands, appalled by this lie, try to get away from her; she squeezes them back down on the armrests.

"Or so I thought." Roger opens a drawer and holds up a tiny plastic cup, the kind doctors ask you to pee into. Elizabeth can't fathom why Roger would have such a thing, and for a second her stupid, addled brain spins with bizarre possibilities. "Human Resources has a new drug-testing policy. You've been randomly selected from our department."

Elizabeth may be more hormones than synapses, but she can see through that: Human Resources wants to know if she's pregnant. Outrage flares across her face. Then she realizes Roger is watching her reaction.

He says, "That's what I thought, too."

Oh God. "What?"

"It's not about drugs."

"Then what's it about?"

"In my opinion?" He purses his lips. "I think you're pregnant."

Kill me now. Please.

"Very pregnant, in fact. Maybe five months."

Her hands spasm.

"Which would put the conception date around... well."

Roger's eyes grip her. It's not fair; he's reviving the memory of their coupling! Sweat pops out on her hairline. She digs her fingers into the armrests with all her strength.

"Given that, I'm looking on recent events in a new light. Such as what you said to me."

He stands.

Oh no.

"It makes me wonder..."

He comes around the desk and drops onto his haunches in front of her.

No! No!

"... if that was in fun..."

No no no no no no—

"... or not."

The sun shines behind him, forming a halo. She bites down on a whimper. In this moment, he is the most beautiful, desirable asshole in the world.

"Stop me if I'm off base here," Roger says softly, "but I'm wondering if that was for real."

She holds out for a full second. Considering the tidal wave of physical need crashing against her, it's a kind of victory. *I tried!* she thinks. Then she grabs Roger's face with both hands and mashes her lips against his.

Jones is halfway across the lobby when a hand touches his arm. He looks around into the pale gray eyes of a blue-uniformed Human Resources and Asset Protection security guard. "Mr. Jones?"

Jones supposes this is the part where he is forcibly escorted off the premises. "Okay, who told you to do this? HR? Because they don't have the authority to fire anyone."

The guard looks startled. "I just have a message for you."

"Oh," Jones says.

"What you did on Friday was a great thing, Mr. Jones. I told my kids about it." He consults a scrap of paper. "The message is that the Alpha team wants to see you. As soon as possible. In the usual place." His eyes flick up at Jones. "Does that make sense? I wrote down exactly what they said."

"Yeah. Thanks."

Jones claps the guard on the arm and walks on. When he's inside the elevator, he presses 12 and 14 together, even though he is sure nothing will happen—surely the first thing Klausman did after Jones trashed his company was to revoke his Alpha clearance. But no: the elevator moves. Jones chews his lip. At the right moment he hits DOOR OPEN and the car slides to a halt on 13, just like always.

Jones hesitates. There are not too many reasons Alpha would want to see him, and even fewer that will be much fun for him. One possibility is they want to bawl him out; another is they want to inflict some kind of horrendous revenge on him, the nature of which they've spent all weekend devising.

But he can't dodge them forever. He leaves the elevator and walks to the meeting room, his business shoes making no sound on the plush carpet. Despite himself, he is nervous. He reaches the door, stops, and wipes his hands on his pants.

Then he throws open the door. An agent, Tom Mandrake, stops speaking so abruptly that Jones hears his teeth click together. "Hi!" Jones says. "How you guys doing?"

Klausman, sitting in his giant leather chair, eyes him from dark, sunken hollows. The man looks ten years older than he did on Friday. He also looks as if he would like to punch Jones in the guts. "Sit down, Jones."

He takes a few steps into the room. "I'm good, thanks."

Klausman eyes him for a moment, then shrugs. It is the worst attempt to feign nonchalance Jones has ever seen. Then Klausman's eyes flick across the room and Eve says, "Jones."

She's not sitting in her usual position, but rather at the foot of the great table, opposite Klausman's big leather chair. Her expression is stony—which is what she told him to expect, at least in front of Alpha. But at this point Jones isn't taking anything about Eve for granted. "I suppose it would be redundant to tell you how disappointed we are."

"Probably."

"Ten years. That's how long this version of Zephyr Holdings has been running. That's how much sweat and blood went into it. You destroyed a decade."

Jones glances at Klausman, who is staring back at him with his arms folded. He doesn't seem to want to join in, so Jones guesses Eve is today's designated attack dog. Well, too bad; he's addressing this to Klausman. "Are you serious? Do you really think Zephyr was corporate Utopia? It wasn't. It was a shit place to work, and a shitty template for a successful company. You screwed the staff too many times, and that was always going to come back to bite you. Well, here it is. *You* killed Zephyr. All I did was show you that it was dead."

"Why you arrogant little prick," Blake says.

"Blake," Klausman says, his voice low.

Eve folds her hands together and leans forward, pulling Jones's attention back. She looks very earnest, and even now, when Jones is reasonably sure she is focused on nothing beyond extracting the maximum personal benefit possible from this situation, he feels a pang of desire for her. "Jones, we didn't ask you here to vent our frustration. We want to determine the best way forward. If word leaked out that the Omega Management System's test-case company imploded . . . well, there would be no way to recover from that. So our objective is to get Zephyr back on track as fast as possible. We . . ." She glances at Klausman. "We want to ask for your cooperation with that."

Jones laughs before he can stop himself. "You're joking."

"There's no one more likely to persuade the staff than you."

He looks around the table. They're as solemn as funeral directors. "Zephyr is not going back. Zephyr is running a new project now: to find out whether a company can be successful without eating its own employees. You all need to accept that. And stop assuming this is a disaster! What if—and sorry if I'm turning anyone's worldview upside down here—what if Zephyr can be successful *and* a good place to work?"

"Oh, Jesus," Blake says, disgusted.

Eve says, "Jones, we are not amateurs. Alpha did not *as-*

sume that cutting employee benefits raises productivity. We studied it. We tried it both ways. We tried it in ways you haven't thought of yet, and that's why we know: letting employees run the company is a *bad idea.* Does Zephyr have high turnover and poor morale? Yes. Do its employees complain a lot? Yes. Would it be more successful if it addressed these problems? No, because at that level, happy employees are not more productive. People don't become receptionists and sales assistants because they love answering phones, and if you give them the opportunity to earn the same salary by working less, you know what? They grab it. This is not a principle Alpha invented because we enjoy being assholes; it is a fact. Maybe you don't like it, maybe *we* don't like it, but we understand it, and we manage it. You, Jones, don't understand it. You took a high but manageable level of employee dissatisfaction and turned it into a rebellion because you believe in a goddamn *fantasy.*"

"Enough," Klausman says. "Jones, I'm only going to ask you once. Will you help me get Zephyr back?"

He feels rattled from Eve's attack, but if there's one thing he's sure of, it's that he's not going to help Alpha. He's surprised they bothered calling him up here to ask, since surely Eve, at least, must know there's no chance he will agree. Perhaps it's a sign of how desperate Klausman is to save his corporate baby. Or maybe—

Oh, he thinks.

He gets it. He looks at Eve, and it almost breaks his heart. She regards him steadily, waiting for his response.

"No," he says.

Then it all goes pretty much as he expects.

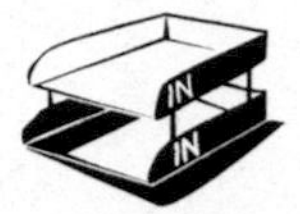

Eve turns to Klausman, spreading her palms. "Daniel, I have to say it. This is just what I predicted."

Blake says, "Jones, think about what you're doing, for Christ's—"

Eve talks over him. "And I'm going to speak frankly, because the circumstances demand it. The blame for this debacle, Daniel, lies at your feet. You allowed Zephyr staff too much freedom, despite what we knew about their levels of dissatisfaction. You selected Jones for Alpha. And now we've spent three days *talking*. It pains me to say this, Daniel, but you are losing Zephyr. We need to take back the company. We need to sack the ringleaders. It has to happen now. And, Daniel, you have to step down."

Klausman's eyebrows jump up in shock.

"I'm not saying permanently. But this is a crisis. It's no time to stand on egos. You started this company, Daniel, but you have to let somebody else save it. You know it's true. If this happened on anyone else's watch, you'd sack them in a second. Not out of spite, not as punishment, but because that's what's best for the company. It's what the investors will demand; it's what our customers will demand. If they hear about this, and if we haven't done something drastic, something major, in response . . . I don't need to tell you how damaging that would be. Alpha wouldn't survive it, Daniel. It couldn't. That's why you need to hand it over to me."

Blake says, "Whoa, whoa—"

Eve says, "Daniel. You know I'm right."

Blake: "This is not the kind of thing that should be decided on the spur—"

Eve: "Blake, you had your chance. It was on Friday, at 5:00 P.M."

Blake: "Oh, come on, what has that got to do with—okay, maybe that could have been handled better, but they took us by surprise. It was—"

Eve: "Unless we do something, we'll be sitting here tomorrow saying we could have done today better. Daniel, I love you. And I love this company. That's why I'm pushing so hard. I'm sorry to say it, but if you can't see this is a crisis, I'm tendering my resignation."

Blake: "That's a cheap stunt."

Eve: "I'm completely serious."

Blake: "You bitch—"

Klausman says, "All right." His voice is soft, barely audible. He doesn't meet anyone's eyes. Jones almost feels sorry for him.

Jones leaves and nobody cares: they're enraptured by the seismic power shift occurring around Daniel Klausman and Eve Jantiss. He walks down the corridor, and, on a whim, enters the monitoring room. There are two techs present, but after the first curious glance, they ignore him.

Jones pulls a chair into the middle of the room and stares at the monitors for a while.

"I don't know what to say to you."

It's Blake, standing with one hand on the door handle. Jones turns back to the monitors. He hears Blake let go of the door handle and come closer, until he can practically feel waves of silent hostility breaking against his back. "You know, Eve is Eve. She saw an opportunity, she took it. I hope she wraps her car around a pylon on the way home tonight, but I get it: she outplayed me. *You,* though—I warned you. I told you what she was like. But you went ahead and let her screw you anyway. You spineless piece of crap, I bet you still think she's on your side. I bet you can't wait for her to come out of that room and tell you everything's going to be all right. Is that why you're hanging around?"

"Blake?" Eve says. Jones sees her reflection in the glass wall. "I know you're pissed and all, but let's not do anything that will make it impossible to work with each other, okay?"

Blake makes a noise that sounds like he's chewing his own tongue. "I'll leave you two to it." His voice is wet with contempt.

Eve closes the door behind him. She comes around and squats in front of Jones. When she enters his field of vision, she is sharing a wide, beautiful smile with the two techs. "Okay!" she says to Jones. "Let's get coffee and talk this thing out."

Jones starts to laugh. It pops out of him without warning and escalates into something uncontrollable, where there are tears in his eyes and a stitch in his side. Eve watches him, her smile growing fractured.

"You," he says, "are unbelievable. I mean that."

"Thanks. So what do you say—"

"We're not going for coffee."

"Ah." She rocks back on her heels. "So it's like that."

"What you said in there about sacking people, was that just for Alpha? Or did you mean it?"

She says softly, "Jones, this isn't a company. What you've done . . . it's sweet. It really is. But it's not workable. You still think there are such things as good companies and bad companies, and there aren't. I'm sorry."

Jones stares at her.

She holds up her hands. "Okay, let's get this straight. I did not pretend to like you. I am not some kind of corporate whore who uses sex to get what she wants." Jones starts laughing again. "I mean it. I care for you. Look at me. Jones, I adore you. What happened in there, that's business. It has nothing to do with you and me."

"It has *everything*—" he chokes on the word. For a second he thinks he's about to cry.

Eve doesn't say anything for a moment. "It will be easier if you help, Jones. You can save a lot of jobs."

"If you sack a single person, I'll tell the whole company about Alpha."

"Jones," she says patiently, "that would only force me to sack all of them."

"You won't do that."

"I will. In a heartbeat. We already have everything in place; all it takes is a phone call. And after what you've done, it might even be easier to start from scratch." She puts her hands together, as if in prayer. "But the best solution, Jones, is to go back to the way things were before. Your friends can keep their jobs. I won't have to move Alpha to a new city. Everyone's happy—well, you know what I mean. Please, think about it. It really is the best outcome."

"I should have told everyone about Alpha the second I found out."

Eve bites her lip. "Jones, you have this idea that they will be glad to know the truth. That they'll thank you for telling them. They won't. They'll hate you. I'm telling you the truth right now, Jones, and are you grateful? No, you're angry and upset and you probably hate me a little. I don't want to threaten you, because I know you're emotional and you're not thinking logically, but if you want to stay friends with any of those people, you won't say a word about Alpha. You'll convince them that they need Senior Management back."

"So that's what's in my best interest. To lie. To keep lying."

"Yes."

He looks around. "Where's that ethics tape? The one you play for nervous investors?"

"Um . . . I think—"

"I'm joking."

"Oh." She smiles, but her eyes flick up and down his face. "Well, that's good. You should laugh about this. It's just business."

This makes him feel like crying again. He forces it down. "If I tell the workers about Alpha, they hate me. And they lose their jobs. If I help you, nobody gets fired."

Eve hesitates. "Actually, I will need to fire certain key people." She sees his expression. "But we can talk about that later. Jones, I know this is tough. But one day you'll look back and realize this was a huge step forward for your career. I have so many ideas for Alpha—I shouldn't tell you this, it's still in the early stages, but I think I can get financing for a village in Virginia. We can build a town, Jones. A town for Zephyr. It'll have a school and a mall and every home will have broadband and an inbuilt meeting room and we'll give them everything, everything they want. All they have to do is live in the town. You say we've been stealing pieces of people's lives, and you're right, you're exactly right. But in our town there won't *be* a difference between work and home, because everyone will be at work twenty-four hours a day, seven days a week, and at the same time they'll be home. You see? They'll work, not because we force them to but because their town depends on it, because that's how they improve their quality of life. Because they're proud patriots of the company." She squeezes her hands together, her eyes shining. "You see, Jones, you can't end things now. We have so much left to do."

Eventually, Jones says, "I need to think about this."

"Of course. Of course you do." She nods. "I'll give you some time. Alpha meets again at noon. Come along, okay?"

Elizabeth sits up. She pushes her hair back from her face. She shifts her butt, which feels as if it is stuck to the top of Roger's desk. She begins buttoning her blouse.

Roger squeezes her shoulder. "That . . . was . . . incredible." He shifts to look up at her, and she can see his gleaming smile without even having to face him. "Don't you think?"

"Mmm." She looks around for her panties.

"I want to apologize. I've been a bit of a shit to you lately, I know. It's just, sometimes, Elizabeth, I get so focused on the politics. You know what this place is like."

She realizes that they are hanging from her left ankle. She bends forward, dislodging Roger's head, and tugs them up.

"I mean, if I'm going to be brutally honest, it's insecurity." He laughs. "You probably don't believe me. But it's true. You made me nervous. I always felt I had to prove myself to you."

She stands and begins fixing her skirt.

Roger sits up. "I guess what I'm trying to say, Elizabeth, is I want to take this further."

She looks at him. She shakes her head.

Roger blinks. "What? What do you mean?"

"I don't want to."

"You don't want to what? Have sex again?"

"You."

"You don't want me?"

Elizabeth shakes her head.

"Why not?" His face pinches. "What's the matter? Was something wrong?"

"No."

"Then what's the problem? For God's sake, what *do* you want?"

Elizabeth thinks. "Gherkins."

When Jones arrives back at Staff Services, he finds himself in the middle of a hockey game. He stands in the doorway, watching people clamber over desks and knock aside chairs. One man bumps a cubicle wall and sends a row of manila folders tumbling to the carpet. His foot lands on one, tearing its cover, and he runs off without looking back.

"Jones!" Freddy comes over, looking happy and excited. "We're playing hockey."

"So I see."

Freddy peers at him. "What?"

"Well," Jones says peevishly, "we didn't overthrow management to play games."

"Aw, come on. It's the first day. We're just having fun."

"Freddy!" someone yells. Jones looks around as Holly streaks past, knocking along a rubber ball with a cardboard tube.

Freddy glances apologetically at Jones. "Things will settle down. They're good people." Then he runs after Holly.

Jones walks to the Training Sales cubicle, which is empty. He sits down heavily and puts his head on his arms.

At first he thought it would be impossible to convince people that they need Senior Management back. Now he thinks it's inevitable. Eve was right: this isn't a company, it's a party. And they will all realize that, sooner or later: they will see nobody is working as hard as they used to, and understand what that means.

"Hello?"

He lifts his head. It's Alex Domini, the man he hired to coordinate the rewiring of the Zephyr computer network. Alex has a sheaf of papers in his hand. Apparently he is the only person actually working in Zephyr today. Of course, Alex is on contract.

"Sorry to bother you. Is this a good time? I have a little problem." He comes into the cubicle, looking sheepish. "The thing is, I can't get to level 13. There's no button 13 in the elevators, and the stairwell doors are locked, so . . . I don't know what to do."

Jones stares. "Why do you think there's a level 13?"

"The wiring. I hooked in a laptop, and there's definitely a network there, between 12 and 14. I just can't . . . find it."

Jones swallows a couple of times. "Level 13 is hard to get to. I'll take you there."

"Ah! Thanks. Geez, I thought I was going crazy."

"It's not you. It's this place." When they reach the elevators, he says, "By the way, how's the rest of the network coming along?"

"It's basically done. Even level 13—I don't know what's there, but it's wired in to everything else now. We more or less just need to turn it on."

"Interesting," Jones says.

Jones is in the level-13 monitoring room when the Alpha agents begin to return. Eve is first to arrive: she walks past the glass wall, heading for the meeting room, then sees him, stops, and beckons. Jones closes the door behind him. "Hi."

"Hi. How are you doing?"

He shrugs. Together they walk toward the meeting room. "Okay, I guess."

She nods. "I don't want to push you, Jones, but—" This is the point at which she opens the door to the meeting room and reveals Alex sitting at the great table. Eve looks at him, then at Jones, then back at Alex. "Who are you?"

Jones says, "He's working on the network."

"What's he doing here?"

"I let him up. He needs to splice some data cables or something. I don't really understand the details."

Alex says uncertainly, "Sorry . . . should I go?"

"Thanks, yeah," Jones says. "We need this room now."

Alex stands. Two more agents arrive on level 13 and come up behind Eve and Jones. Eve doesn't move, so there's a logjam: Alex waiting to get out, agents waiting to get in, and Eve blocking the doorway. Her eyes flick between Alex and Jones.

Jones says, "Well?"

"We're not going in."

"What? Why not?"

"Because," she says, "you're trying to be clever."

"What's going on?" says Mona.

Jones says, "I don't know what you're talking about."

"I'm relocating the meeting."

"What?" Jones yelps. "You think he bugged the room or something?"

Eve says, "This is not a good start to our new working relationship, Jones."

"What did I do?"

"Everybody out. And someone get *this* guy off level 13."

On the way back to the elevators, Eve grips Jones's arm just above the elbow. She whispers, "You *know* I was looking forward to sitting in the big chair."

Eve inspects two meeting rooms off the lobby before she finds one that satisfies her. She pulls the blind over the little window in the door, eyes the security camera in the corner of the room, then calls level 13 on her cell. "Just so we're clear," she says, "until you hear back from me, nobody is to be in the monitoring room but you. *Nobody.*"

"This is nuts," Jones says. "Klausman wouldn't have made us traipse down here. What if someone barges in?"

Eve hesitates. "Mona, can you wedge a chair against that door?"

Mona looks startled. "I'm not sure . . . okay, I'll see about that."

"We have a perfectly good meeting room on level 13."

"Jones," Eve says, "shut up."

Blake says, "Eve, as much as I hate to agree with Judas here—"

Eve slaps the table with the palm of her hand. Everyone jumps. "We're here. We have a meeting to get through. Let's go."

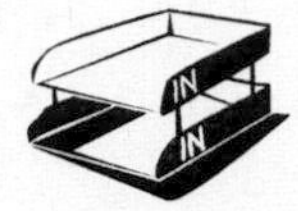

Freddy is passing by his desk when he sees something weird on his computer screen. He detours into his cubicle to peer at it. For the last few months, Freddy's desktop taskbar has sported a little computer with a red cross through it. Now, there's a yellow balloon with the message: ZEPHYR INTRANET IS NOW CONNECTED. SPEED: 100.0 MBPS.

"Hey," Holly says, coming in. "I thought you were getting me a coffee."

"Check this out." He reaches for his mouse. But before he can activate his e-mail, a new window pops up. First it says STREAMING UPDATES, then it says COMPLETE, then it disappears and something else comes up.

"What..." Holly says. She trails off. They stare at the screen.

"In terms of regular projects, well... do we still want to go through these?" Tom Mandrake looks at Eve, who doesn't react because she is watching Jones. Then she realizes and nods sharply. "Okay. Well, Project 442 is the study on how removing reminders of the outside world from the workplace affects worker productivity. You might remember, there were some interesting early results in this area."

Mona nods. "They stay at work longer."

"We're also seeing downtrends in personal calls. Unfortunately, I ran some of this by one of our psychologists, and he said it sounded like some of our subjects could be developing dissociative identity disorder."

Blake says, "They're going schizo?"

"It's not schizophrenia. It's more like split personalities. One for work, one for home. We've had a few, well, slightly alarming incidents. People getting calls from their family and not recognizing their voices. That kind of thing."

There's a moment's silence. Then an agent on Jones's left says, "Well, that could be anything. These people could be predisposed."

"I'm not saying we should pull the study," Tom says. "It's just, I think it could be a serious medical problem."

Jones feels Eve's eyes crawling over him. And suddenly it's all he can do to keep from laughing.

"Step one, talk to our insurer," Blake says. "We need to make sure we're covered if anyone goes postal because of this."

"Stop," Eve says. She's still looking at Jones. "Stop talking."

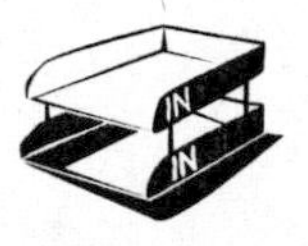

A few minutes ago, Staff Services was filled with shouting and noise from the hockey game. Now it's silent. Throughout the department, as on the floors above and below, people cluster in cubicles and stare at computer screens.

Blake says, "What's the matter?"

Eve doesn't answer. But she's worked it out. Jones can see it in her eyes.

"Okay!" Jones says. "My turn?" He adjusts his tie. "First up, I'm pleased to report that the network is back."

"What are they doing?" somebody says from behind Holly. She can't answer. She can't breathe. She has worked for Zephyr for four years, and in all that time the company never made sense. She thought it was her.

The words tear themselves from her chest. "We're a *study.*"

"One of the reasons this is good news," Jones continues, "is you can now access Alpha's project files from any computer in the building. They're on network drive R. Another is you can get a live feed from the cameras without having to visit the level-13 monitoring room. There's sound and everything. I'm told the picture's a little jerky, but still—" This is as far as he gets before Blake drags him out of his chair.

Freddy clicks through drive R. At first he gets nowhere, because everything is organized by project name. Then he finds a directory of employee files, which contains one called CARLSON-F. Inside is a cross-reference of every project Freddy has apparently been involved in. There are five. The first, Project 161, is titled WITHHELD REWARDS AND MOTIVATION. Beneath that, in INSTRUCTIONS, it says: BLOCK ALL PROMOTIONS REGARDLESS OF PERFORMANCE.

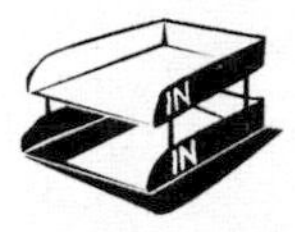

It's Gretel's first day back at work. She is feeling a lot better; people aren't hammering the switchboard today. She has a feeling that she might even be able to sneak out for a proper lunch.

The board blinks at her. "Good afternoon, reception."

"Gretel? It's Holly Vale, from Staff Services. Can you come upstairs?"

"I'm on the phones."

"I know. But there's something you need to see."

Elizabeth emerges guiltily from Roger's office. Her body is tensed, ready for the accusation: *What have you been doing in there?* But it doesn't come. In fact, the department is curiously quiet. She looks up. There's nobody in sight.

She does a double take the first time she passes a cubicle. There are five or six people crammed in there, clumped around a monitor. None are making a sound. Curious and a little bemused, she comes up behind them and stands on tiptoe to peer over their shoulders. She sees the screen. At first it makes no sense. Then it does, and her hand creeps down to her abdomen.

Blake gets Jones by the shirt lapels and shakes. Jones's head bounces against the carpet. *"What have you done?"*

"Let him go," Eve says, on her feet.

Blake takes his hands back as if Jones is infectious.

"This is what we're going to do," Eve says. "We're going to level 13, right now. We'll take it from there."

Freddy discovers a file for Megan, and inside is her home phone number. He pushes through the crowd of people to get to his phone and dials.

"Hello?"

"Megan? It's Freddy Carlson." There's a pause, so he adds, "From Zephyr?"

"Oh! Sorry, of course! I just didn't expect to hear from you. What's going on?"

"Well," Freddy says.

It's a tight squeeze in the elevator, but the entirety of Project Alpha gets into it. In the close quarters, they mostly avoid Jones's eyes, except for Blake, who stares at him with outright hostility, and Tom, who looks plaintive. Halfway up, Tom says, "You haven't really, have you, Jones?"

"Don't be a dick, Tom," Blake says.

"But why? Jones, why would you do something like that?"

"Because they deserve better," Jones says. "And because I don't."

Nobody responds to this. When they reach the monitoring room, they stare at the monitors in utter silence.

Then Eve screams.

It's short and sharp: a sound of pure frustration. Everyone jumps, including Jones. Blake, sounding shaken, says, "Jesus, Eve."

"Did you think I was *kidding*?" she yells at Jones. "My God, did you?"

"No, Eve."

She yanks her cell phone out of her bag. "You watch those monitors. And keep this in mind: this is your fault. I warned you what would happen if you told them. You're doing this."

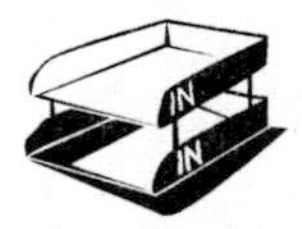

Nobody is angry; they're too stunned. "It's a joke," says an accountant on level 7, but nobody responds. It doesn't feel like a joke. They look at their desks. Their in-boxes, piled high with fruitless tasks. It feels like Zephyr is making sense for the first time.

The voice-mail lights all come on at the same time. A murmur sweeps through the building. Hands reach for phones.

"Hello to all staff from Human Resources and Asset Protection."

The voice is female, and light in tone. Most Zephyr employees don't recognize it. But Freddy's hand tightens on the handset, and Holly feels something in her gut contract.

"My name is Sydney Harper. I have some exciting changes to announce at Zephyr Holdings today, so please give this voice mail your full attention. As you know, last week most of Senior Management resigned. This has, obviously, thrown out our organizational structure, so Human Resources has worked hard to come up with an effective solution. After extensive consultation, both within Human Resources and the remaining members of Senior Management, we believe we've come up with a plan to maximize our resources during this difficult transition period.

"Effective immediately, all positions are vacated. Employees may apply for their current jobs, or, if they wish, another position. Full details are posted on the Jobs Board. Good-bye."

The message ends. Stunned employees put down their phones. They turn to each other, but nobody has any answers. Slowly, they rise from their desks and file toward the elevators. The young ones don't understand; they think it's exciting. "So I can apply for any job in the company? Any one I want?" The others exchange worried looks. That's not what they heard. What they heard is that every employee has just been sacked.

The Jobs Board is a large cork bulletin board fixed to one wall of the Canteen—or what was the Canteen before Catering was outsourced. It has long been a Zephyr Holdings policy that all vacant positions must be advertised on this board, in order to ensure that the hiring process is open and transparent; also it made the people interested in leaving their current job open and transparent. Employees who approached the board could feel the eyes of anybody nearby swinging onto them. They could hear rumors being birthed. In recent times, however, the Jobs Board has been a blank canvas, a morbid reminder of how bad things are. Then, of course, Catering was outsourced, the Canteen closed down, and nobody had much reason to look at it anymore.

But now a black tack fixes a lone piece of paper to its center. It is brief and to the point.

THERE ARE NO VACANCIES AT THIS TIME

—Dept. of Human Resources & Asset Protection

Then they get angry.

Eve sits down heavily on the carpet: one second she's standing, the next she's on her butt. The other agents mill around uncomfortably, looking at each other.

"Well," Blake says. "That's that. Congratulations, Jones. You just got everyone fired."

"Don't even try," Jones says.

"I can't wait to see you try to explain this to them. That's going to be really funny. I'm going to stick around to see the look on your face when you realize they hate you for it."

Jones looks at the monitors. "I'm sure there's enough hate for everybody." In the lobby, a group—perhaps "mob" is the right word—watches as a man begins to throw himself against the stairwell door.

This elicits a murmur of alarm from the agents. Mona says, "Should we get Security up here?"

From the floor, Eve says dully, "Security is not going to be on our side, Mona."

Tom says, "We haven't done anything illegal. There's nothing wrong with what we did."

Jones snickers.

"How strong are those doors?" Mona asks.

Everyone gasps.

"Not strong enough, I guess," Jones says.

The sun sets on Zephyr Holdings. The building glows orange-yellow, as if on fire. The glass flares, appearing to dissolve.

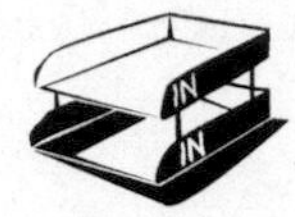

Men and women pound up the concrete steps. The stairwell fills with their raw emotion; it rebounds from the walls and redoubles in intensity. "We should kill them!" somebody shouts. *"We should kill them!"*

Mona starts a thin, high-pitched whine and doesn't stop even when Blake gets on the phone and dials 911. He tries to shush her as he tells an operator that assistance is required *right now,* that people are trying to *attack* them. Some of the agents hurry out of the monitoring room—to barricade themselves in offices or hide under desks, Jones guesses. He kneels down next to Eve. Her hair is hanging over her face. He carefully moves this aside, and sees to his surprise that she is crying.

"No, I mean there are *hundreds* of them," Blake says to the phone. *"Literally hundreds, do you understand?"*

Eve looks at Jones. "They're going to get in here."

"I know."

She takes his hand. "You have to stop them. Please. Jones."

"How the hell do you think I can do that?"

"Please." Her body trembles. "Jones, please, they're going to hurt us."

Jones says nothing.

She cries harder. *"Jones, please don't let them touch me."*

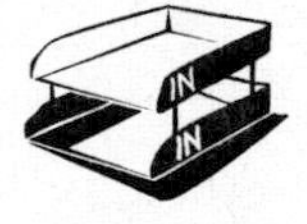

Level 13 is not marked as such, of course. The door says MAINTENANCE. But it's after 12 and before 14, and if you're looking for it, it's not hard to spot. A man with his shirt-sleeves rolled up over bulging biceps—perhaps until recently a frequent user of the Zephyr gym—is the first to reach it. He tries the handle, but it's locked. He slaps his hand against the door in frustration. From the other side, there is a startled yelp. The man turns and yells down the stairwell. "They're in here!"

Blake paces back and forth across the carpet. When he smooths back his hair, his hand trembles. Abruptly he grabs at his eye patch, pulls it off, and tosses it onto the carpet. The skin around his eye is gray and shiny. Something—or someone—crashes against the stairwell door, and Blake jumps. "We need some kind of barricade," he says, his voice tight. "Something to . . ." He turns. "Jones. Jones. What's your plan?"

Jones looks up. "What?"

"Your plan. Come on. Yes, okay, you got us. Alpha is over. Congratulations. Now how are you getting out of this? You wouldn't have done this unless you had a way out for yourself."

Jones feels sympathy for him. Not a lot, but some. "Sorry."

Blake stares. Then he laughs. It comes out high and cracked, and breaks off when there's another crash from the stairwell door.

Eve curls into a ball on the carpet. Jones thinks about suggesting that she move. It wouldn't be a good idea for her to be here, under the bank of monitors, when the horde bursts in. That would make a bad situation worse.

He strokes her hair. "I don't think Zephyr is externalizing anymore," he murmurs, as the stairwell lock splinters and the door bangs open.

He hears Mona scream. And somebody else—male or female, Jones can't tell—lets out a high, strangled shriek that he will never forget. "We're just businesspeople! *We're just businesspeople!*"

Elizabeth walks to the corridor and presses for an elevator. She turns back to Staff Services, for one last look to remember it by—but there's nothing to look at. The people she worked with are already gone, seeking vengeance, and the interior decoration is nothing special. It's not even level 14, which at least had a distinctive feature in the Berlin Partition. There is nothing significant here for Elizabeth to remember.

Maybe that's why she feels good about leaving. When the elevator arrives, she enters it with a spring in her step. The farther it descends, the higher her mood lifts. *Good riddance!* she thinks. She feels like laughing.

She used to fall in love with her customers. What kind of person does that? Elizabeth wouldn't describe what she feels toward her embryo as love, not yet, but she knows that feeling is growing. By comparison, her workplace infatuations are—well, there is no comparison, is there? When she thinks about the person she was four months ago, she doesn't even know who that was.

She wonders what she will miss about Zephyr Holdings. This place has dominated her life for most of the last decade. It has largely defined her. But sifting through her memories, the one that stands out is the time she sat in a bathroom stall and realized she was pregnant. So, as the elevator doors slide open onto the parking lot and the ramp and the sunshine beyond, she decides the answer is: Not much.

APRIL

THEY CLAP LOUDLY, passionately, and for far too long: they keep going even when the lights come up. It's a large room filled to capacity, so the applause rolls around like thunder. Jones, who knows he's not a rock star, feels embarrassed. He steps away from the podium and walks into the audience, where people rise from their seats and converge on him with a mixture of admiration and horror on their faces.

Today they are from a whole range of companies, and their name tags glimmer as they press in from three sides. He gets the usual questions—asked while eyes flick over his body for some sign of the injuries—and delivers his standard answers, which elicit mass groans of sympathy and exhalations of disgust. Then a woman at the back says, "Steve, I have a question. How do you sleep at night, knowing you caused all those people to be hurt?"

All eyes swivel to her. When he finds his voice, Jones says, "Hello, Eve."

"I was going to come up before you went on," she says, *clack*ing her way down the corridor. She's carrying a long black coat and wearing a thin gray skirt so narrow it's amazing she can walk, yet is somehow having no trouble keeping pace with him. "But then I thought, no, I don't want you changing it because I'm there. I want the full Steve Jones experience."

"I thought you moved to New York," he says. They arrive at his little dressing room and he begins packing up his things.

"I flew back just to see this. You must know why." Her eyes search his. She looks, Jones has to admit, stunning. Her hair bounces; her skin glows; you wouldn't think that four months ago she was in traction.

"I have no idea."

"I'm on the speaking circuit, too. I'm doing the exact same thing as you, only in Manhattan." One corner of her mouth curves. "Well, maybe not the *exact* same thing. There may be certain details we don't agree on. But it's the same basic take-home message: 'Don't piss your workers off so much that they bust into your office and beat the crap out of you.' " She laughs. "Oh, also, I charge more."

Jones stops packing. "*You* are speaking about *ethics*?"

"At the end of the talk, when I tell them about the riot, we turn the main lights off so it's just me on a stool in a spotlight. It's so quiet, nobody even breathes. Then I'm done and the regular lights come back up, and I see this *ocean* of shocked faces. It's like their worst nightmare. It's like the most appalling thing they've ever heard."

After a second, Jones laughs. "I don't know why I'm surprised."

She's watching him carefully. "Are you pissed?"

He considers. "What you're doing now is not really relevant to me."

Her lips press together. "How about Blake, then? He's selling cars now. Nice ones," she adds, to Jones's expression. "If you want a good deal on a Merc, call him." She tilts her head. "Or maybe not. Then there's Klausman; he retired. Moved to northern California, I think. I haven't heard from him since we beat the class action."

"How much did that cost? Just out of interest. I heard you had about a dozen lawyers."

"Look, Alpha did nothing illegal. I kept trying to tell you that. The only thing we were guilty of was giving those people jobs."

"Fake jobs."

"There's no requirement that jobs be meaningful, Jones. If there was, half the country would be unemployed. That's why we won the case."

He zips up his bag. "Well, I'm glad to hear you're all doing so swell. Now, if you'll excuse me, I'm meeting Freddy and Holly."

Eve's eyebrows shoot up. "Don't tell me they *forgave* you. Wow. I wouldn't have. But then, I guess Freddy and Holly didn't end up in a hospital." For a moment, her face twists. Then she smiles. "But! I did get a free nose job out of it. What do you think?"

"I was wondering what was different." He hefts his bag. "Okay, I have to go."

When he reaches the door, Eve says, "You know, I tried to get in touch with you."

He looks at her. "I know."

There's a silence, during which Eve seems to be waiting for Jones to say something. When he doesn't, she lets out a laugh. "To be honest, I had an ulterior motive for coming out here. I wanted to see how I would feel about you." Her eyes flick between his. "To see whether I wanted to kill you or... not." Again Jones says nothing. "Want to know which it is?"

"Not really."

"Oh, come on. I know you still think about me. I think about you."

Jones says, "Eve, I have no interest in you whatsoever."

This is clearly not at all what she expected: her face registers surprise, then doubt, then finally her features harden into a mask. All this happens in about half a second. "I mean, when I say I think about you, it's just, I feel bad for you. I know it must piss you off that Blake and I are making good money, while you... well. But what can I say? That's how business works. Nobody gives a crap about ethics. That's why people like me will always be successful."

"You have a funny definition of 'successful.' "

She frowns. "Huh?"

"Still lonely?"

Eve blows air between her teeth. "I was never lonely. I just said that to make you feel better."

Jones snickers. "It was good to see you again, Eve. Really."

He leaves the dressing room, his bag over his shoulder. He is almost at the exit, where Freddy and Holly will be waiting for him—he can't wait to tell them about *this*—when Eve calls out, "Hey, Jones. Don't blame me when America loses its corporate base to countries that aren't so hung up on *labor conditions*, okay?"

He turns. "I don't blame you for anything. Except being you."

Eve thinks about this for a moment. Then she grins. "Thanks," she says.

Acknowledgments

I AM ETERNALLY grateful to those people who read my crappy first drafts and told me what they think. I know it's not easy to read three hundred pages of unbelievable characters and inexplicable plot developments, then craft an insightful, helpful response that doesn't also make me want to jump off a bridge. But somehow these people did it, and it's thanks to them that I managed to claw my way toward something that finally resembled a novel: Beth English, Roxanne Jones, Gregory Lister, Lindsay Lyon, and Dennis Widmyer.

Charles Thiesen, my mentor (or I'm his, I forget), read more drafts than I can remember and played cheerleader when I needed encouragement, and oracle when I needed advice.

Kassy Humphreys gave me a ton of great ideas exactly when I needed them, and, as if this wasn't enough, let me plunder huge tracts of her career for inclusion in the book. As she said, "It *would* be funny if it wasn't my life."

Luke Janklow, my agent, continues to be the most dependable, supportive, and all-round awesome guy in the Universe.

It's thanks to Bill Thomas, my editor, that the final version of this book bears little resemblance to the one I sold him. That's a good thing, trust me. He helped turn a book I was happy with into one I loved.

And Jen, my wife, is perfect. Always.